Crosswind

The WWII Adventures of MI6 Agent Katrin Nissen

A NOVEL BY

KAREN K. BREES

Black Rose Writing | Texas

First printing

ISBN: 978-1-68513-091-6
PUBLISHED BY BLACK ROSE WRITING
www.blackrosewriting.com

Printed in the United States of America
Suggested Retail Price (SRP) $22.95

Crosswind is printed in Baskerville

*As a planet-friendly publisher, Black Rose Writing does its best to eliminate unnecessary waste to reduce paper usage and energy costs, while never compromising the reading experience. As a result, the final word count vs. page count may not meet common expectations.

To the four of us

ACKNOWLEDGMENTS

Every book has a starting point, and *Crosswind* owes its beginning to the information graciously provided by Lori Bronars, Librarian for Life Sciences at the Marx Science and Social Science Library at Yale University. Ms. Bronars gave my protagonist, Professor Katrin Nissen, a credible background and answered all my questions about the state of botany/horticulture at Yale in 1940 and the status of female faculty at that time.

Prof. Dr. Simone Fühles-Ubach at the Institut für Informationswissenschaft, Technische Hochschule Köln did some serious digging to find out the correct means of address for female professors in Germany during the time period of the novel. I am grateful.

It's true. Louis' Lunch really does make the best hamburgers in the world. If your travels happen to take you to New Haven, stop by.

Thanks also to Faithful Reader (FR) Joyce Miller for slogging through yet another of my manuscripts, pointing out inconsistencies, and helping make the second, third, and fourth revisions incrementally better.

My developmental editor, Cate Perry, took what I thought was a pretty good book and showed me how to make it a thousand percent better. Thanks, Cate. The result sparkles!

Finally, thanks to my publisher, Reagan Rothe, Creator of Black Rose Writing. The team at Black Rose is nothing short of wonderful, and the Black Rose family of writers are a great group of people. I'm happy to belong to the group.

Crosswind

FOREWORD

Katrin Nissen is not one woman. She is a composite of many women who fought during World War II and risked their lives in service to their country and to the hope of a better world. Her character and exploits have been drawn from the chronicles of real women who fought on the side of the Allies. Theirs was a different struggle, as they fought alone, without benefit of a squadron of fellow soldiers by their sides. Using their wits, their knowledge in diverse fields, relying on instinct, and trusting in luck, they did their jobs. Not all of them would survive, but all had committed to a cause bigger than themselves. They fought for freedom.

I hope you enjoy Katrin's story.

Monday, June 10, 1940

Italy declares war on England and France
Norway surrenders to Germany

CHAPTER ONE

Somewhere in Berlin

Dieter Weiss might not have been on the run his whole life, but enough of it to know it was time to start looking over his shoulder again. His first trip back to Germany since he'd left almost eighteen years ago hadn't gone the way he'd expected, but then, not much ever did. He'd been preoccupied, letting his mind wander to what he'd say to his sister when they finally met, but as he drew closer to the bakery, he shifted his thoughts from Kristine to the present and started paying attention. He'd sensed it more than anything. It was that gut feeling that something was off. He'd learned to trust that feeling. He was still alive because he had.

Call it a sixth sense or a vague warning of impending doom or even a little voice from somewhere deep inside. It wasn't fear, but fear wasn't far behind. During his training, his instructors had drilled into him the importance of listening to his gut when it told him to stop, look, and listen. In that moment, when the senses shift to a heightened state, the body is getting ready for an adrenaline infusion to prepare for fight or flight, because humans, depending on the situation, are either predator or prey, and any prey animal is only a fraction of a second away from flight.

Something was haywire, and Dieter decided not to continue with the drop until he could find out what that *something* was. He didn't walk up to the door and enter the bakery. Instead, he paused at the display window, checking out the pastries and deciding which one he fancied, but his mind wasn't on the cream cakes. He was watching the street reflection in the plate glass window. A black Mercedes 260D sedan was pulling up to park directly across the street from the bakery, and the occupant or occupants were obviously planning on keeping watch over who entered and left. So that was it. Dieter's instincts, in this case, his hearing, had picked up on the sound of a car engine slowing down before parking where cars didn't usually park, and now he turned away from the window, put his hands in his pockets, and casually continued down *Unter den Linden*. He was just another man out for a morning stroll.

Stopping in front of a clothing store, he looked at the display of men's summer attire. The car hadn't moved, so he continued on his walk. A long block later, he turned left, walked two more blocks, made another left, and approached his apartment building from the back. His movements had been deliberate and controlled, but his heart was racing. He was safe, but for how long? It was time to make a tactical retreat and regroup. The additional small apartment he'd rented in the event of just such a turn of events was ready and fully equipped for him. Should he collect his belongings and move across the street to the bolt hole, or should he just continue on with the routine he'd established and wait to see what happened? He weighed his options.

His assignment hadn't been complicated. Every other Monday, he was to deliver office supplies to the various departments at the university and pick up any new orders. That would be the opportunity for the mole in the physics department to slip him any microfilm inside a hollowed-out pencil that he'd hand to Dieter, along with the supply requisition form. Then, stopping at Wolff's bakery for a morning pastry, Dieter was to hand the film to Ulli, his contact, in the handful of coins he'd use to pay for his breakfast. It was all simple enough, nothing suspicious about any of his actions, and he had fallen into a comfortable routine. Routines, as he had just been reminded, are subject to change. The automobile could have been mere coincidence, but perhaps caution was the better choice. He could always move back to his regular apartment if things returned to normal. Decision made.

From the safer confines of his bolt hole, even as he considered which of his favorite disguises to adopt while he waited, his gut was telling him he should leave Berlin while he still could, postpone meeting Kristine until the world was a safer place, and take the microfilm to an alternate site. That's what he should do, but it wasn't what he wanted to do or what he was going to do. He'd started this assignment on his own terms, and he'd finish it the same way. *Or it would finish him.* He shook off that thought. He'd give himself two days to find out what had happened at the drop to set the black Mercedes after him. Two days. Then he'd leave.

He'd been in Berlin less than two months, not nearly enough time to do what he had really come to do. He hadn't expected things to fall apart so quickly. Kristine was in Berlin, and while he knew where her office was, he couldn't very well saunter up to the reception desk of the Ministry for Public Enlightenment and Propaganda at Number 8 Wilhelmstrasse and ask to see his sister. He was so close to meeting her, but he'd been waiting for the right moment, biding his time, and now there wasn't any more time. He'd have to make his move soon, but finding out her home address had turned out to be a problem. Personal residences of Himmler's staff weren't that easy to run down. He didn't have her telephone number. He needed a break. Just a little bit of luck. His mind flashed to his father in Rostock. Gerhardt would be able to provide her home address, but he'd never taken anything from him before and he wouldn't now. *He'd die first.* Dieter kept watch on the street, and he hadn't been idle while he waited. Each morning at 10 o'clock he'd gone to the bakery, his makeup in place, curly brown wig secured to his scalp, the frumpy dress with the padding to make him appear twenty pounds heavier belted around his spare frame, and his props—the pram he pushed with the doll that was bundled inside and the shopping bag he carried over his arm—had insured he wouldn't be bothered in his quest to discover what had gone wrong at the drop and hope against hope that Ulli had returned.

This morning, as with the others, he flipped open the compartment in his ring and transferred the microfilm to his pocket so he could pass it to Ulli with the money for the pastries. Shortly, the plump mother with the baby carriage was waddling down the main drag to Wolff's Bakery and Delicatessen, where this whole mess had begun. Predictably, a black Mercedes—perhaps the same one—was parked across the street. The distinctive model and vintage of the vehicles the Gestapo preferred made them instantly recognizable, and that was the intent—to instill fear, and by extension, manipulation and control, and the Gestapo were experts at it. If you could make people fear you, you controlled their minds, and if you controlled their minds, you controlled their actions.

Dieter Weiss wasn't immune to fear, but he craved the adrenaline rush that came with it. It didn't cripple him. No, quite the contrary. It made him feel alive, and besides, outsmarting opponents by operating right under their noses was something of a game. How close could he come before he had to pull back, pull away to save his life? Each time he tried, he was emboldened, and he pushed a little more the next.

Today was a case in point. He knew he should just get the hell out of Berlin, but he had to know what had gone wrong, he had to move the microfilm along to its next stop, and he had to find his sister, which, he kept reminding himself, was the main reason he'd taken this assignment in the first place. From the time he'd found his father's letter clutched in his mother's lifeless hand and had seen Kristine's photograph neatly tucked inside the envelope, the search had consumed him. He'd give himself two more days, then he'd come out. He might be reckless, but he wasn't stupid, and he knew that luck didn't hold forever. Just two more days added to the two he'd already allotted himself. Two more days couldn't hurt—if he was careful.

But then, Ulli was the most prudent person he knew, and where had he gone? On his previous trips to the bakery, Dieter hadn't found Ulli at his regular station at the cash register, so Dieter had just made his purchases and left. With time slipping away, he couldn't afford to wait any longer. Today, after he made the usual pleasantries at the bakery, selected a loaf of bread, a salad from the deli, and picked up the newspaper, he took the risk of inquiring in his trained, female stage voice where Ulli was. *Was he sick? When would he be back? Such a nice man. Always with a smile and a little joke.* Dieter's concerned face offered encouragement for the woman at the till to continue the conversation, but she merely made a pointed glance at the line of customers waiting and thanked him for his purchase. Dieter smiled his agreement, gathered up his purchases, and pushed the pram back to his bolt hole, passing by the black Mercedes that was now parked across the street from his apartment and in front of his safe house.

Dieter cursed. The presence of the Gestapo could only mean one thing. What had he done wrong? He couldn't think of a thing. He hadn't done anything wrong. *This time.* This time he'd been careful, extremely careful. It must mean that they had Ulli, and he had talked. But what could he have told them? Ulli didn't know where any of his contacts lived. He didn't even know their names. Ulli was just a conduit. He knew nothing and could tell the Nazis nothing, although they'd be dead sure of that before they let him die in peace.

Somehow, he'd been followed, and this was going to complicate matters. If he'd had the company car, things would have been so much easier, but the scheduled quarterly maintenance was underway, and that meant he was either on foot or a patron of the bus line.

In a way, his safe house was a prison of his own making, but it was one he could still leave in relative safety. He knew he should cut his losses and leave, but he needed just a little more time, and so, instead of bailing, he waited, and while he waited, he skimmed the newspaper. Luck. They called him *Lucky*, and now, he was lucky again. He found two items of interest. Front page news, of course, was that Heinrich Himmler, Reich Commissioner for the Strengthening of Germanism, would be hosting the conference, *Vegetation Mapping for the Third Reich* at the University of Berlin from June 17-19. He set the paper down and considered what that meant. Vegetation? Plants? What the hell were the Nazis doing having a meeting about plants? Probably some sort of cover for something else. It didn't matter. He didn't care. Kristine would be there. Himmler wouldn't let an opportunity to have his picture taken pass him by. It might be the chance Dieter was waiting for, but it was a week away. Could he keep up his charade for a week? It was too long. The fun of the game was beginning to wane.

He picked up the paper again and rifled through the rest of the pages until he got to the Society page where he hit paydirt. There would be a reception for the press covering the upcoming Vegetation Mapping Conference to be hosted by Kristine Trautmann, staff photographer for Heinrich Himmler, at her home on Kollwitzstrasse the Saturday preceding the conference. So there it was. Finally. Everything he needed in one tidy edition of the press. He had her street. He tossed the paper aside and reflected on this bit of luck. Kristine was making all the right moves and getting every bit of publicity she could to keep herself important. She had a plan. He had a plan. The waiting was over. He'd scout out her residence on his next morning outing. Everything was falling into place. Everything would work out. At the right time, he'd be able to get back into his old apartment and take the letter that was still on the dresser. Once he had that, he could leave.

The source of his delay was the surveillance vehicle parked on the street. Surveillance was perhaps the most mind-numbing activity of police work, and yet it required the ability to do seemingly nothing for hours while constantly being aware of one's surroundings and detecting the slightest change in normal patterns. It also required extreme bladder control. To that end, drinking endless cups of coffee worked to one's disadvantage. That fact of physiology worked to Dieter Weiss's advantage, for it seemed that the Gestapo officer in the car outside the apartment building could not postpone nature's call any longer and had sped off at precisely 4 o'clock that afternoon to find relief. It was what Dieter had been waiting for. The watcher had become the watched and patience had paid off, but the agent wouldn't be gone long, knowing full well the consequences if his prey either showed or escaped during the brief absence.

Dieter needed five minutes. If his luck held, he'd get what he needed from across the street and be back before his nemesis returned. He raced down the stairs, crossed the street to his apartment house, and sprinted up the three flights to his dwelling. Key in hand, he unlocked the door and made straight for the bedroom, where he grabbed the letter from the bedstand, jammed it in his pocket, and made the return trip in well under four minutes. It was barely enough time. The car had returned between the time he had closed the front door behind him and his collapse on the chair by the window, where he caught his breath. Lucky. That was as close as it gets. He sure as hell didn't want to try to shave another second off the clock, but he still had the touch.

Dieter pulled the envelope out of his pocket to reread the letter for the hundredth time. His father's confession. He'd write a brief note on the back of the photo and hand both the letter and the photograph to Kristine when they met. Then she'd know what a bastard their old man was. It was justice, long overdue. He took off his ring and opened the secret compartment to replace the microfilm, then dumped all the change from his pocket onto the table. He spread the coins out and looked, but the microfilm wasn't there. He turned the pocket inside out and shook it, and then the panic took over. The microfilm was gone.

Tuesday, June 11, 1940
First RAF attack on Turin.
Whitley bombers hit Fiat factories

CHAPTER TWO

Louis' Lunch
202 George Street
New Haven, Connecticut

"Katrin, we have a situation," Gene said, setting down his hamburger so he could blot a grease spot on his chin with a paper napkin, while regarding his lunch with something approaching affection. "This is how a hamburger should be made. Ingenious idea. Grilled vertically to sear in the juices, served on toasted white bread and garnished with sliced cheese, tomato, and onion. This is gastronomic perfection." He inhaled deeply.

I reached across the table and attended to another spot on his cheek with my own napkin. "You appear to be wearing your gastronomic perfection as much as you're eating it." The man was hopeless. Gene was one of those men who looked middle-aged when they were only in their mid-twenties, although the upshot of that was that they didn't change all that much as the years rolled by. I really didn't know how old he was. There was a touch of grey at the temples, and, while his face was free of wrinkles, it did have jowls that seemed to take on a life of their own when he shook his head. Those, plus the mournful brown eyes, gave him the appearance of a friendly basset hound. He was looking more rumpled than normal today, however, and that usually meant trouble for me.

"Interesting choice for a situation room," I said, looking about. We were in Louis' Lunch, birthplace of the hamburger—a fact dutifully noted by the Library of Congress and enthusiastically appreciated by the loyal clientele. From its beginnings on the back of Louis Lassen's horse-drawn cart on Meadow Street back in 1895, Louis' Lunch was now arguably the most popular eatery downtown. Seating was limited, and most people simply shouted out "To go!" as they approached the cash register, placed and paid for an order, and then retreated outside to be called. Somehow, Gene had snagged one of the few cramped booths and was ignoring the pointed stares from those jealous of his good fortune.

"Situation room? No, that would be the Oldsmobile. This is the briefing room. I'm working away from the office these days." He returned his attention to the potato salad on his plate. "Beef and gin. Queen Victoria attributed the greatness of the Empire to beef and gin." He narrowed his eyes. "Hitler is a strict vegetarian. He denies his own nature. This," he raised his hamburger sandwich and waved it in an arc, releasing more gastronomic perfection in the form of grease that dripped onto his shirt, "is why we shall prevail."

"Gene, pardon my French, but you look like hell. When did you last sleep? You've got bags under your eyes that qualify as luggage, and judging by the wrinkles, you've been sleeping in your work clothes. I'm not making a judgment, just an observation. What gives?"

He gave me one of those irritating, dismissive finger flicks. "Small potatoes. Speaking of potatoes, you going to eat the rest of yours?"

I held onto my hamburger as I pushed my plate towards him. If I'd set it down, he would have thought it was fair game. "Help yourself, but when you've got a minute, why are we here?"

I waited while he made short work of my potato salad. Watching the man eat was like watching feeding time at the Bronx Zoo. He obviously hadn't summoned me here to talk about my legitimate job, not that my spy work was illegitimate, of course, but Gene didn't know a pansy from a petunia, so I could be pretty sure he didn't want to talk about Yale or my botanical research or my never-ending quest for tenure. Nope. It was spy stuff for sure, and if he ever stopped inhaling his food, I'd find out what and where and the rest of the details. So, I sat and waited for him to spill the beans.

Finally, he paused, fork midway to his mouth. He considered the food briefly, then set the fork back on his plate. "I need your help. Under the radar, as it were."

"Isn't it always?"

Gene tossed the napkin on the plate and pushed it aside. "I'm caught in the middle this time, walking a tightrope."

"Explain."

"Nothing new. Still Donovan and Hoover slugging it out over who gets to run us. I've thrown in my lot with Wild Bill and J. Edgar has taken exception. MI6 is working overtime, and we're just adding to their load. We need our own agency to handle these types of operations. Hoover is digging in his heels, as he wants the FBI to retain control, and that means he'll remain in control. But what's happening is way beyond their scope." He picked up his fork again and impaled an unfortunate remnant of hamburger with an unnecessary expenditure of effort.

I waited again.

Gene released the meat, set the fork back on the plate again, and arranged it so it lay parallel to the knife. He gave the fork a last nudge, then looked up. "They aren't trained, equipped, or capable of managing both domestic and foreign affairs, but he's such an arrogant bastard, all he can see is his own pinafore."

I pursed my lips. J. Edgar's penchant for female dress was the worst-kept secret in Washington. "Understood. Our own agency. It *would* be nice to have a home, Gene, some place that claimed us. Like Yale. I belong there. They know me. One day, I may even get tenure, if I manage to survive these little excursions you keep sending me on. Think about it. *Dr. Katrin Nissen, Professor of Botany*. *Full Professor*, I might add. Doesn't that sound nice?" Sure sounded nice to me, and I thought about what it would mean for me professionally—my other professionally, that was. For now, we were in spy mode, and he wasn't listening. I might as well have been talking to my hamburger, which, by the way, Gene was now eyeing. My little daydream evaporated into the ozone, and I resumed eating. Gene resumed talking.

"Wild Bill Donovan is Roosevelt's pick to head a new agency that will deal with all our clandestine activities, and they're on the right track. General Donovan's a soldier—the most decorated soldier from The Great War—and he's got common sense, which is a commodity in short supply these days. So Hoover and Donovan and Roosevelt are now in a big pissing match, and I hope Donovan's got the biggest dick—sorry, bladder—because we're going to get involved. The writing is on the wall, if they'd only stop to read it. This is only beginning, and it's going to get a hell of a lot worse before it gets better, and it won't get better if we don't stop turning a blind eye and a deaf ear to what Churchill needs. Hitler isn't going away. We need this. MI6 needs us. Great Britain needs us. We will not be able to sit this out much longer." He eyed his plate and dragged it back in front of him, scowled at the napkin, and stuffed the rest of the hamburger in his mouth.

"When will all this get settled?" I wished I could help him. Gene was usually as calm and collected as the King. I couldn't remember a time when he didn't seem in control of everything. It's what gave the rest of us our confidence, but now, for the first time since we'd met when I'd just gotten off the boat from Denmark all those years ago, he looked old and uncertain, and I didn't like it one bit. This couldn't continue. Whatever war he was fighting on the home front needed an armistice, a final victory, a *something*.

And it had damn sure *better* happen soon. But all I said was, "From what you're saying, it seems as if everybody's got their heels dug in, and nobody's willing to budge." It was apparent that too much ego was involved, and it was going to take some kind of catalyst to get things moving. In these kinds of matters, though, it wasn't likely the catalyst would be something good.

"When? I don't know, but it had better happen quickly. Hoover says *no*, Donovan says *yes*, and I say, 'just let me do my bloody job and get on with it.' So I am. When the dust settles, I hope it settles on the right side of all this. Meantime, we're running solo, with the Brits our main line of support." He scraped the plate with his last morsel of toast.

Gene was right on that account. We were moving closer and closer to the inevitable. It had been one week since the massive evacuation at Dunkirk, and the Brits were essentially the only roadblock to Hitler. We knew Roosevelt was doing what he could to help Churchill behind the scenes, but the U.S. government's official position was that we were staying out of Europe's troubles. I had no control over what our government did or didn't do, and I couldn't help Gene with his own battle, but I did have a question, and so I reached into my pocketbook and fished around until I located the telegram he'd sent to set up this meeting. I dangled the paper in front of his face. The message, in Gene's typical fashion, was brief to the point of curtness. *High Noon* was all it said. He never disclosed anything that anybody else would ever be able to decipher, but we had our code and I had followed instructions. Louis' Lunch at high noon. "Gene? The situation you mentioned?"

He sighed heavily and shoved his plate aside, then lifted a shopping bag off the attaché case that was wedged on the bench between his hip and the wall. He handed me the bag, and I peered inside. "Socks?"

"Shartenberg's was having a sale."

And just like that, we were back in the present, with Hoover and Donovan and Roosevelt delegated to the wings, waiting like vultures for the outcome of whatever it was we were about to face. Gene extracted a manilla folder from the attaché case and removed a photograph and dossier, which he then handed to me. "Just set the bag down." He flapped his hand in the direction of the floor, then rested a chubby thumb on the photograph. "This is Dieter Weiss. He's gone missing in Berlin, and you're going to find him."

"A lot of people are going missing in Berlin these days," I said. "Whoa. Wait a second, Red Rider. Back up. *I'm* going to find him?"

"Your hearing is impeccable. Anyhow, yes, many people are going missing in Berlin these days, but Dieter is ours. I recruited him myself, and he's been a valuable asset, but he didn't show for a drop. He's simply gone off the radar. Weiss is a good man with some highly specialized talents. He's quite the master of disguise, so that may hinder your efforts to find him, and he's also quite skilled at deception, but then, aren't we all?" Gene frowned. "You'll work it out. The worry is that it's been five days now, and no trace of him. There are lives at stake here, in addition to the loss of essential information he's been supplying. He has a contact at the University of Berlin in the physics department. The guy is part of an elite team of researchers working on Hitler's nuclear program. The Germans are on to something big, and we need to know what it is."

"You need a physicist, not a botanist," I said.

"Point taken, but I don't have a physicist. I have you. Besides, trust me. Have I ever let you down? Left you hanging? Of course not," he answered his own question.

I had to give him credit. Gene was a master of deflecting concern. He didn't address it, he just ignored it until it died a slow, painful, solitary death. I studied the photo. A young man, mid to late twenties, pleasant smile, good teeth, close-cropped brown hair, and eyes so blue they were almost violet. According to the dossier, Weiss was average height, medium build, medium complexion. "There's nothing to make him stand out. Just those eyes." I handed back the file, where it lay on the table between us, midway between the salt and pepper shakers and the water glasses.

Gene ignored my response. "The eyes. Yes. He gets them from his mother. She was quite a beauty, I hear. A film star back in the days of the Silent Screen, but she had a voice like a stevedore. She didn't survive once the talkies came on. Killed herself."

"Okay, life is tough and only the strong survive, but getting back to our *Situation*." Damn, there I'd done it. *Our.* I was already in Gene's snare, just waiting for him to reel me in, to mix my metaphors or whatever they were. I gave the slightest of head shakes—just enough to indicate, if not concession, at least a willingness to continue the conversation. "So, what happened? Or what do you think happened?"

Gene smiled. He had this shy little smile, like a little boy who'd done something wrong, not too wrong, just wrong enough to be bad and wasn't worried about being caught. He knew he had me, but I was going to make him work for it.

"You didn't ask me here to discuss the mother."

"No, I didn't. Although it's quite a story for another time." He lowered his voice. "Dieter scored big time when he made that university contact. We need this guy. And that's why I need you." He handed back the dossier. "Keep this. Find him."

I pushed the dossier back. "Why me? I know absolutely nothing about physics, and besides, I'm up to my eyebrows in research. Come on, Gene. I'm getting ready to publish and make my move for a full professorship and tenure. There's got to be somebody else you can send."

"There isn't. And there's no time to train somebody new. You're it." He ticked off the points on his fingers. "You're the best suited to the job. You speak German like a native. You're a Dane, which is almost like being a German. The Nazis are fond of the Danes."

"It's not mutual."

"You're a scientist, after all," he said, ignoring my comment. "You know how to conduct an investigation, interview people, ask questions, and you will do it all in the name of horticultural research." He leaned back and folded his arms across his ample stomach, daring me to disagree.

"You want to run that last part by me again? The part about horticultural research?"

Gene winked at me. "I knew I'd get you with that. It's brilliant! I called in every favor I could on this one. You'll want this." He pulled another folder from the case.

"You got any more paperwork in that thing? It's full as a filing cabinet."

"Just the essentials. Take a gander."

It always happened. He wove his little webs like an overweight, predatory spider, knowing full well I'd eventually get trapped. My curiosity always overcame my common sense. Inside the folder was an envelope, quite large, actually, and inside the envelope was a personal invitation written on highly embossed stationery. The University of Berlin, Faculty of Horticulture, was requesting the honour of my presence and participation to deliver a paper on my research on the propagation of hardy perennials at the conference, *Vegetation Mapping for the Third Reich,* to be held at the university June 17-19. The invitation was formal, as was the grammar, *Althochdeutsch,* Old High German. The favour of a reply was requested.

"Don't worry about the reply," Gene said. "It's already been taken care of."

"This isn't an invitation. It's a summons." I felt as if somebody, and that would be Gene, had pricked me with a pin and all my air had escaped. I shook my head, trying to find a way to end this discussion in my favor. The couple at the next booth were also having trouble with their own discussion, it seemed. Their voices had been increasing in volume for the past fifteen minutes, keeping pace with their beer consumption. Their relationship appeared to be on shaky ground. In addition, they were giving me a headache, but at least their noise level served temporarily to drown out our own conversation.

"Yes, well, you know the Krauts. Not very adept at the social graces—'*you vill do this und you vill like it, ja?*'" He permitted himself a chuckle. "You'll do just fine. They have no idea what you're capable of." The dossier slid my way again.

"No." I pushed it back. "My research interests are a hundred and eighty degrees away from the current fashion in Nazi Germany. They've got some very, very strange ideas, in case you haven't been paying attention. And when I write up this year's sabbatical study, they'll know it."

"Yes, well, that's about to change."

"Excuse me?"

"We can't have you going to Berlin as an adversary now, can we? That won't do. Your department has already agreed that this is a professional opportunity not to be missed, and the details have already been worked out. You go with their blessings and their instructions to glean everything you can from the proceedings." Once again, the folder was on my side of the table, but this time, Gene plunked his hand down on top of it. The folder wouldn't be traveling again.

The loud couple at the next booth had finally had enough beer and argument and had left, but my ears were still ringing. The lunch crowd was thinning, and so were my chances of winning this skirmish. I tried one last time. "Gene, you don't just up and change your theoretical base like...like..." I searched with desperation for a logical comparison, and the shopping bag offered up the best I could manage, "like a pair of dirty socks. This is my foundational study. This will frame my entire career. I can't change it. I won't change it, and you can't make me change it." I pried his hand from the folder and shoved it back.

He ignored me and took one last folder from the case, placing it on top of the traveling dossier. "You sound like a petulant three-year-old. It's not becoming, Katrin."

"Not becoming? Not becoming?" I was speaking through clenched teeth, and if I could have figured out how, I would have growled at him. "I'd like to show you what's not becoming. Do you have any idea what a year's worth of research looks like? Do you? My office has stacks of notes. Stacks. Everything's ready to be written up. Each of those piles represents—is a testimony—to countless hours of work, and you're telling me to chuck it all in the name of Dieter...Dieter..."

"Weiss," Gene supplied.

I could feel my cheeks getting hot, a sign of my rising blood pressure. "Do you understand just how much you are asking of me?"

"Yes, Katrin. I do, but I'm not asking any more than you can give, and there is nobody else."

"I lose everything I've worked for. I'm tossing my career down the tubes." I had a sense of time suspended. Voices rose and fell around me, plates clattered, and somewhere in the kitchen, a glass fell to the floor and shattered. I pressed my fingers to my temples.

"Perhaps, but you're overacting just a little, don't you think? Besides, you only lose if *we* lose. You only lose if *they* win. I'd like to think we had some say in that."

My mind raced through a thousand reasons why I could not, would not, do this thing, but in the end, I knew, as I had known all along, that I would. "Gene," I kept my voice as low and controlled as I could, "you bastard."

"Point taken, but game, set, and match." He slid the folders over one final time. "Your tickets and other essential documents. Also enough *Reichsmarks* to see you through, and two additional passports, should you have need." Those mournful eyes looked at me intently. "I sincerely hope you won't have need of them."

"I'll need clothes." As bargaining chips went, this one was pathetic, but if I had to compromise my principles, I could at least make a fashion statement.

"Of course, of course. I told you that Shartenberg's is having a sale. Get what you need and send me the bill. That reminds me. Hand me the bag of socks, will you?"

"You knew I'd agree."

"But of course. You just required a little softening up. I knew the lunch would do it. Anyhow, your accommodations are all settled. You'll be staying at the home of Professors Marta Müller and her husband, Erich von Reichstadt. She's in horticulture. You two should get along famously." He leaned across the table. "She's a rabid plant sociologist." He waggled his bushy eyebrows, looking for all the world like a rabid gerbil.

"Dear Lord."

"That's right. You heard me. You can bone up on her area of interest if you need to before you go, but here's the kicker." He was so pleased with himself he beamed, elevating his jowls to half mast, a sure sign of elation. "Professor Erich von Reichstadt is a professor of physics and, even better, head of the department. Bit of an odd duck, but he's your entry into the department, so work your feminine or professional wiles on him. Choice is up to you."

I groaned inwardly but kept my game face. "Right. Just one more thing, a matter of curiosity." I picked up the files. "I read the journals, and I know for a fact there's been no prior announcement of this conference. Did they just throw one together?"

"Pretty much. It's one of Himmler's little schemes, designed to showcase the Nazi's concern with ecological issues. They're determined to show the world they're nature's friends, but make no mistake, Katrin. The university is a dangerous place to be these days, as is Berlin itself. Anyone and everyone with career aspirations has allied themselves with the Party, and that includes Müller. She is not your ally."

I nodded. Allies. Circumstances made allies, and circumstances could change those allies into enemies. Just thinking back a few months, I considered what the lifespan of a warning might be, and I remembered a not so chance meeting with a woman named Margo Speer, sister of one of the most dangerous of us, a man called *Ronin*. A freelancer. She warned me then that he was active. Was he still? I looked at Gene and merely said the name.

"Possibly."

Gene was right. Danger was everywhere.

But politics and the university—there was nothing new there. I'm a veteran of those wars and familiar with those dangers. "All right. All I have to do is attend the conference, impress them with my research, which really isn't my research, find Dieter, and find his contact in the physics department. Anything else you want me to do in my spare time?"

"Katrin, I understand that your assignment would be easier if our mole had been in the horticulture department. Sorry about that. You'll do fine."

"Couldn't scare up a physicists' conference, I take it."

"We're dealing with Himmler, and, no offense, but everybody has some knowledge or awareness of plants. It's good common ground. But physics? It's not all that charismatic a field. Plants are universal. Physics is... well, it's... I don't know."

"Not exciting?" I offered.

Gene threw his hands in the air. "Nobody's going to get excited about a conference for physics. The Nazis want world attention, so that's basically why they've settled on plants. You'll be fine."

If he told me I'd be fine one more time... "How long do I have?"

"You'll have seven days in Berlin plus two days' travel time. Then you come out. The dossier spells everything out in as much detail as we have. Dieter was working as a salesman. Office supplies. One of his contracts was the university. You may be able to turn up something with that. And there's a longshot, but it might prove fruitful. Dieter has a half-sister. He's never met her. He knows about her, but as far as we know, she doesn't know about Dieter."

This entire scenario was seriously reminiscent of *Portia Blake Faces Life,* one of my favorite soap operas. Real life imitates art more often than we realize.

"They share a father, or rather, the same man fathered both of them," Gene said. "The father's name is Gerhardt Trautmann, and he owns a brewery in Rostock. Dieter hates him for betraying his mother and abandoning the family. At any rate, the sister's name is Kristine Trautmann, and she's a photographer working with Himmler."

"Himmler?"

"Yes, your host for the conference. One and the same."

"Small world. Would Dieter go to her if he could?"

"Your guess is as good as mine, but Kristine is a staunch Party member. Dieter wouldn't know if he could trust her. Be careful, there. Oh, I almost forgot the most important thing." He pulled a signet ring from his finger and handed it to me. "This ring, or one like it, rather, belongs to Dieter. It's how his contact first recognized him. It may bring your man out of the shadows if he sees you with it. Just a thought."

The ring was masculine. An embossed golden griffin leapt against an ebony background. "Distinctive."

"Yes. I had this one made from memory. It's modeled after the city emblem of Rostock, Dieter's hometown."

I had to smile. Gene was like a father hen. He sent his chicks out into the cold, cruel world but fretted the whole time they were gone. "I know, Gene. I'll be fine."

"Katrin."

I looked up.

"If Dieter is alive, find him. If he's been turned, eliminate him."

I nodded. There was nothing else to be said. I slipped the ring into my coat pocket, Gene snapped the attaché case closed, and our meeting was concluded. We plowed through the last stragglers of the lunch crowd and then walked in silence, under the canopy of the elm trees, to my apartment on Trumbull Street. The day had been oppressively humid, and now thunderclouds were moving in.

"There's a storm coming," I said.

"Whichever one you're speaking of—that one," he pointed at the towering cumulonimbus cloud almost directly overhead that was now tall as a mountain, "or the one we're both entering, it's been brewing for a while."

We parted company at my doorstep. He tipped his hat, and I watched him shamble off down the street, attaché case in one hand and his bag of socks in the other. As I turned the doorknob, the first flash of lightning creased the sky. I shivered, even though the air wasn't at all cold, and thought that, if I believed in omens, that would sure be a humdinger.

CHAPTER THREE

40 Trumbull Street, Apt. 3C
New Haven

The thunderstorm took its time developing and sent out a few test bolts of lightning before it decided to get down to business. The wind came first, a howling banshee that bent the branches of the elms almost to the ground, then the full serving of thunder and lightning, and finally the rain that fell in torrents and hail that pelted the automobiles and the umbrellas of those still unfortunate enough to be caught in the downpour. The buildup had lasted a good deal longer than had the storm itself, which almost seemed anticlimactic. If Gene's forecast were correct, this current storm would pale in comparison to the wrath that would soon be unleashed and that would undoubtedly cause more damage than any natural disaster had ever thought of doing. People say nature is destructive, but man is much more dangerous than nature and perhaps even more unpredictable.

From my desk by the street window in the living room, I watched the aftermath, as the fat drops turned to drizzle and the torrent of water rushing through the downspout turned to drips that spread across the grass on the tiny square of our front lawn. The sun was now shining through the jagged filaments of the spent, dark thunderheads, and a curtain of mist rose from the sidewalk as the dampness evaporated from the concrete. And just like that, the storm had passed. I had left the window open a crack, just enough to let in a little air and keep the rain out, and now I opened it the rest of the way. The clean air filtered in. After the rain, everything always smelled so good, as if the earth had been reborn.

The contents of Gene's dossier were spread out before me, and I was devoting a large block of time this afternoon to memorizing the essential information, since none of this paperwork could travel with me. I began at the beginning, which meant studying the profiles of the cast of characters I would meet during this assignment. The Agency had provided me with color photographs, an unusual expense that reinforced the urgency of this little assignment. I was currently working on the profile of Frau Professor Doktor Marta Müller, my hostess in Berlin. Unlike men, all women, married or single, displayed their marital status in their titles for all the world to see, and it didn't matter what country they lived in. Marta was *Frau Professor Doktor,* which translated literally to "Mrs. female professor doctor." In English, it sounded silly, but in German, it was traditional, proper, polite, and expected.

Marta's photograph, apparently taken at some faculty function, revealed a dark-haired and dark-eyed woman who wore glasses and used a cane. The attached biography noted that she was in her mid-fifties, was a full professor in the Faculty of Horticulture with a research interest in plant sociology, had a keen intellect, and a suspicious nature. I underlined that last part. Good to know. She had joined the National Socialist Party, but had it been out of patriotism, or was it just a good career move? Her reasoning might make a difference in our conversations when we talked shop.

Female professors were not common in the German university system and full professors even less so. Her status was a testimony to her accomplishments in her field and most likely also to some important family and political connections. Plant sociology was a relatively new area of research, but it wasn't the exclusive domain of the Nazis. There were members of my own department who were involved with it, and they were discovering some fascinating things. The crux of this line of inquiry was that many plants, like many people, prefer to live in groups with others of their kind. They have friends, other plants they get along with, and enemies, other plants they don't especially want around. Studying how plants manage to keep the unwanted ones away was an emerging area of study in the related field of plant communications, and researchers were looking into how the resident plants might have the ability to release certain chemicals into the surrounding soil to make the ground less suitable for the newcomers to take root, sort of like erecting a fence to keep out the neighbor's dog. This was a defensive strategy and seemed to be a safe topic for discussion, so I made some notes that might prove useful.

Marta was done. I turned her page over and picked up the next, Herr Professor Doktor Erich von Reichstadt, Marta's husband and head of the Physics Faculty. His photograph showed a man of about sixty, with blue eyes, sandy brown hair turning to grey at the temples, and an angular face with a square jaw. He bore some resemblance to Ichabod Crane. He was considered tactful and occasionally absentminded. He was not a member of the National Socialist Party, and I was interested in why he had not joined. Finding some common ground for conversation with von Reichstadt would be more challenging than with Marta.

The members of the Physics Faculty involved in the nuclear research program were next in the pile. I didn't have to memorize their life histories, just be able to recognize them and put names to their faces. This would take a little time but was doable. The ability to commit large blocks of information to memory is an acquired skill and had been my most difficult hurdle back in spy school. When time is of the essence, rapid memorization is essential, and we had been taught that the key to rapid memorization is visualization and association. You can't memorize things in isolation. There have to be relationships of one sort or another. Enter *Snow White and the Seven Dwarfs*.

Walt Disney had released the film three years before, so the old Grimm Brothers fairy tale was still fresh in my mind. It was a perfect fit. I was Snow

White, and the seven physicists were the dwarfs. Or dwarves. I never understood that. English is a much more difficult language than my native tongue, Danish, or German either, regardless of what the rest of the world thinks. Anyhow, von Reichstadt, as the head of the Faculty, the German term for Department, was a logical choice for Doc. *One down*. Eric Weber, as the youngest member of the team, was eager to make his mark. He had a brilliant mind and a gregarious personality. *Happy Weber.* That was *Two.* And on it went, until I had populated the entire cast, linking each name to a dwarf. I'd need to spend some time reviewing these before I was confident.

Then I came to my quarry, Dieter Weiss, our agent who had disappeared in Berlin. I could easily visualize Dieter Weiss without referencing his photograph, but Gene had said that Weiss was fond of disguises, something that was going to make a difficult task somewhere between impossible and totally impossible, unless I caught a break. I sat back and drummed my pencil on Dieter's nose. There seemed to be three scenarios. In the first and best scenario, I find him. He has either been ill or injured, is on the mend, and resumes his work. We have a nice conversation, I can attend the conference and also have plenty of free time to look up my mentor, Karl Förster, and take a side trip to Czechoslovakia to view the site where a species of low-growing *rudbeckia* (black-eyed Susans), had been discovered in 1937. I preferred that scenario. If I were honest, finding the *rudbeckia* and visiting Förster had been at the back of my mind during my dueling match with Gene. That scenario meant Dieter wanted to be found. It was also the least likely at this point. Too much time had elapsed. This was not going to be a cakewalk.

The second scenario was that, after exhausting all avenues, I simply couldn't find Dieter Weiss. This could mean he didn't want to be found or couldn't be found because he was dead, under deep cover, or in prison or a concentration camp. The bottom line here would be that he had gone off the radar either willingly or not, and I would have to return home having failed. It meant no field trips for me. That was, unfortunately, a very possible outcome, but one I refused to accept at the onset.

And then the third scenario. I find him and discover he has switched sides for whatever reason or reasons and is now working for the opposition. This was the most distasteful of the three possibilities. If it came to pass, I had orders to eliminate him. This was arguably the least pleasant aspect of the job. When I'd first signed on, I'd promised myself that if taking a life ever got easy, it would be time to quit.

Physically, killing is not difficult. In fact, it's quite a simple action, and we had been trained in a variety of methods to accomplish it. For some of us, the act is an exercise in power. For others, it's nothing more than a means to keep on living and eliminate a threat. It's more than that, though. It's putting everything in the balance scales—one life against countless others that will most certainly die unless the threat to their existence is eliminated. When all is said and done, the rationalizations don't help that much, and we all carry the scars and the burdens of what we've done. Some of us carry them better than others, but carry them we do.

If Dieter couldn't be found, which was scenario two, or had been turned, which was scenario three, my next task would be to make contact with the physicist who was our mole in the nuclear research program and advise him to lie low until a new office supply person, who would be named Rolff, according to the dossier, contacted him. MI6 had access to the supply company's personnel department, which was convenient and reassuring. It was about the most, and arguably, only, reassuring part of the entire project. Dieter joined the pile with Marta. I felt confident I knew all I could know about him at this point.

And finally, the last person in the dossier, Kristine Trautmann, Dieter's sister, or half-sister, to be precise. There was little family resemblance between them. Dieter had taken after his mother and Kristine, their father. She was also in her mid to late twenties, attractive, her brown hair cut quite short, her brown eyes a contrast to her fair complexion and freckles. Trautmann kept to herself, usually wore trousers and long-sleeved shirts, seldom wore jewelry, and was a vegetarian. She was a Party member and Himmler's new staff photographer. She, like Dieter, was originally from Rostock, a seaport town on the Baltic, where her father, Gerhardt Trautmann, owned a beer brewery. There were no other siblings.

The next question to consider was how much Dieter knew about his sister and whether he would actively seek her out. Could he trust her? How loyal to Himmler and the Party was she, in the face of possibly learning that her brother was an agent working for the other side? There was no record of them ever having met, although Dieter was aware of her existence, her location, and her current employment. That information had been given to him when he had accepted his current assignment. I caught myself chewing my lip again, a sure sign I was apprehensive, because I knew that if I didn't turn anything up on my own and was forced to contact her, I would need to tread carefully. There was no way of determining whether I could trust her or even be safe, if I *could* arrange a meeting. That was all I could learn about Kristine. And that was everything. Every person I would need to find or contact was in this tidy little pile. *I hoped.* Tomorrow, I'd review it one more time and then destroy it.

Finally, two hours after I had started work on the dossiers, I was finished. The realization, as I examined the two passports that Gene had given me, that I was the only blonde, blue-eyed member of the entire group struck me. The only stereotypical Aryan in the mix was there to ensure that the Nazi Aryan ideal never came to fruition. The irony was, for want of a better word, ironic.

In addition to sporting my likeness, the first passport had been issued to Astrid Andersson, a Swede, and the second to Tereza Novak, a Czech. I agreed with Gene. I hoped I would not need either of them. I took the passports, the 1,000 in *Reichsmarks*—a generous amount for any expenses I would incur, and my travel tickets to the bedroom, where I set them on the dresser. I'd need to add my own passport and jam the others into my money belt. This fashion item always traveled with me, securely fastened around my waist, hidden by my slip and skirt. Too many agents had lost their cover and some their lives for leaving evidence behind in hotel rooms or boarding houses when they went out. Once I snapped the clasp on that belt, those passports, the money, and anything else that became essential during this assignment would be my constant and very close companions, except for when I bathed, and even then, they'd be right at hand.

It was time for a break. I'd gotten more done today than I thought I would, and there would still be a little time to start on the presentation overhaul before John got home from the university. I needed a rest and a bit of a diversion, and it was time for today's installment of *Portia Blake Faces Life.* Portia, like *Helen Trent,* another of my soap opera favorites, was a scrapper and my kind of gal. She was a widow with a ten-year-old son, Dickie. Her husband, Richard, had been killed by the criminals he was trying to bring to justice, and Portia, "a beautiful and courageous woman," was an attorney battling the forces of crime, injustice, and civic corruption in Parkersburg, your typical American small town that was, in reality, a simmering, festering hotbed of nefarious doings. In today's episode, backtracking in time, Portia revisits the telephone call she received from a mysterious woman who warned her not to let her husband leave the house. And, of course, her husband had left the house. This didn't end well for him. It struck me that the husband's situation seemed to bear a strong similarity to that of Dieter Weiss. I hoped he hadn't made an error like that—leaving his hiding place and walking into an ambush. Sometimes the most ordinary action, such as leaving your home, can prove fatal in our line of work, just as it did for Portia's husband. Usually, though, not much happens in these fifteen minute sojourns into fantasy. A phone call and a lot of chatter. That was all for today, not much of a diversion and not much of a rest either, because I couldn't stop thinking about Dieter.

As I finished straightening up the stack of papers on the dresser, my eyes traveled to my left hand and my wedding band. It was a detail that I never looked forward to dealing with, but it was necessary. I twisted the ring from my finger and placed it in its special niche in my jewelry box, where it would wait for my return. In the meantime, the cheap costume jewelry substitute with the ornate rose, the ring of an unmarried woman who wished she were married, would be its replacement. I was now, to all outward appearances, that unmarried woman with questionable fashion sense. By the time I boarded the plane, my metamorphosis would be complete, and I would truly be that person. It was the only way to survive. One minor slip, one inadvertent reference to who I really was, and I would be in danger. I had lost a good friend that way, once. He'd let his guard down and talked too much and to the wrong person. One never forgets something like that. *Or shouldn't.*

The cuckoo clock on the wall chimed 3 o'clock. The carved wooden figures of the man and woman chased each other around in a circle for a bit and then disappeared back into the house. They were probably married. He'd stay inside the clock if he knew what was good for him.

The last item on the agenda was the presentation I'd be giving. The slides I'd labored on for so many months wouldn't have to be changed, but the commentary that accompanied them needed some political revision to satisfy Herr Himmler's requirements. I'd been chewing on my pencil, and I must have chomped down a bit too hard, as I could now taste the graphite. It was bitter. I wiped my mouth with the back of my hand and, sure enough, there was a telltale black smudge. Trying to think like a Nazi wasn't easy. At the very least, one could die from graphite poisoning. Tossing the pencil aside, I got up to fetch a washcloth from the bathroom to give my face a good scrub and nearly tripped on the stack of books I'd set down next to the desk chair. Undoing and redoing something for the umpteenth time was taking its toll, and I had an irresistible urge to give the books a kick. But then I'd just have to pile them up again, and I'd probably end up hurting my foot in the process. I wanted to kick those books, I wanted to kick Gene, and I especially wanted to kick Dieter Weiss, except I'd have to find him first, and that was the problem, wasn't it? I settled for a shove with the toe of my shoe. It was symbolic more than anything, but I felt better.

Shortly, I was back at work, having substituted two sticks of Wrigley's spearmint gum for the pencil. As I stopped to ponder an appropriate turn of phrase, I found myself transferring the gum from one cheek to the other, like an agitated hamster. There was a certain rhythm to the process, and it seemed to be working. I'd hit on an angle that just might work and possibly help me salvage my career while I completed my assignment. All I needed were five slides from my presentation that fit into my plan. Five slides that would be five bullets in my private little war against Hitler. If I did this right, I'd have my own *blitzkrieg* and there wouldn't be a damn thing they could do about it. With half an hour or so until John got home, it was looking as if I might get this done today.

CHAPTER FOUR

New Haven
Katrin and John's Apartment

"This is new," my husband remarked upon opening the front door and finding me sitting cross-legged on the living room rug, drinking a Manhattan, and staring at the orange and the orchid I had placed side by side on the coffee table.

"If it's not 5 o'clock, it ought to be," I said.

"No, that part you've got right. It's the uh—altar setup."

I nodded. "Yes. I'm trying to think like a Nazi." Lifting the maraschino cherry from my drink, I gave it a cursory glance and popped it into my mouth. "I think the cherry is all right, most likely an acceptable fruit, but I'm not a hundred percent sure. I haven't researched it. I'm not a hundred percent sure of anything right now."

"I'm a hundred percent sure that if we were in court right now, I'd go for the temporary insanity defense. What exactly are you doing?"

My husband was a law professor at Yale, senior partner in his own law firm, and a fellow agent. From time to time, we worked together. Life got interesting then, not that it wasn't interesting enough in the times between.

There are situations where words fail to explain anything, but I gave it a try. John has always been a good listener, and I appreciated that in him. He rarely interrupted, and when he did, it was usually because I'd gone off track, so I launched into what I hoped would be a reasonable and intelligible explanation. "To say it's complicated would be the understatement of the century." I gave a dramatic sigh, and not entirely for effect, because this drama was too bizarre. "Go fix your martini, make us a snack, and I'll do my best to make sense." I hauled myself up and followed him into the kitchen, not a very long trek, since the apartment was compact and the kitchen and living room sort of flowed into each other. Someday, when our lives slowed down a bit, I wanted to have a home in the country, with a garden for vegetables, a greenhouse for flowers, and chickens. I like chickens. That peaceful time, however, didn't appear to be going to happen anytime soon. If anything, our lives seemed to be speeding up with each passing year. It was a conversation we were going to need to have, but not today.

"Those," I pointed back to the orange and the orchid, as I settled myself in my accustomed chair at the kitchen table, "are weeds. If you can accept that, then the rest of the story is simple."

John paused with the refrigerator door open. The coolness was a welcome change from the oppressive heat of the day. The thunderstorm had cooled things down for a bit, but the temperature had been steadily climbing since it had passed. I detected a visible, slow shake of his head. "Weeds." There was that head shake again. "Sorry, hon. No takers here. The round orange thing? That's an orange. A Valencia, I believe, and that plant is the orchid I got you for your birthday. They don't charge that kind of money at the florist's for a weed. Maybe you'd better back up a bit and start at the beginning."

"Okay. Time to back up. Right." I took a measured, calming breath. "It's just that I think that I almost get a handle on it, and then, poof, it's gone, and I'm back to square one. Believe me, if I hadn't had lunch with Gene today, I wouldn't be sounding this crazy." The rhythm of the martini shaker gave a sort of orchestral accompaniment to this recital, and I considered what to say next.

While I was thinking, John remarked, "Gene had a busy day. Breakfast with me—two crullers with powdered sugar, two cups of bad coffee, and a telegram from MI6—and then lunch with you. But please, continue. My story isn't half as fascinating, and we can talk about it later. You were saying something about weeds?"

"I thought I detected chocolate on Gene's shirt front. The man is a food magnet. Anyhow, yes. Weeds. They have entered politics. Truly. I am not making this up. Everybody in the department at the university is on the ecology kick, and so are the Nazis. They, the Germans, I mean, created the term in the last century, and the Nazis have been developing the concept in their warped fashion ever since. On the surface, it all seems peachy. Stop invasive plants, only plant native plants, exterminate what isn't native, period, but it's become a metaphor for the Nazi drive for," and I delivered the next words in my best impersonation of newsman Edward R. Murrow, "*purification of the fatherland by eliminating all foreign intrusions.*" I stopped to take a sip of my drink, then got up and went to the pantry for some crackers. I was getting hungry.

"Weeds," John repeated. "Your assignment is weeds."

"No, that's my cover, but the background is that basically, *all* foreign intrusions are weeds. And this extends way beyond plant life. This means anyone who isn't 'rooted in the blood and the soil', meaning only Germany and its population of native Germans should exist, just so long as they aren't Jews or gypsies or political opponents or whatever else the Nazis don't like. Himmler's the one pushing this agenda, and his front man is Reinhold Tüxen, botanist and plant sociologist. And now, I have been recruited to sing in the chorus, when I present my research at Herr Himmler's horticultural conference next week. Gene's even got me an embossed invitation. John, this is going to kill me." I reclaimed my chair and took a savage bite of my saltine.

"I certainly hope not." His tone was light, but a crease had appeared on his forehead between his eyes. He was unscrewing the lid on the olives, or trying to. It was almost impossible to do this unless you had the grip of a wrestler. Finally, he turned it upside down, gave it a couple of hard smacks on the floor, turned it right-side up, and whacked it on the bottom. Miraculously, it unscrewed on the next try.

"Where do you learn these things?" I asked.

"I am a man of many talents." He snagged two olives with a toothpick, added them to the martini, and motioned for me to continue.

"Where was I? Oh, yes. Everyone is taking sides, and the popular side today is on the same side as Herr Hitler and the gang. There are opponents, of course, but their voices are being drowned out. Karl Förster—he's a botanist living near Berlin—is at the forefront of the voices of reason, but he's outnumbered. I'm afraid it won't be long before anyone who dares speak up will be silenced. We've even got the Nazi sympathizers here and not just at the university. The loudest voice is Jens Jensen, a Dane. Cripes. *A Dane.* He's a landscape architect, too. I am ashamed my country hatched him. And that's all they're arguing about in the department. It's getting serious. Jensen seems to have undergone some sort of conversion experience. He became convinced that native plants should be the only plants cultivated in the garden. It sounds innocent enough, maybe a bit eccentric, but it's taken on an aura of mysticism. Native plants and native people had a connection—a positive, spiritual connection that non-native plants and non-native people could never have. And, getting back to the beginning, since the orange and the orchid are not native to *America,* they are weeds and should be exterminated, according to this twisted logic. It would be laughable if it weren't so deadly serious."

John had finished constructing his martini and was now staring at the olive-laden toothpick he'd dropped into the glass. "No, there's nothing laughable about it at all." His voice didn't betray his thoughts, but that furrow was still there on his brow, and his motions were just a little too deliberate. I could tell what he was thinking. He was worried. So was I, but worry doesn't solve anything. Action does, and we both knew it. It was as if we had come to some silent understanding, and he soon shifted gears and began rummaging in the pantry. "I'm listening. Hold on. Where're the pretzels?"

"Behind the peanut butter." I waited until he'd emerged from the little closet with the pretzel bag securely gripped with his teeth, while he juggled the martini in one hand and the peanut butter in the other.

"What are you doing?" I asked.

"Dipping the pretzels in the peanut butter. It's quite good. So, native plants and native people."

I would never understand the food habits of men. He put the strangest combinations together. Peanut butter and tomatoes, whatever. I watched him—memorizing his movements, filing them away for a time when we'd be far, far apart and for how long, nobody knew. But, here we were, talking about pretzels and peanut butter while the world outside was going to hell. It seemed important and necessary to cling to this last bit of normalcy before we had to leave. I hoped there'd be another pretzel and peanut butter time when this was done. I pushed the thought away.

"Yes. Native plants and native people. It was a convenient association. The Germanic types were rooted in the soil. The Jews were nomadic. They had no roots. They were weeds. And, lo and behold, a rallying cry for the Nazis was born. It wasn't surprising when the Nazis embraced Jensen. They don't seem to think that conquering other countries in their quest for *lebensraum,* makes them the non-native plant in their *new* living space."

"They'll make any associations that they think will work for them."

John was spot on with that. Truth had no place in the Nazi military arsenal. If even plants could be drafted into their army, what was safe? Nothing. This foray, though, felt like a professional attack, hitting me where I lived, and I was liking the idea of striking back. *If I could just find a way.* I must have been totally transparent, because I felt John's gaze on me. I looked up.

"Don't get involved, Katrin. Do the job. Get in and get out. Keep your focus. How long are you going to be there?"

That was silly. I never got involved. Well, hardly ever, and only when it was absolutely necessary. Actually, the peanut butter on the pretzels looked rather appetizing. I stole one from his plate. "The conference is just a cover for me, of course—a simple, effective cover that will turn my world upside down, but it's necessary to track down a missing agent. And that's the long way around the reason I'm going to Germany. Dieter Weiss, one of ours, has gone missing. My task is to find Dieter or find out what happened to him. He's an interesting case, and he's not going to be that easy to find. He's a rather complex fellow."

John made one of those noncommittal grunts that could mean just about anything, but I took it as a sign of interest.

"He ran away from home when he was fourteen and joined the circus. I'd heard about people who did that, but Weiss actually did. He's had a bit of a bad deal. His mother committed suicide, his stepfather beat him mercilessly whenever the fancy hit him, which was fairly often, and the kid finally made a break for it. He's been on his own most of his life, even when he had a family, such as it was. He's only twenty-six. I've got to find him. Problem is, he's fond of disguises and he's a risk taker. That's going to make it tough." I took a healthy swallow of my Manhattan. "I am not going to get personally involved. Don't look at me like that." John took the glass and poured me another two fingers of hooch, which I accepted with appreciation.

"So, for the cause, I shall extol the virtues of Himmler, Tüxen, Jensen, and Karl Seifert—he's Himmler's 'Reich Landscape Attorney'. His nickname in the Party is Mr. Mother Earth." I took another pretzel.

We sat together at the table and munched our pretzels and drank our drinks. "That's my *Tale of Two Cities—New Haven and Berlin*. I've got seven days there plus two travel days, total time, to answer your earlier question. That's not much, but it's what I've got. Gene was firm on that." There wasn't a whole lot more to say. "What about you?"

"I leave in the morning for London."

The man was a master of understatement. I'd gone on for twenty minutes with my story, and he gives me one short sentence. "How come you always get to go to London and I don't?" I was still feeling somewhat sorry for myself, but it would pass.

"Well, let's see." John gave me one of those husband-type looks. "First, my last name is Breckenridge. That's pretty English. Also, unlike certain people, I don't speak any other languages except American English, and I've got enough difficulty trying to figure out what the Brits are saying sometimes. They tend to mumble. Outside of that, I don't know. You'll need to take it up with Gene, but be careful what you ask for."

"You and I both know that won't get me anywhere. Anyhow, back to the topic at hand. What will you be doing in London?"

"Actually, I was not being one hundred percent honest with you," he said, smearing another pretzel in the peanut butter.

"Damn." That was the third time 'one hundred percent' or a variation of it had been part of the conversation in the past half hour. "Talk. Now."

"You're not coming home to stay after your assignment. Just do what you have to do, and when you're done, be ready." He leaned back in his chair. "We'll be working together on this next one, but I don't know the when or the where. There's something big in the planning stages, and Britain is soon going to need us desperately. Something critical is on the horizon, and MI6 is pulling all of us in to help."

He touched my cheek and kissed me. Damn. This was serious. And wait just a minute. He'd never answered my question. He wasn't going to. He'd never told me what he was up to. And now this. John wasn't prone to spontaneous outpourings of affection. In other areas, he was extremely affectionate, but that's a private matter. My curiosity was piqued, but he wasn't saying anything more. When I finally spoke, it was the age-old plea of women. "Be careful, John." And then he laughed. It was a deep, rich laugh that warmed me all the way through.

"Yes, dear. I'll be careful." He rose from his chair, screwed the lid back on the peanut butter, and turned on the radio. Glen Miller and his band were playing "In the Mood." No more worries. No more cares. Tomorrow would come soon enough. We had tonight, and God willing, we'd have a lifetime of tomorrows. It was time to dance. And dance we did, as if tomorrow would never come.

Wednesday, June 12, 1940
3,000 British and French troops surrender to Major General Erwin Rommel at Saint-Valery-en-Caux

CHAPTER FIVE

University of Berlin

"Your request of six female students for the brochure photo has been denied. You have been allotted two."

"But Herr Kaltwasser, this is about balance." Kristine created an arc with her hands. "The women on one side, the men on the other, and all serving as the frame for Herr Himmler."

"You have been allotted two. If that is not to your liking, perhaps *none* will get the point across." Herr Kaltwasser handed her the requisition form with *denied* stamped across it.

Kristine Trautmann gritted her teeth and accepted her supervisor's decision with as much grace as she could muster. She'd requested twelve blond, robust university students—six women and six men—to serve as the frame or halo which would surround Himmler as he posed on the steps of the university hall. She'd been plotting out the Greek god concept, even though Himmler's body shape wasn't all that godly. Still, if she could artfully arrange the students around him, they'd provide the necessary camouflage. Kristine had been supported by her first boss, but now her vision was being forcibly revised, in keeping with the growing trend to reduce the number of women in the professions and education to allow them the opportunity to fulfill their proper roles as wives and mothers, with the focus on motherhood. This breeding program for women was a disturbing trend that seemed to be gaining favor in the Party. Still, it was important to remain on the good side of everyone who could either help her or hurt her. That much was obvious, and so she accepted the new composition of the group with sincere thanks. An old saying of her mother played in her mind: "When you dance with the devil, the devil gets to lead."

There wasn't all that much freedom for creativity in this new position, as she was finding out. The interview had gone well, her portfolio had been approved, and she had been hired. Why was everything turning into something difficult? How can you keep people under such a tight rein and expect them to perform? Those were questions better not asked. She returned to her desk to sketch out a new arrangement for her student models.

This was her third assignment. After she had successfully completed it, her work would be reviewed, and she would either move up in her position or be terminated. So far, she'd proven her abilities in the two small assignments she'd been given, but there hadn't been much that could have gone wrong. She needed an opportunity to show what she was capable of, but overcoming the bureaucratic mindset of her boss was going to hold her back. She set her pencil down on the sketch pad. Perhaps that was the intention. It was so hard to know what to say and what not to say. She slapped her hand on her desk in frustration, an act that caught the attention of Herr Kaltwasser, who responded with a frown and an obvious notation on one of his forms.

Her first assignment had been at the propaganda conference in the Eifel, a mountainous region in the western part of Germany. As a newly hired member of the photography staff, she had been required to attend the three-day event and learn the importance of using her craft and skills to advance the cause of the National Socialist Party. The second part of her assignment had required her to capture the essence of the conference on film, using both candid and posed shots. She had had more freedom in that task than she was experiencing now. The mountains had created the perfect backdrop for her concept of showcasing the power of nature as an ally of the Party. The storm that swept in on the second night was a bonus, and she caught the intensity of the wind-tossed trees against a lowering sky. It was quite dramatic, and when Himmler had been shown what she had accomplished, he had been impressed, as had Herr Engel, her supervisor.

The second assignment had proven more difficult. She'd been told to attend the next speech given by der Führer, Adolf Hitler, and film its majesty. She'd recorded his every powerful gesture on film, along with shots of the captivated throng cheering and intent on his every word. Her closeups of Hitler and the men and women in the crowd had focused on their eyes and the intensity of the event. Again, Himmler and her supervisor had been impressed. But then, Herr Engel had been replaced by Herr Kaltwasser. And now, nothing was the same, and her third assignment, covering Himmler's Vegetation Mapping Conference, was turning into a nightmare.

Professional photographers must work with both natural and artificial lighting, but most will tell you that natural lighting, particularly during the Golden Hour, which occurs just after sunrise and just before sunset, gives the best results. The light flatters most skin tones. It is soft and there is a pleasing golden or reddish aspect to the photos. Mid-morning and evening also work well, but the harsh overhead light of high noon and afternoon can turn the most gifted photographer's efforts into a disaster. It was this last situation, the looming disaster, that Kristine was attempting to address. She knew she was expected to produce perfection, regardless of the circumstances, and also that Himmler's work schedule was sacrosanct. She'd been notified that Herr Himmler would only be available for the outdoor shots from 12:30 to 12:45. This was the absolutely worst time of the day, and yet there was nothing to do but agree and try to work a miracle.

. . .

"Your biggest problem, Kristine, is that you want everybody to like you." Ilsa had said this with a smile, back in those happier days when they'd first been together, and it was accurate to some extent. Kristine wanted people to appreciate her work. It wasn't so much about her as it was about that, but then her work was an extension of herself, so Ilsa was probably right. She usually was, but with Kaltwasser in control, Kristine knew she'd never be able to let her guard down for a minute. She had to succeed. This third assignment was the end of her trial period. For whatever it was worth, her position would be secure, at least for a while. These days, nothing was permanent.

At twenty-six, Kristine Trautmann was the youngest person on staff. She'd been thoroughly investigated and confirmed to be one hundred percent non-Jewish with no detrimental character traits or previous unsavory associations. She'd been careful, and it had paid off. Tall and slender, with short brown hair and brown eyes, she didn't fit the ideal Aryan model, but few did. Her preferred manner of dress, trousers and long-sleeved shirts, gave her freedom of movement as she worked around her lights and backdrops, moving electric cords and lugging whatever equipment needed to be hauled from place to place. Today, she'd hauled some of that equipment to the front steps of the university entrance, where she planned on photographing Himmler. And so, here she was, two days before the deadline to submit her work to the printing department for the conference brochure, wandering around the exterior of the university with her light meter and measuring tape, trying to conjure up some magic.

Himmler's photo would grace the cover of the conference program, but first she had to deal with the issue at hand. There had to be somewhere on the grounds of the university where the light would cooperate. All she had to do was find that place, and her search took her on a circuitous route around the campus, until she found herself right back where she had started, at the university's main entrance on *Unter den Linden* at Prinz Heinrich Palais, named for Prince Henry of Prussia, brother of Frederick the Great. She wanted to scream. She'd been all the way around the courtyard twice, and the answer had been the same both times. There was no other suitable place for the big photo shoot. It was going to have to be here. She ran her fingers through her hair. Perhaps canopies? Streamers? What could mute the harshness of the noonday sun? She sat down on a bench to work this out and was deep in thought when a male voice intruded.

"*Entschuldigung.* Excuse me, I couldn't help but notice that you seem to have a problem. Is there anything I can do to help?" Dieter Weiss offered that crooked smile that usually got him whatever he wanted, but Kristine didn't even see it.

"I'm sorry? What?" She looked up to find a young man standing next to her, a concerned expression on his face.

"Your problem. Is there anything I can do to help you solve it?"

"Is it that obvious?" She looked at the light meter in her right hand and the measuring tape in her left. "Of course it is. I must look like some sort of madwoman." She gave her inquisitor a quick glance. He was about her age. Pleasant looking. A bit thin.

Very blue eyes—almost violet. She could envision a portrait with those eyes as the dominant feature, but the smile was a distractor. Regardless. There was no time for taking on a new project. "No. No, thank you. I'm just sorting out a logistical concern. Thank you all the same." She turned her head away, dismissing him. It was apparent he was interested in her and not her problem. Men. They were all alike. Uniformed or not, all they wanted was a chance at sex.

"Kristine." It was all he said, but it was enough.

She turned her shoulders so she could face him. "Do I know you?"

Dieter studied the face of the young woman he had finally met. She still resembled, to a considerable degree, the young girl in the picture. "No, you don't know me. Please, if I may, my name is Dieter Weiss." He took one deep breath and continued. "This is going to sound nuts, but I promise, first off, I am not nuts and I mean you no harm." He paused, waiting for some kind of reaction, but Kristine just stared at him, and so he continued. "I rehearsed over and over what I would say to you when we finally met, and now I can't remember anything I had memorized." He took the envelope from his pocket and handed it to her. "This will explain better than I can. Please, read it. I'll wait. There's time enough for that." He looked at the bench and extended his hand. "May I?"

She gave him a quizzical look. "Be my guest." She moved to the side, increasing the space between them, then slipped the letter from the envelope, all the while watching him. Within the letter was a photograph. "This is a picture of me. Where did you get this?"

"Please, Kristine." He shook his head. "Read the letter. I promise it will explain everything."

She shrugged but did what he asked, and when she had finished, she carefully refolded the letter and returned it, along with the photograph, to the envelope. "Now I'm afraid I'm the one who doesn't know what to say." Her eyes searched his face.

"The timing is all wrong, I know," he said. "Nobody trusts anybody right now, not even people you know, and here I am, a stranger, asking you to trust me when I tell you I am your brother, based on one letter and a photograph." He tried once more, a twinge of desperation in his voice. "I wish I had more proof, but you can talk to your father. That's all I can offer. He will tell you that I am not lying, that he wrote the letter, that he was married to my mother, and that I am his son. If there were time, I would come back tomorrow, after you'd had a chance to speak with him. But there is no time, and this will be our only meeting. Please believe that what I tell you is true."

"If you were Gestapo, you'd most certainly have a better story, hard evidence, and definitely a more flattering photograph of me."

"Undoubtedly."

"But why now, after so many years? What do you want from me?" Her eyes narrowed in suspicion. "Is this some sort of loyalty test?"

Dieter gave a sad smile. "I don't want anything from you, at all. I just wanted to meet you—*had* to meet you—before I left. I've gone through so many different ways we could have had this meeting. I am sorry it had to be like this." His gaze was intense, the last vestiges of hope in his eyes.

"You have to admit, this is difficult to believe."

"Yes. I know." He turned to stare at the concourse where students were going to and from classes. "All right," he said, turning back to her. "I've got it. Ask me something. Anything that I would know if I am telling the truth. That's what they do in the movies to find out if somebody is a spy. You know, 'Who's the pitcher for the New York Yankees?' or something like that. At least, it happened in one movie I saw."

"You're serious."

"As serious as I've ever been in my life. Please, Kristine."

"All right." She gave him a hard look and then seemed to soften. "Let me think." She looked again at the letter. "Okay," she said, "All right. What did Papa call his fishing boat?" She folded her hands in her lap and waited.

Total disbelief spread across Dieter's face. "Papa? Fish? He hates the water. He wouldn't go near a boat to save his life."

Finally, Kristine smiled. "I believe you," she said at last and touched his cheek. "This is so unbelievable it has to be true." She said the words with something like wonder. "I have a brother." Her smile broadened. "I have a brother!" Then she paused. "Are there any more of us?"

"You know, I don't know. Anything's possible, I guess, but that's something else for you to take up with your father. What I do know is that you are my sister and the best thing that's ever happened to me."

Kristine mouthed the word *sister.* "But how did you find me? Did you talk to Papa?"

"No, I didn't and I won't, but it wasn't all that hard. I mean, well, there's quite a lot more to the story, but once I knew you were in Berlin, I just kept at it, and finally I saw your name in the paper for this," he waved his arm around the courtyard, "and hoped you'd show up. And you did! That was easy. Figuring out what to say when I saw you was the hardest part."

"I never would have thought..." Kristine had run out of words.

"You're the only family I have now, and I hoped you'd want to know about me, so I followed you here from your home, trying to find the right time to talk to you and hoping I'd remember what I had planned to say. I haven't seen our mutual father, Gerhardt, since I was ten, and I don't care if I ever do again. I just needed to let you know that you have a brother, for whatever good he is."

"Dieter." She repeated his name. "Dieter. It's a good name. We have so much to catch up on. I want to know all about you. Where do you live? We can have dinner tonight. I can stop at the market. We can—"

He put his arm around her shoulder. "I'm sorry, Kristine. We can't. At least not now. There's a great deal more I would like to tell you, but I can't stay. If you like, I will write when I am safe."

"Safe? Why aren't you safe? Dieter, there's obviously something very wrong. Let me help you."

"No. There isn't anything you can do for me. Honestly, there is nothing I would rather do than stay and talk. I will write to you. Kristine, I'm sorry. I wish

I could stay. I really do, and I hope we can meet again in easier times." He rose from the bench and kissed her forehead. "I will write." He threw those last few words over his shoulder as he hurried away and disappeared into the crowd of students on the concourse, leaving Kristine with her instruments, the envelope, a thousand questions, and a brother that she'd never known existed, who had appeared out of the blue and who, just as quickly, had vanished from her life.

▪ ▪ ▪

The best place to hide is in a crowd, and if Dieter could have hired a marching band and a football stadium to ensure he got back inside his bolt hole safely, he would have. All he had, however, were his wits, his talents for disguise, and a good, working knowledge of his neighborhood.

Two months ago, when he had first moved to Berlin, he had taken the time to get familiar with his neighborhood. He'd studied every aspect of his surroundings. He'd checked out the side streets and the alleys, the dives and the markets, the homes with easy access on the ground floor, and the vehicles of the tradesmen who lived within a square mile. Now, he was putting that knowledge to use, because time, that most precious of commodities, had nearly run out. He'd delayed as long as he could and then had delayed a little more. But he had done what he had come to do. He had found his sister.

There was precious little he could be proud of in his life, but he had finally met Kristine, and he was proud of her. He had forgotten to tell her that. He would remember to do so in his first letter to her. Their meeting had been, above all, a new beginning in a time when so many other things were coming to an end. He'd found the one person he could finally care about and who would care about him.

It would have been better if there'd been more time. She'd been so excited, planning their dinner and their newfound lives, but it had all been so rushed and so one-sided. She still knew nothing about him, but in their brief conversation, she had said that she wanted to know more. After he'd been gone for a while, if she began to doubt what he had said, she could read the letter again and know he was telling the truth. She could talk to her father. Gerhardt couldn't deny the existence of his son, and there was no denying the picture was of her. One day, maybe not too far in the future, if the fates allowed, they'd have that dinner she had wanted, but it would have to wait. As soon as he'd reclaimed the microfilm in the morning, just that one more thing, he'd be on the next train out of Berlin.

He'd been moving along with the flow of students, but now he left the safety of the group and returned to the pram he'd left parked against an outbuilding. The doll, prominently visible as what it was and not an abandoned baby, waited under the bonnet, alongside the shopping bag that held his disguise. Everything was as he had left it. Luck. His luck still held. He redressed quickly. Nobody paid him the slightest attention. University districts drew the eccentrics, along with the studious.

As he walked, he massaged the tight muscles in his neck and considered strategy. He realized his pace had quickened, and he forced himself back into character. In the morning, he would need transportation, money, and a plausible reason to enter his old apartment without attracting attention. Hopefully, that would also mean he'd get out in one piece, as well. He was clinging to the shred of hope that the microfilm was on the floor in the bedroom and had somehow come out of his pocket when he'd put the letter in it. It was a long shot, and if it weren't there, it was gone for good, but he owed it to Gene. He had to do this one last thing. The only other possibility was that he'd lost the microfilm during his mad dash to or from the apartment. If that were the case, the odds of finding it were nil. How it had happened wasn't his concern. Finding it and getting it safely away were all that mattered.

CHAPTER SIX

Aboard the Yankee Clipper

In the end, I didn't buy a new wardrobe. I didn't need one. I certainly wouldn't be attending any fashion shows or cutting a snappy profile on the streets of Berlin. I was just being difficult with Gene. I felt bad about that, so I settled for some hosiery and a new briefcase, neither of which were luxury purchases. I was out of stockings, and my old briefcase had literally worn out and given up the ghost. The tape that I kept slapping on the catches to hold them shut was not working all that well. If I were going to make any kind of impression on my fellow botanists, at least I could arrive with my equipment in one piece and without having to constantly scoop my papers up off the floor.

Once again, I hauled the trusty Gladstone suitcase that had come with me from Denmark to America out of the closet, plopped it on the bed, and opened it up. The hinges gave a faint sigh of complaint, and I gave them a reassuring pat. The interior was lined with a lavender silk that had faded over the years to a pale blue, but these few signs of wear didn't affect the Gladstone's usefulness. One day, the lining would fray into threads and need to be replaced, but the suitcase was still holding up, overall, and I was fond of it. It was an old friend, and I'd traveled with it more times than I could count.

I never wasted much time packing. When one is apt to be called away on short notice, one develops a sort of routine, and stuffing everything into a suitcase isn't a time-intensive task. Apart from my clothes, which comprised one business suit, my pretty blue polka-dot dress and jacket, a couple of skirts and blouses, underwear, a nightgown, robe, and my fuzzy slippers, I had also planned for a variety of activities essential for passing the time and alleviating boredom. Agatha Christie's new novel, *And Then There Were None (Ten Little Indians),* and Raymond Chandler's *The Big Sleep* found themselves nestled together in my handbag. I also had my current knitting project. I was always starting something but rarely seemed to finish anything. If I got bored, I could watch the film they'd show in flight, *Gone with the Wind.* It wasn't the same setup as in the movie houses, but it was a pleasant diversion. They hauled out the projector, lowered the screen, and it was showtime.

One day, when I'd travel for pleasure again, I promised myself I'd slather the Gladstone with those travel stickers to show all the places I'd been, because in my line of work, that's not something we advertise. Pity, too, because I've been to some exotic locales. With John now in London, the house felt empty, and I was anxious to get underway. Shortly, the packing completed, the unadorned Gladstone joined my new briefcase and my stuffed-to-the-brim handbag at the front door to await the taxi that soon arrived. I was off to the airport to get reacquainted with the *Yankee Clipper*.

The first transatlantic flight of the *Clipper* had taken place only last year, and I'd been on it, along with Wild Bill Donovan, Gene's friend, who'd needed the fastest way to get to Europe to confer with the Brits about the turmoil that was brewing. That fastest way was the *Clipper*. The Vikings had taken two weeks to cross the Atlantic, the *Queen Mary* took four days, but aloft on the *Clipper*, we'd be across The Pond in twenty-four hours, and that included stops for refueling. Perhaps one day, we would be able to cross in a matter of a few hours. Life was speeding up, and it seemed to accelerate more and more with each passing day. If this transatlantic commuting were going to become a habit, though, I might seriously consider getting my pilot's license. At least, it would be good for domestic travel.

My second trip on the *Clipper* had been only three months ago, and now, here I was again, doing my best impression of a bouncing ball. If Hitler couldn't be stopped soon, perhaps we'd be kept overseas until he was. For now, it was a marathon commute. We boarded at Port Washington, New York, for the first leg of the flight, landing at Shediac, New Brunswick, to refuel. Then, on to Botwood, Newfoundland, to top off the tanks for the flight to Foynes, Ireland, in County Limerick, coincidentally, the birthplace of Irish coffee. It was there that I would bid farewell to the *Clipper* and board my flight to Berlin. I was thinking that I should just surrender, quit the university, and become a full-time nomad. A little voice inside whispered, '*you are,*' and I had to agree. There was no stability, no security, nothing of the familiar anymore, and it was both unnerving and exhilarating at the same time. Nobody cared about my feelings, however. Well, maybe John, but I knew he was enjoying his own adventure, whatever it might be, and, to be honest, I was enjoying mine.

Anyone can become a professor of botany, not just anyone, of course, but more people than can do what I was doing now, and that was a fact. So, if my departmental nemesis, Cynthia Lawton, wanted to pounce upon my academic work in my absence, more power and good luck to her. What she didn't know, was that if I weren't successful in my current endeavors, neither would she be with hers in the long run, for what we were doing was essential work. While the naysayers were preaching peace at all costs, appeasement to maintain the status quo, and were willing to offer up small pieces of humanity to satisfy the Teutonic overlords whose goal was world domination, those of us on the front lines were giving everything we had to *keep* everything we had.

It felt good to be on the front lines. It also felt good to be aboard the *Clipper,* cruising at the breakneck speed of 188 miles per hour. Flying was for the adventurous. We were the pioneers, and our pilots were the best of the best. The *Clipper* was essentially an air boat, and we took off and landed from the water with a boat shuttle to and from shore. Apart from radio navigation, which used two radio signals that pilots could line up until the signals merged, giving them a precise location, most of the tools used to transit the skies were the same ones used by sailors from the earliest times. Celestial navigation used a sextant to measure angles from the sun, moon, planets, and stars to the horizon to chart and keep on a course. Dead reckoning allowed pilots to plot a course from a known position using speed and heading, and they could estimate drift, how far they might be off course, from observing sea currents. Our pilots could do it all, so we could relax.

And relax, we did. The seats were comfortable and converted to bunks for the night portion of the flight. Also, the food was top notch. I think the Agency was trying its best to take care of us on the outgoing flight, knowing full well that many of us might not be present on the incoming. And so, one does learn to live in the moment, because that's all there ever is.

The stewards in their snappy white coats with black trim, their black slacks, and the white napkins draped over their arms had announced that dinner was being served in the dining area, and I didn't waste any time taking my seat at the table adorned with the white tablecloth, full setting of silverware, and the good dishes. I was thinking that the only thing the table lacked was a flower in a vase when a steward appeared with one that held a single rosebud and set it by my plate with a smile. And then the food came. Recruited from various four-star hotels, the chefs put on a five-course feast. The roast beef was done to perfection, the baby carrots in a honey glaze were just crunchy enough, and the baked potatoes with all the trimmings were delicious. The salad, a mix of fresh greens and tiny tomatoes, was served with a light raspberry vinaigrette. Dessert was a hot fudge sundae, complete with whipped cream, a cherry, and a vanilla wafer on the side. The glass of champagne was an elegant touch.

Pleasantly full and once again back in my seat in the main cabin, I searched in my handbag for my knitting. To the casual observer, the handbag is designed to accommodate my knitting and the accoutrements of femininity, but the padded leather trim that encircles the base and runs up the sides is the nesting ground of my stiletto. It fits securely in one of the side leather pieces, and there's a spring mechanism that can transfer the knife from its case to my hand in less than a second. It's come in handy at least twice, that I can recall. Currently, it was off duty but ready, nonetheless.

I was attempting to knit socks. After I saw Gene trotting off with his bag of socks, it seemed important to contribute to the cause. A noble undertaking, considering that the British forces were in need of clean footwear, but I wasn't having much luck. My needles kept taking turns dropping off my lap, and I seemed to be constantly fishing around the floor with my foot, trying to locate one or another of them. They often seemed to end up by my seat companion's feet, and my frequent apologies for bothering her began our somewhat stilted and mostly one-sided conversations.

The woman was a puzzle. I had her pegged as an Englishwoman, with her peaches and cream complexion, aquiline nose, strong chin, and thin lips, but she sported a hairdo with those twin hair rolls above her ears that said she was German. She had perfected the look that only the entitled can bestow upon the rest of the world, and I wondered about that. How do you get those eyebrows, those lips to convey such disdain while pretending to care? There was that supercilious arch to the eyebrow, the modulated voice in low tones that pretended to listen but really wasn't, and all the time, doing everything biologically possible to transmit the belief in superiority. I found it fascinating, although annoying, but I kept up my cheerful chatter for the hours of our flight when we were awake. As I struggled to knit and purl my way across the ocean, I determined to engage my seat companion in conversation once again. There was nothing to be lost and, as every agent knows, perhaps something to be gained. I gathered my thoughts, as I once again gathered up the yarn that was doing its best to take over my lap.

"Do you knit?" I enquired.

"Do I knit? No, I don't *knit*."

She delivered this response in the same tone as if I had asked her if she had athlete's foot. It was obvious I had chosen a poor conversational opener, and so our forced acquaintanceship continued across the Atlantic, as my needles or yarn intermittently found their way to the floor. It was evident we were not destined to become friends.

My thoughts then returned to my reason for flying the *Clipper* in the first place. "*Where are you Dieter?*" I tried to picture someone who was lost or running from danger. I'd never been blessed with children, although there was still time for that, but in some obscure way, Dieter had become something of a child figure to me. He was young, had had a troubled upbringing, and perhaps had found himself in way deep over his head. What would a person in this situation do?

I wondered. I could see his face in all its detail, a handsome young man with that pleasant smile, and I realized I was looking for someone who, quite possibly, couldn't be found. Perhaps he didn't want to be found. I wished I had the gift of second sight, but all I had were my instincts, and while they had served me well in the past, I wasn't picking up on any signals regarding Dieter Weiss.

The questions, a litany for the lost, repeated themselves over and over in my mind. *What had happened to Dieter? Was he alive? If alive, where had he gone? If he were dead, had he fallen victim to an accident? Been murdered? Had his cover been blown? Had he talked before dying?* A vision of him wandering the streets of Berlin, some sort of spectral amnesiac, passed through my mind, and I dismissed the idea as melodramatic, as well as unlikely. If Dieter were alive, he was probably in hiding, in fear for his life. Then again, I kept coming back to the possibility that perhaps he didn't want to be found. Where to begin? The most logical course of action would be to first check out Dieter's apartment. It wasn't that far from where I'd be staying. I would just need an hour or so, something that should be easy enough to scare up. If that didn't pan out, and I had little hope that it would, I'd go to the drop to see what was cooking or rather, baking, there. That also wouldn't take long. But if I turned up empty, I wasn't quite sure what the next step would be. I could try the sister. I toyed with the idea of checking out Dieter's place of employment. It seemed like a long shot, but if nothing else worked, there wasn't anything to lose.

I'd also been wracking my brain trying to come up with a logical or even an illogical reason for visiting the Faculty of Physics. If this were the movies, I would somehow walk right in without a care because everybody in the main office would be out to lunch. I'd turn a corner and find myself just outside the door of the nuclear research lab. It would be unlocked and unguarded. I would walk right in and essentially trip over the physicist I needed to find. If life were only like the movies. That place was probably locked up tighter than Eleanor's corset. Professor Erich von Reichstadt, Marta's husband, would be the logical person to work on. Maybe I could accompany him to work one morning. Time would tell, but time was in short supply. Regardless, I couldn't leave any avenue unchecked. I was impatient to get started.

Our plane, now fully fueled after our stops at New Brunswick and Newfoundland, set out on the last leg of our journey across the wide Atlantic. The stewards came around late in the evening and turned the seats into bunks for those who wished to get some sleep. The *Clipper* had separate dressing rooms for men and women, so while my seat was being flattened, I hoofed it to the women's changing station.

My standard travel dress was a navy blue shantung outfit. It was at least four years old, but it didn't wrinkle, and after sitting on a plane, train, or in an automobile for hours on end, arriving at one's destination looking like an unmade bed isn't professional. I folded it with care, arranged it in my handbag with my undergarments, and changed into my cotton nightgown with the pretty blue flowers, my matching robe, and my fuzzy slippers with the pom-poms and padded back to my seat, now transformed into my bed. I climbed over my recumbent seat companion and into my own sleeping quarters, tucked my robe and the blanket, thoughtfully left on top of the pillow by the attentive steward, around me, after stashing my handbag between the pillow and the window, and closed my eyes.

It's not that easy to sleep on a plane, but I did my best, until the turbulence began in earnest in the middle of the night. As the wind buffeted us, I could feel the plane increasing its altitude, as the pilot sought calmer skies. Occasional flashes of lightning lit up the night, but in our soundproofed metal cocoon, we could not hear the thunder. It was a game of cat and mouse, and for all its majesty, the *Clipper* was the mouse. It was a crafty and a swift mouse, though, and eventually outran the storm.

The plane rose and fell through this stormy night across a windswept ocean. It dipped in the skies just as a Viking ship must have done in the waters below in days long gone. I dozed fitfully. My seat companion, however, wasn't dozing. She was out like a light and snoring to beat the band. I was in awe of her decibel level, but in between her snorts, I managed to drift off. In my dreams, hands reached out to me—hands brushing my face, hands with voices that screamed for help, other hands encircling my neck. I woke in a cold sweat, disoriented. The damn yarn had fallen out of my handbag and was in a pile across my chest, with the tendrils reaching up towards my face. Hands? Not exactly. More like tentacles. Regardless, I was now wide awake. I jammed the yarn back in the bag. The cabin was dark, as was the night outside my window, clouded over, devoid of stars. I sat up and stared out into the vast nothingness of sky above and around me, knowing full well there was endless ocean below. A bit later, I finally slept, not stirring until the first rays of sunshine streamed in through the window and touched my face. Once again, the storm had passed.

I folded the blanket and took my bag to the dressing room to get ready for the day. When I returned, my bed had once again become my seat. I took a light breakfast of coffee and a croissant in the dining area, and I could now see, through broken clouds, the mainland far below. Somewhere down there were the answers, if I only could find them. Shortly, the pilot banked to the right, and we began our descent to Ireland.

Thursday, June 13, 1940
Paul Reynaud, Premier of France, broadcasts a final appeal for American intervention

CHAPTER SEVEN

Berlin With Dieter

The overweight mother left the bolt hole for the last time. Today, the shopping bag contained a pair of overalls, a rough cotton work shirt, a tradesman's cap, a pair of work boots, and, from the makeup box, a dark brown handlebar mustache. In the alley behind Martin's *Bierhaus,* a working-class bar three blocks from Dieter's apartment, he shed the trappings of motherhood and joined the workforce.

Martin's was the usual stop for the after-work crowd before they headed home to wife and family. It was also packed at lunch and reasonably well-frequented throughout the rest of the afternoon. In short, it was a good place to provision for the final push, and Dieter spent a few minutes checking out the vehicles parked along the street. From the three vans available, he briefly considered the benefits of the All-City Electric and the Custom Woodwork vehicles and finally settled on Gunther's Locksmith Service. His selection made, he entered the bar, where it was standing room only.

He ordered the house specialty, beer, and struck up a conversation with the fellow next to him. Taxes were too high. Food was getting more expensive instead of cheaper. His wife was spending too much money. Dieter gave a sympathetic ear, downed his beer, patted his newfound friend on the shoulder, and left the bar with a new wallet. Within a minute, he'd hotwired the van and was out of sight. By the time the thefts had been reported, he hoped to be long gone.

Dieter pulled up in front of his apartment, opened the door, and gave a respectable stretch. He removed his cap, scratched his head, repositioned the cap, and then retrieved his toolbox from the back of the van. He gave the gutter and the sidewalks a cursory glance, but, as he'd expected, there was nothing to be found. Clipboard in hand, he climbed the few stairs to the front door, made himself seen checking an address on the registry against something on his clipboard, rang his own bell, waited a minute, then let himself in as if someone had opened the door from the inside. He closed the door behind him and then ran for all he was worth up the flights of stairs to his apartment. Perfect. It had gone off without a hitch. His luck still held.

Finally, he'd done something right. That was a plus entry on the tally sheet, but not every entry on the ledger was of equal importance. Still, the bottom line, the final accounting was all that mattered. He just needed one more plus than minus, because his opponent was running his own numbers.

Stop and assess. It was another rule of the spy game that provided a measure of security in dangerous situations. Even when time was short, it was essential to stop and assess, then move quickly and decisively, but he didn't. Once inside, heart racing, his eyes first swept his lodgings and then, on impulse, he chanced a quick look out the window and that was enough. Another mistake, and this time, not a small one. The Gestapo agent stared back.

Idiot. Why the hell had it done it? An amateurish mistake and no way to erase the damage that had been done. He'd counted the steps from the bolt hole to the front door of his apartment. One hundred and sixteen. It would take less than a minute for the Gestapo agent to cover that territory. Desperate now, and with the net closing in, Dieter entered the bedroom, his one last hope of finding the microfilm, and then, luck. One more piece of luck. The microfilm lay on the floor by the closet. He snapped open the compartment on his ring and stuffed the film inside at the same time a sharp rap at the door announced that time was up. Again came the insistent knock, heavier this time. There was no back door and no window. It had been a bad choice for an apartment. One more mistake. The only way out was through the front door and hope he got lucky one more time. He reached into his trousers pocket and his left hand closed around the handle of the switchblade. He moved to the door.

The game was nearly over. His opponent was closing in, and Dieter was trapped. Absent a miracle, Dieter Weiss knew the next few seconds would determine whether he lived or died. His mind raced through escape options and came up empty. There was no shelter to be found in the hallway. No utility closet to duck into, no corner to turn and hide. There was only one chance. Flight wasn't possible, so Dieter prepared for the fight of his life.

"*Open This Door*!"

It was not a request. It was an order given by a man accustomed to both giving them and having them obeyed without question, but Dieter hadn't been all that good at obedience his whole life, and he didn't see any reason to start now. There was no point in playing dumb, asking who was at the door and what they wanted. The Gestapo officer wouldn't buy it, and Dieter wouldn't insult either of them by pretending the ruse would work.

If one of them were to walk away from this, Dieter planned to do everything in his power to make sure he would be the one who would, but he'd made yet another mistake. He'd left his service revolver across the street. The equalizer was a hundred and sixteen steps away. It might as well have been a hundred and sixteen miles. He hadn't thought to pick up the gun as insurance when he'd made his move. Now, forced to rely on the switchblade, he'd run out of options and out of time. Why the hell had he chanced a look out the window? He had no answer. It was just one more impetuous act, a lack of mental discipline, and from the moment he had locked eyes with the Gestapo agent, he knew this was the last act of the play in which they'd been cast.

His training had stressed one basic fact: you either control a situation, or the situation controls you. If you've lost control, the odds of regaining it diminish with each second until you've passed the point of no return. It appeared he had passed that point, but faced with the almost inevitable outcome, he still had to try. There was no other way out but through that door, and he didn't control the door.

"Yes, I am coming!" He turned the doorknob and stepped immediately to the side, giving himself a slim tactical advantage.

"You will come with me." Stated calmly and with authority, the words were most often the prelude to the hearer's death. Inevitably, they brought first a chill of fear and then either an attempt at flight or resignation. The first course of action was invariably fatal. The second was Dieter's only hope, and so he nodded meekly to the man with the Luger P08 pointed at Dieter's heart. In the instant that he nodded, the SS officer blinked, and Dieter thrust the knife into the man's chest, seeking his heart. His aim was true, and the man fell, dead, but as he did, the gun discharged, and Dieter's hand instinctively went to his side. He grimaced with the surge of pain. The pistol, having done its work, lay before him on the carpet. He bent to pick it up, the action sending another jolt throughout his body. He reached for the doorjamb to steady himself, and when he let go, the impression of his hand, painted with his blood, remained on the wall.

His mind now shifted to damage control. *Stop the bleeding.* That was the first thing to do. He went to the kitchen, took a towel from the drawer, and pressed it to his side. This was not good. If he'd just been standing a bit more to the side, he could have avoided the gun. He hadn't stepped far enough. He shook his head at his error, and even that motion caused the pain to intensify. That line of thought wasn't productive. He needed to stop the bleeding.

Time and luck—each seemed to be deserting him. There wasn't much time left if he couldn't stop the bleeding, and so he pressed harder until his fingers ached. As for luck, well he wasn't dead yet, although it was a distinct short-term possibility. How much blood could he lose before it became critical? He didn't know, but he did know that he needed help, and there was only one place he could get it. With another towel, he made a pressure bandage using the ties in his closet, then donned a jacket and slipped the Luger in his pocket. Stepping over the body, he staggered from the hall, down the stairs, and to the van. Sitting behind the steering wheel hurt like hell, but he forced himself to concentrate on driving. At least he'd done one thing right. He'd been the one to walk away, and once darkness fell, he had a chance. He had to hang on until he could get to Kristine. If he hadn't used up all his luck, he just needed to get lucky one more time.

CHAPTER EIGHT

I Invade Germany

I bid the *Clipper* farewell in Foynes, Ireland. Inside the terminal, the busiest place was the Irish Coffee Spot. It was a wee bit early for my thinking but not for the cheerful crowd enjoying a sip or two or twelve. I settled for a regular cup of joe and a scone while I waited to board the connecting flight to Berlin. The boarding process didn't take that long, as there weren't that many of us on this flight. Travel to and from Germany was not all that easy these days.

Adolf "Der Führer" Hitler had big plans for Tempelhof airport, portal to Berlin and Nazi Germany. He had big plans for all of Berlin, which he was planning on renaming *Germania,* after he'd gotten the Third Reich firmly in hand. The current Tempelhof airport had only been built in 1927, and, as airports went, it was functional and even had an underground railway linking it to the city center, about two miles away, but it wasn't majestic or imposing enough to satisfy Hitler. All of his civic improvement projects were designed on the grand scale to the tenth power. The new Tempelhof would be able to accommodate a hundred thousand people during the Luftwaffe's air shows and military parades, and a proposed stadium there would seat a million. He even wanted it to have a waterfall. Symbolism was of prime importance to the Nazis, and Tempelhof had gotten its name from the original occupants in medieval times, the Knights Templar, who'd spent much of their time handling the Crusades.

Symbolism didn't stop with the name. The entire airport complex was intended to give the impression of an eagle in flight, with the curved hangars evoking the eagle's outstretched wings. The curved roof above the hangars was more than a mile long. It was apparent that brick by brick and stone by stone, Berlin, in particular, and Germany, in general, were rising from the ashes of The Great War like ill-tempered phoenixes. When others had balked at the cost, Hitler had declared that the enormous scope of the project was necessary for national prestige. The message was clear. Everything about the airport was massive and a testament to order and efficiency. When completed, the building complex would form an entire city district. For now, though, the old Tempelhof was the only one in use. The new edition was being used as a facility for building combat aircraft and munitions. The workers were slave laborers, prisoners taken from conquered lands. Some were still children. Few would grow old.

There is something almost sinister about a construction project that's been put on hold. A sense of abandonment, a promise not kept. Awaiting my turn to deplane, it was my sincere hope that Herr

Hitler's promises would remain largely not kept, and I intended to do my part to help.

Symbolism. The Nazis had gone overboard with the symbolism motif, as it continued all along the exterior of the terminal, and arriving passengers were subjected to the full treatment. Red and black, the colors of blood and the soil, provided background for the ever-present swastikas. Blood and soil might be warm, but there was nothing warm about these colors. They were cold as the stone eagles that stood guard at the ends of the approach colonnade. Watching. Waiting. It looked for all the world like a movie set for a horror film. "Odin's bird," I murmured. Typical of the Nazis to commandeer the principal god of Norse mythology.

"I beg your pardon?" My seat companion, the same charming woman I'd crossed the Atlantic with, was fumbling with her handbag and gave me a sideways glance.

"The eagles." I pressed my back against the seat so she could see out the window and pointed to the carved stone. "The eagle is Odin's bird."

"Yes, well, it's our bird now," she replied, arranging her furs and adjusting the clasp that fastened the dead animals around her neck. The remnants of their beady little black eyes stared vacantly at me.

"Of course." I smiled at her, but she had already lost interest in me and was rummaging once again in her handbag. All for the best. This was neither the time nor the place. She intrigued me, though. Was she what or who she appeared to be? She'd come from America, and her destination was Berlin. Like me. For all I knew, she was engaged in similar work. There would be no way to discover the truth, although it's all part of the *small world* syndrome. We tend to meet the same people or the same kinds of people as we go through life, just because that's the way it is. We move in the same social or economic or political or religious circles as our peers and so we have a higher degree of probability of meeting others occupying similar notches than those who don't inhabit our particular worlds. Take, for example, the world of espionage. How many of us are there, actually? Exactly. Not all that many. So, it's not unusual for our paths to cross from time to time. There was no way of knowing who she might be, however, and so I began gathering my own belongings, which included tracking down one last knitting needle and sticking it back in the handbag and then unfolding my coat that I'd been using as a pillow.

"Welcome to Germany." The stewardess delivered her greeting in a mechanical monotone, more like an order than a welcome. Indeed, I had to admit I wasn't feeling all that welcomed, and a line from Goethe came to mind: "Enjoy when you can and endure when you must." I picked up my bags and prepared to endure.

Outside, the stairs had been wheeled into place and the first passengers deplaned. Finally, as the line continued its slow progress towards the door, my travel companion vacated her seat. As I moved a few inches closer to the aisle, a minor but much-appreciated victory, the air freshened. I stole one last glance out the window and saw that there was now an automobile on the tarmac with five Gestapo officers waiting alongside, watching the passengers make their way down the stairs. When I reached the doorway, I tightened the grip on my briefcase. Just as I stepped onto the asphalt, one of the men threw down his cigarette and moved towards the plane. The others fell in behind him. I bit my lower lip. Air travel was nerve-wracking enough, the raptor gaze of the eagles had done nothing to alleviate that stress, and now this. What did they want? More to the point, *who* did they want? I was confident they weren't after me. *Almost.* But then the man in front of me first stiffened and then bolted across the pavement. It was a futile action.

"Halt!" It was a guttural command, but the man just ran as if the hounds of hell were at his heels. Just as quickly as it had begun, it was finished. The crack of a pistol being fired, muted by the whine of the plane's engine, did its work and the man fell to the ground, his knee shattered. I realized I had been holding my breath, and I now exhaled, along with the death hold I had on my briefcase and handbag. With the rest of the passengers, I quickened my steps. No one stopped to watch as the Gestapo dragged the man to his feet and propelled him to the waiting car. It was like a scene from a badly directed movie, but it was all too real. *Was he one of us?* I wondered, but I forced my eyes to fix on the entry doors of the terminal. "Welcome to Germany," I muttered.

I wanted to get out of the airport before somebody else's number was up. The next obstacle was Customs, but with my papers in order, I passed through quickly, and quickly couldn't be quick enough to suit me. My companion in fur hadn't been as fortunate as I. She'd been detained and was now unleashing a barrage of insults at the official. "Do you know who I am?" she thundered. The commotion turned heads and also brought the Gestapo running, apparently what the woman wanted. After a brief check of her papers, they snapped to attention. She directed one parting insult at the customs official before ordering the officers to carry her bags. That they did made me quite happy I hadn't engaged her in any further conversation.

The last step of this gauntlet was locating my hostess, Frau Professor Doktor Marta Müller, and she was easy to spot, given the neatly lettered white card that said *Nissen* that she was holding, along with a bouquet of blue Forget-me-nots. Marta Müller was a study in brown, and at nearly six feet in height, she was a tall study in brown, and that meant we might be able to see eye to eye, literally. It wasn't often I found someone my height. Her suit was brown, her shoes were brown, her handbag was brown, and so was the hat perched atop a tangle of wiry, brown hair. The only interruption in this monochromatic color scheme was her black and silver cane, upon which she seemed to rely. Her face had an elfin quality, and the fine lines around her mouth that bespoke a nicotine addiction conspired to pull her face downward towards her pointed chin. I noticed her eyes were also brown, the color of caramels.

"Fräulein Professor Doktor Nissen?"

"Frau Professor Doktor Müller?"

And with the formalities of introduction complete, she thrust the bouquet at me.

"*Blumen*," she said. "For you!" She gave a decisive nod.

I shifted my bags to free up a hand to accept the flowers. The tiny blossoms of Forget-me-nots are so perfect in their symmetry with their delicate blue petals, yellow throats, and a dot of red at the center. They symbolize exactly what their name says. More symbolism in a morning heavily laden with it.

There is a German legend that tells the story of a knight and his lady out for a stroll along the Danube. The strong current had uprooted some blue flowers and was carrying them along. The woman cried out, wanting to save the flowers, so the knight dove into the water to bring the flowers back to her, but the current was too swift. Before he drowned, he threw the flowers to her, calling, "Forget me not!" And so the flowers got their name. It was a thoughtful flower to give as a welcome gift, although I hoped it didn't mean one of us was going to die. "*Myosotis sylvatica,*" I smiled at her. "Thank you, Frau Professor Doktor Müller. I've always loved Forget-me-nots. And they are native to Germany."

"Yes, they are." Another bob of her head. "And you must call me Marta. We will talk more after you have eaten and rested. My car is waiting, and it is not far to my home. The airport is most convenient." She bobbed one more time, and we started towards the main doors. We hadn't gotten far when our forward progress was halted. The press had the doors blocked and were interviewing the woman in fur with her highly official companions. I strained to overhear.

Marta leaned on her cane to get a glimpse of the goings on. "That looks like Frau Wagner."

I noticed the pride in Marta's voice, but my blank look prompted some further explanation. "Frau Wagner is a personal friend of der Führer. Her father-in-law was Richard Wagner, the composer. The Führer always attends the Bayreuth Festival. Wagner is his favorite composer."

That rang a bell, for sure. The Bayreuth Festival was an annual affair devoted exclusively to Wagner's work. What I hadn't known, however, was that Hitler was a fan of Wagner. They were two peas in the same pod. Wagner had penned an essay he entitled *Judaism in Music* in which he asserted that the Jews had no connection to the essence of the German spirit and, because of this, could only produce shallow and artificial music. The question was, did Hitler like opera, or did he simply like somebody who shared his own beliefs? It was a tough call, but the clincher, at least in my mind, was in the symmetry of the titles of Wagner's autobiography, *Mein Leben (My Life)* and Herr Hitler's *Mein Kampf (My Struggle)*. Kindred spirits and not a nice couple of fellows.

Curiouser and curiouser, I thought, feeling something like Alice in Wonderland. Scratch the horror film. This was a whole new category of strange. Finally, the crowd cleared, and the woman and two of her escorts with her bags departed to a waiting automobile. I stole one last look behind me and saw the customs official being escorted away from his station by the third Gestapo officer. It didn't seem likely he would be returning to work. *One week.* I would be here one week. It was beginning to seem like a lifetime.

CHAPTER NINE

Berlin, Day One

"And here we are," Marta said, turning onto Wissmannstrasse. We pulled to a stop at the third house on the right, a stately three-story home with mature trees, well-tended flower beds around the house and the walkways, and, from all appearances, a peaceful haven on the outskirts of Berlin.

"Your home is beautiful," I said, gathering up my flowers and bags.

"It's been in the family a long time. I hope you will find it comfortable. I'll let you get settled and then have a lunch tray sent up to your room. You can rest until dinner. You must be exhausted. I know I'm always a wreck after traveling." Marta led the way up the walk, her cane tapping a rhythm on the brick path. We climbed the few steps to the front door, and, once inside, she paused at the foot of the staircase. "Your room is on the third floor. The last door on the left. It's the one closest to the bathroom." She gave me a knowing look. "If you'll just wait here, I will get Barbara, our cook, to help with your bags. Heidi, she's the maid, has her day off today." She set off for the kitchen, in search of Barbara, and turned back to me just before disappearing around the corner. "There will be two other guests. Two more trips to the airport this afternoon! You will meet your colleagues at dinner. I hope you enjoy your lunch."

Barbara was a hefty woman with wire-rimmed eyeglasses, a steel-grey bun, sensible shoes, a no-nonsense attitude, and an apron that bore witness to her profession. She hoisted the Gladstone as if it were weightless and set an athletic pace up the two flights of stairs, not even pausing for a quick breath at the landings. I had a feeling that it was understood her kitchen was off limits to the rest of the household. When we arrived at the door to my bedroom, she deposited the Gladstone on the floor, gave a curt nod of her well-coiffed head, and trudged back to her domain.

The settling-in process wasn't difficult, as it consisted of placing the Gladstone on the cedar chest at the foot of the bed, my handbag on the dresser, the briefcase on the desk, kicking off my shoes, and flopping down on the bed to rest until lunch arrived, which it did precisely twenty minutes later, announced by a short knock on the door. I left the comfort of the bed and opened the door to find a tray just outside on the floor. If Barbara had delivered it, I had no doubt but that she was already back in the kitchen. I carried my feast, and feast it was, inside. A small dish of potato salad, a plate of schnitzel with noodles, two rolls with butter, a healthy slice of Black Forest cherry torte, and a cup of coffee. I devoured every morsel.

While my lunch was digesting, I took the brief interlude to review my notes for the presentation I was to give next Tuesday. I had done a bang-up job on nearly everything, if I did say so myself, and I'd done it in less than twenty-four hours. Still, I wasn't happy with where I'd placed my comments on propagating the *rudbeckia,* the black-eyed Susans, so I did a little shuffling and reordering of the pages. I reread what I'd changed, and it seemed to flow better. It was the best I could do, given the amount of time I had had to do it, so I shoved everything back in the folder and set it on the dresser to check one more time when I'd returned from my afternoon out. The clock was ticking, and I had no intention of resting until dinner. I slipped back into my shoes, grabbed my handbag, and set out to begin my search for Dieter Weiss. I stopped by the kitchen with my tray to save Barbara a trip back upstairs and to thank her for the lunch. I also let her know I'd be gone for a bit. It seemed the polite thing to do. Another curt nod. She was well into preparations for tonight's dinner and also tomorrow's lunch. Homemade egg noodles were drying on a rack, the aroma of bread in the oven filled the room, and two chickens lay on the butcher block. Marta had left for her second airport run, so I set out on my quest.

Public transportation was frequent, fast, and reliable in Berlin, and it was only a five-minute walk to the bus stop on *Unter den Linden*, the main drag that runs from the City Palace to the Brandenburg Gate. Originally a bridle path, it was used by Elector John George of Brandenburg to get to his hunting grounds in the *Tiergarten*. Back when John George had been around, he'd stocked the Tiergarten, the Garden of Animals, with an assortment of wild game, in addition to the resident deer. The Tiergarten isn't as big as New York City's Central Park, but it's a respectable size at over five hundred acres, with lakes and woodlands and gardens and paths that meander through it. It's always been a popular place for families and picnics and just getting away from the hustle and bustle of the city. It would be nice to take a picnic there this weekend, if my assignment were progressing smoothly. It would also be a good place for a meeting with my physicist when I found him.

A mere ten minutes after boarding the bus, I pulled the cord and was deposited at the university with a three-hour window to find out what I could. It would either be enough or not, and there might be few other opportunities, regardless of the outcome. I stood, getting my bearings and a feel for the neighborhood. Familiarizing oneself with new surroundings is important, and Berlin had a sense of newness about it, as much had changed in the fifteen years since I had last visited. *Under den Linden* was still a beautiful boulevard, a wide street where graceful Linden trees had once lined both sides, but most were now gone, having been cut down when the rapid transit railway system, the S-Bahn, had been constructed. Change was evident everywhere.

The sense that I had just entered a movie set kept recurring, and the swastika-emblazoned banners draped from countless windows only reinforced that feeling. It was more than the political display, though;

it was in the very air one breathed. Germany was different. Actively reshaping its identity, it was creating a new society with strict rules for membership. I was a guest, hand-picked for what I could offer, but my status could change at any time, and I knew it. The National Socialists, with Adolf Hitler as their leader, were like a vise, slowly and inexorably tightening their grip on the populace, controlling every movement, monitoring every word. Some would even suggest perhaps every unspoken thought.

I straightened my shoulders and set off on my quest, but finding Dieter's apartment on a working-class side street turned out to be a piece of cake. He'd wanted some place open and accessible, and, as I observed upon entering after using my picklocks to open the door, barebones. No frills at all. Also, no occupant. I stepped inside and immediately was hit with the realization that some desperate struggle had occurred here. Blood was everywhere, and especially by the door, where a bloody handprint on the wall testified to the horror that had occurred here. There was the unmistakable metallic odor, the splattered walls, the sodden carpet. It was all very fresh. Only around the perimeter had the red begun its transition to brown. I stepped around and over it as best I could on my way to the kitchen, where I found the remains of a cup of coffee moldering on the small kitchen table. Next to the coffee was a plate with a partially eaten piece of toast and a newspaper propped against the sugar bowl. The paper was dated June 6th. It didn't fit. From all appearances, Dieter had left in a hurry on that date. Had he then come back, perhaps some days later, and surprised someone in his apartment? Had someone surprised him? Had Dieter even been involved at all? From the amount of blood loss, it seemed likely that someone had died here, perhaps only hours ago. If it had been Dieter, his body had been taken away. If it had been someone else, the body had also been removed. Regardless, where was Dieter now? How he had left and in what condition could be well-nigh impossible to find out. The Gestapo didn't give daily body counts to the local newspaper. I'd found Dieter's apartment, but it hadn't given me any answers, just more questions.

The rest of the three-room apartment, while not moldy, had been gone over meticulously and not at all neatly. When? Again, there was no way of knowing. Cushions on the sofa had been slit open and tossed onto the floor. The sofa back also had been cut open. Furnishings in the small bedroom had been given the same treatment. Drawers had been pulled from the dresser and table and flipped upside down. The coffee cannister had been dumped on the kitchen counter, and there was a fork next to it that someone had used to rake through the grounds. The only picture had been removed from the wall and also flipped. Had they had found what they were looking for? No way to know. The closet door next to the entry was open. Two shirts and two suits lay in a heap on the floor, pockets turned inside out. The two pairs of shoes had had their innersoles ripped out and tossed aside and the heels pried from the leather sole. Then, I noticed the odd thing.

In spy school, they had taught us to look for the odd thing—the thing that doesn't seem to fit, doesn't quite belong, or the thing that is missing. It doesn't have to be something big; in fact, it is often something quite small, and that is why I noticed the closet held two shirts, two suits, and two pairs of shoes. There should have been two ties. There were no ties. The underwear, undershirts, and socks had been the only occupants of the dresser drawer. No ties anywhere. Odd. I stood, hands on my hips, and gave the room one more look. There was nothing left to see. It was time to leave. I closed the door behind me, wiping the knob with my handkerchief. There was nobody in the hall, and I met no one on the stairs.

From the foyer, I checked the street for anything that might be out of place. Nobody was standing by storefront windows reading a newspaper or casually smoking a cigarette. No cars were parked by the apartment house or in the close vicinity of it, and traffic was flowing smoothly. I waited until the traffic lights had changed twice, but no vehicle seemed to be circling the block, so I exited the building. My next destination was just around the corner, Wolff's Bakery and Delicatessen.

Wolff's was a small, family-owned shop dating back to the days of the Weimar Republic. The current proprietors were Ulli and Helmut Wolff, and, as one of the chattier paragraphs in my dossier had informed me, they prided themselves on giving each customer their undivided personal attention, a practice that often resulted in a long queue of patrons waiting to order their items and pay for their purchases.

Regardless of the inconvenience, tradition prevailed, and that was why, ten minutes after entering the store, I found myself still fourth in line. Eventually, I reached the finish line, and it became my turn to be entertained by Helmut.

My order was simple. Using the code provided in the dossier, I requested one loaf of the pumpernickel rye, without seeds. Helmut did not reply. There was a moment of silence. His jovial smile remained fixed firmly in place. He nodded and asked me to wait while he searched the racks in the holding room. There must have been quite a few racks to search, as he was gone a good two minutes, but he did return, shaking his head.

"I am so sorry. I know we had one loaf, but it hasn't been a popular item lately. I don't know when we will have more."

So, there it was, confirming what Gene had told me. Dieter, the one loaf, hadn't shown up to make his drop. "I appreciate your checking for me," I said. "Is there perhaps another bakery nearby that might have what I'm looking for?"

"No, I'm sorry." His face wasn't registering sorrow, however. He looked scared to death, but he continued. "We are the only ones who can make this. I wish I could help you." There was a note of desperation in his voice and his eyes betrayed a deep worry.

"I understand. Thank you, anyway." I turned to leave but noticed that a black Mercedes 260D, the favorite automobile of the Gestapo, had pulled up outside and two men were getting out of it. They had the unmistakable aura of authority. I shot a glance at Helmut, whose eyes gave an almost imperceptible shift to the right, towards the back holding room.

Well, that explained the delay. Damn and double damn. I snaked my way through the ever-lengthening line, putting it between me and the front door, before entering the holding room and bolting out the back. I ran full bore down the alley, my breath coming in short, stabbing gasps. Finally, I forced myself to slow to a gentle stroll before turning back onto *Under den Linden* two blocks down. I was safe for now, but how long my luck would hold was up for debate. This was an unwelcome turn of events. I walked quickly to the first bus stop and caught my ride back to Marta's.

The return trip was thankfully uneventful. No Gestapo boarded the vehicle and dragged me away, and that was a relief. It was possible, even likely, they didn't know who I was. Helmut didn't know who I was, so there was no way my name had been used. I forced myself to slow my galloping thoughts and go back through the series of events that had transpired since I had left Marta's house. Of course, it was a given that I had been watched from the moment I had deplaned at Tempelhof, but each evasive maneuver I had made this afternoon, starting from when I'd left Marta's home should have given anyone tailing me the slip. Nobody had boarded the bus with me on my way to town. Nobody had gotten off with me when I reached my stop. I'd strolled through the university, turning frequently to see if anyone was interested in my meanderings. Nobody. Not a soul. I'd checked all around as I'd neared Dieter's apartment, and I was certain I was not being followed. It all came back to the bakery.

Separate and analyze, I reminded myself, and so I did. The first thing was determining what I had done that would have raised suspicions. The second part was making sure I had logical answers to counter those suspicions. My manufactured reputation, courtesy of Gene, was one mark in my favor. My "*Heil Hitler!*" salute in response to Marta's greeting was another positive. The only way I had stomached that one was to remind myself I was playing a role. It had helped, but not overly much. I also had had my fingers crossed on the hand that held my flowers. That should have cancelled it out. Anyway, those were two positives. What else? I'd told the cook I was going out. Just the fact of telling her should have reinforced my harmlessness, but it also could have alerted her to inform somebody about my plans.

No, I hadn't done anything that could have been construed as being overtly suspicious, at least not until the breaking and entering, but I was fairly confident no one had seen me. The corridors in the apartment house were empty. So was the foyer. Everyone was at work. It had to have been the bakery. What had happened to give me away? Helmut was trusted. But then, trust can be broken. And where was Ulli? He was supposed to have been at the cash register, guarding it as if it were his own personal Fort Knox, or so I had read. Perhaps the Gestapo had him and the price for his life was for Helmut to turn informant on his agents, for Dieter wasn't the only agent using the bakery. What else? Helmut had left the front and gone into the back room. He had been gone long enough to place a phone call and then keep me in the store until the Gestapo arrived, but then he had given me a way out. I closed my eyes. My head was spinning.

If Helmut had been compromised, other agents were at risk. I had to get word to Gene. There was nothing to be done but find a reason and a way to send a telegram without sending alarm signals to my hostess or anyone else here. I almost chewed my lip but settled for drumming my fingers on the dresser, where I was standing while going through this marathon mental examination of conscience.

Then the fog cleared, and a logical answer came into focus. I could use my research as a valid and sensible reason for my sudden and urgent need to send a communication back home. I'd been doing a final check of my presentation and realized I'd forgotten to update one vital piece of information. I had discovered that one of the reference citations was outdated and must be corrected before I spoke on Tuesday. Yes. Given the German obsession with correctness and order that would work. I went downstairs.

"Last trip for today!" Marta said, as she gathered up her purse and two shopping bags. "First to the butcher's and then to the airport for the last collection. Is there anything you require?"

My timing was perfect, but then I'd been listening from the stairs until I heard Marta bustling about, a clue she was getting ready to leave. "I took a stroll around the university grounds this afternoon. It was a good chance to relax, so, yes, I do need something, if it's not too much trouble. I was reordering my notes and realized I had forgotten to properly cite my pollination statistics." I did my best to convey a look of appropriate concern. "Would you be able to send a telegram for me? The librarian at the university can provide what I need easily and quickly. I know it's an imposition. I can come with you."

"Oh, no. No need," Marta said. "Just write it out and I'll take care of it. It's no trouble. The telegraph office is not far from the butcher's shop. I'll just drop it off, do the shopping, and pick up the reply either before or after the trip to the airport."

I gave an audible and totally genuine sigh of relief. "Thank you so much. Just give me a second, and I'll jot down what I need." I ripped a sheet of paper from the notepad on the stand by the telephone and used the pen there to write: *Pollination stats. New source required. First in list is out of date.* I handed her the note. "Just let me know what the cost is, and I'll reimburse you when you return." I gave her a sincere smile.

"Very good," Marta said, scanning the copy. "All right then. And now, you must rest." She made shooing motions with her hands, and despite everything, I agreed.

"You're right. I am really, really tired." I returned to my room, stretched out on the bed, closed my eyes and slept until it was time to dress for supper. This evening would be the first public appearance of the ring. My first scenario, that I would find Dieter and this would all have been a tempest in a teapot hadn't panned out. I hadn't found Dieter yet, and if what I had seen today was any indication of his health, it wasn't good. Scenarios two or three were becoming more and more likely with each passing minute.

There was a radio on the dresser, and I switched it on. I turned the knob, looking for music, and I found gold with Otto Stengel and his Dance Orchestra. "Don't Say Goodbye" was playing, and I hummed along as I changed into the cream blouse with the cap sleeves and high neckline that showed the ring on its chain to good advantage, my slightly flared six gore aquamarine chambray skirt, and my black pumps. When one is close to six feet tall, high heels are not in the wardrobe closet. A light application of face powder from my trusty compact with the secret compartment, currently empty, and a touch of lipstick from the tube, also with its own hiding space and also currently vacant, completed my first night's ensemble.

I descended the stairs to meet my fellow houseguests and presenters at the conference, Herr Professor Doktor Stefan Bauer, who would be delivering his talk on fungi, Herr Professor Doktor Jürgen Winkler, who specialized in bacteria, and my host, Herr Professor Doktor Erich von Reichstadt, the odd man out, being a physicist. Horticulture is a diverse field, and the lines separating it from biology or genetics can get blurred. As far as I knew, though, physics hadn't entered the horticultural umbrella, so the conversation was centering on beer, as evidenced by the already half-empty glasses in hand. The gentlemen had wasted no time, that was for sure, and they turned to acknowledge my presence as I entered the parlor.

"*Guten Abend,*" I said. "I am Fräulein Professor Doktor Katrin Nissen."

Their responses were enlightening. Winkler set his glass down and made a stiff bow. I wasn't sure, but I think he might have even clicked his heels together. He was slightly beyond middle-age, more stout than thin, but with the physique of a man who might have had an athletic past. His nose appeared to have been broken on more than one occasion, perhaps a consequence of some time spent in the boxing ring. His round face and ruddy complexion bespoke someone who enjoyed both alcohol and the outdoors in equal proportions. "*Guten Abend,*" constituted the sum of his remarks. He reclaimed his beer.

"*Guten Abend.*" This greeting came from Bauer, young, trim, and obviously fit. He also set down his drink and accepted my outstretched hand of greeting, shook it once, and let it drop, as if he were a fly fisherman engaged in catch and release, although he gave a slight wink before he also returned to the beer.

And finally, von Reichstadt, who smiled warmly. "*Guten Abend.* I am Herr Professor Doktor Erik von Reichstadt. Please, join us." Von Reichstadt appeared older than his photograph. His shoulders seemed a bit more stooped, his complexion had a greyish tinge, and I noted that his hand, the one not occupied with his beer, had a slight tremor.

Join them, I did. The conversation began somewhat awkwardly, as we sought safe ground. In deference to von Reichstadt, we didn't talk shop. In deference to all of us, we didn't discuss politics. That left the weather. It had been quite warm and sunny. Exhausting that, we settled on a topic we could all contribute to without fear. Beer.

Beer is the elixir of life, and the only things Germans love more than talking about beer are drinking it and brewing it. Beer didn't originate in Germany, which, as a horticulturist, I found intriguing. It traces its roots to pre-agricultural times in the middle East, but its cultivation soon spread. People liked the way it tasted, and when the monasteries in southern Germany began the first breweries around the first millennium, the future of beer in Germany was assured. In the early days, beer was safer to drink than water and even children drank it. It became firmly cemented in the culture and became a staple in the German diet. Simply put, beer is to Germans what wine is to the French and vodka to the Russians.

Ingredients-wise, beer is uncomplicated. Hops, malt, and water were the only ingredients originally allowed, according to the *Reinheitsgebot,* or purity law, with yeast coming along later. Once people agreed that beer was here to stay, Bavaria became home to a good portion of the beer produced in the country, and for good reason, a fact that Jürgen Winkler was driving home to us. That's when we began to talk shop, even though we hadn't planned on it.

"While hops is not native, of course, there is a certain type that grows mostly in a region of Bavaria north of Munich called the *Hallertau,* a region famous for producing some of the finest beer in the world." He took a healthy swallow that finished off what remained in his glass. "So, the fact that it grows so well here must indicate that it does indeed belong."

I couldn't resist. "Naturalization for desirable plants—just like naturalization for citizenship for desirable people."

"Novel perspective, but yes. The female hops plant, *Humulus lupulus*, produces a cone-shaped flower, and the small, yellow pods inside the flower contain oils and resins that give this beer its flavor, aroma, bitterness, and stability. There is something unique about the genetics of this hops plant and its flower that haven't been duplicated anywhere else." With his mini-dissertation on hops completed, Winkler went to refill his glass.

We filled our plates with the cold meats and cheeses set out for us and continued to debate, with enthusiasm, the merits of three Bavarian beers. Pilsner was my choice. Pilsner is a pale lager and takes its name from the Bohemian town of Pilsen, where it is brewed. It's got a crisp taste, which I prefer. Dunkel, a dark Bavarian beer with a stronger, maltier taste was Winkler's beverage. The malt used in brewing beer generally comes from barley, but wheat is also used, and that is why Bauer was extolling the virtues of his wheat beer, Hefeweizen, another product of Bavaria.

Our meal contained everything Germans love. In addition to beer, there was bread, another German passion. Having lived in the States for so many years, I had almost forgotten how important bread is to Europeans. There was bread for breakfast, bread for lunch, bread for dinner. Bread came in the form of rolls or loaves. It was something not lightly dismissed. It's an essential component of every meal, and there were more varieties and textures of bread than would seem possible. Tonight's sandwiches were liverwurst on *Schwarzbrot,* a dark, almost black rye, and they were quite tasty and chewy. Winkel made a dramatic gesture, holding aloft his dark Dunkel with the dark bread and declared himself the victor of the beer comparison discussion. I couldn't help but think that beer would have been a far better choice for a national emblem than the swastika. It's definitely healthier and makes people friendlier. Eventually, the conversation wore down, and so did we. Not too long after we had finished with supper, we retired to our rooms.

The reply to my telegram was waiting for me on the table by the foot of the stairs, and I paused to open the Western Union envelope. The paper inside contained three concise lines of text—two merely gave a current reference to pollination statistics that would fit my data, and the third, a brief, *librarian says hello!* let me know my husband was safe. The reassurance was comforting. As always, Gene had come through. The man was, quite simply, a genius. Once again, back in my room, it seemed only appropriate to make the necessary correction to the citation in my presentation to justify the errand. I took the folder out of my briefcase one last time.

There comes a time in dealing with an article for publication, a presentation, or even a book one is writing, that familiarity breeds not just contempt but something akin to abject hatred and utter loathing, and this was coming close to defining my feelings towards this stack of paper. Still, one more time through was the right thing to do, and I leafed through the pages once more, checking for omissions and any corrections that required my attention before tackling the citations at the end.

It shouldn't have come as a surprise, and it didn't. Somebody had gone through my presentation while I had been out. I think I would have almost been disappointed if they hadn't, but they'd made an amateur's mistake. The pages I had transposed were now repositioned to be numerically consecutive. The German compulsion for order had tripped up whoever had done the deed. Nothing was missing, but somebody had most certainly gone through everything. I set the papers down and considered what had happened, as if it were an academic problem which, in a sense, it was. My presentation research was solid but not groundbreaking in any sense—I certainly hadn't planned on sharing anything that might help the Nazis at their conference. I wasn't in danger of being exposed as a fraud, and the work wouldn't benefit anyone. At least, I couldn't see how it would. And first they'd have to translate it. I'd written everything in Danish for my own convenience partly, but also for just this eventuality. It would take time for someone to get everything translated. This was vexing. It would be nice to know who was doing this and why. There was nothing to be gained by this, unless someone was trying to make life difficult for me or make me look incompetent at the conference. That would make it a personal attack, not a professional one.

Who? For the first part of the puzzle, the only people I had met since I had been in the house were Marta, Erich, and Barbara, the cook. I'd only just met Winkler and Bauer, but their interests were in a different area. I couldn't fathom why they'd be plowing through mine. Still, they had been in the house long enough to have done some snooping, if that had been their intent. That didn't mean there weren't others who could be the culprit. It was a large house, and there was Heidi, the maid, and I suspected there was a housekeeper, as well, and who knew who else there might be. A gardener? I couldn't know.

For the second part, only two explanations seemed logical for motive. Either somebody wanted to sneak a look at my research for professional gain, or somebody wanted to find out if there was anything else to learn about me for whatever reasons. Was there a Gestapo plant in the house? That was a possibility. Possibly even a probability. The professional snooper at work was not unexpected. People have been stealing other people's research forever, although, with the public airing of my work coming within the next few days, there wouldn't be much time to learn enough to credibly add to a weak paper to improve its reception at the conference. No, it seemed more likely and more plausible that this was a deliberate, if clandestine, loyalty check. In the current political climate, trust was a bygone commodity, and nobody, foreign or domestic, could be pure enough. Everyone was under surveillance, and everyone was under suspicion. It made me appreciate my adopted country all the more. One could speak one's mind. Would it ever be this way in Germany again? Not anytime soon, the way things were heading.

It was distressing, but I reordered the papers as they belonged, replaced them in the briefcase, and set the case down by the bed. In my line of work, one expects to have one's personal space violated—sometimes on a regular basis. After all, it's part of what we do. We insinuate ourselves into places, peoples' lives, and whatever else we need to in order to get the job done. Regardless, the snoop had found nothing incriminating. I just wished that whoever had done the deed had been a bit more careful with the lock. There were still some basic rules to the game. We were professionals, and regardless of the side, there was still a certain adherence to a code of honor. Destruction for its own purpose didn't belong. I ran my hand across the leather. There was now a nasty scratch on my brand new briefcase, and I think that bothered me more than anything.

CHAPTER TEN

University of Berlin

Kristine Trautmann had spent all of Wednesday morning at the university, blocking out every photo she needed to set up for the three days of the conference. The first item she'd tackled was the background, where she focused on eliminating distractors that would ruin a good shot. She'd made a list of signs to be removed, trash cans to be relocated, two benches and three planters in the line of sight of the main entrance to the auditorium, and the automobiles parked in random places—the wrong places.

Then there were the additions she needed to make. The planters, once moved to the outer walkway, needed to contain native plants. She'd ask Kaltwasser to approve delivery from a local nursery. If she were going to get past Kaltwasser's *Denied* stamp, she'd need to put a small explanation by every request. It was time-consuming, but necessary. The setting needed to be perfect. This was drama, and she needed staging. But what if he denied everything? No, that wasn't possible when she was essentially creating a propaganda poster. She'd explain that she needed someone from that department. If only Kaltwasser would approve her requests, it would be a feather in his cap. Yes. That was the angle to work. She'd appeal to Kaltwasser's vanity, and she would request that he ask for Ilsa, as she'd be the most qualified for the job. It would also mean they could work together again, and, for the first time in quite a while, she felt everything might possibly turn out all right.

Finally, just to be sure she hadn't overlooked anything, she'd spent all afternoon going over everything she'd done that morning. By evening, totally worn out, she was finally ready to head home, where she'd get the dark room set up for what promised to be a marathon developing session after the shoot. She needed to keep her focus on the job, but the unexpected insertion of a brother into her life was making it difficult to concentrate on her work. It was still hard to believe, but she had the proof in the letter her father had written to his first wife, where he'd apologized for everything he'd done, asked for her forgiveness, and sent her a picture of his daughter, Kristine.

What had prompted the sending of that letter? Loneliness? Guilt? Something else? How could he expect that sending one letter so many years later would erase the hurt and betrayal? It's not as if he were hiding a traffic ticket. He'd had another life. The next time she went back home, she would make him tell her everything. For ten years, she'd had a brother living so close to her, and she'd never known about it. Of all the emotions swirling around her mind and heart, anger seemed the strongest, accompanied by a sense of deep hurt not too far behind. It did explain some things, though. All the times her father had been away from home, sometimes for weeks at a time. It was his work for the brewery that had made him travel so much. At least that's what her mother had told her, and perhaps she had believed it. How much had she known? Had she known anything at all? Her mother had died last year, so that door was closed. Her father had led a double life for ten years. It hardly seemed possible. If someone had asked her to imagine the kind of man who would do such a thing, Gerhardt Trautmann wouldn't even make the list. For want of a better word, he was just too ordinary and not all that handsome a man, either.

Her own life had been so normal. He'd been a good father, although too controlling most of the time, the reason she seldom visited. Every time she went home, it was as if she had never left, and the arguments began again. But she did love him, and she thought she knew him, although now, it was evident she didn't know him at all, and she never had. We don't even know ourselves, it seems, so how can we be sure of someone else? Secrets. She thought again of Ilsa. Secrets. She had them. Everyone had them.

And now it was Thursday. She'd heard nothing more from her brother, but then it was too soon. *Her brother.* Those words sounded strange, foreign. At times, she wondered if the encounter had even occurred, but the letter assured her it had. Would she ever see him again? There was so much she wanted to know. Perhaps together they could sort out the past, but Dieter was gone, and he hadn't said why he had to leave, just that he did. The urgency in his leaving was confusing, but she had to let it go. Those thoughts were for another time. The job at hand was all that mattered right now, and so she turned her attention to the details of getting the risers in position for the first shot which would feature Himmler, surrounded by the blond halo of students, gazing worshipfully at him, while he struck a pose of leadership.

She'd lost the first battle of the gender equality war. There would be no six women, but she was determined to challenge Himmler's instructions that the two women she'd been allotted be positioned at the bottom step of the riser, beneath the men. The only way to be successful entailed using the Party's own words to plead her case, and so she'd reviewed her notes from the propaganda conference she'd just attended and committed a few relevant items to memory. When Himmler arrived, she intended to be prepared, and she was.

"Everything is symbolism, Herr Himmler," she explained. "Everything is propaganda." Himmler had dug in his heels, but she pressed on. "At the propaganda conference, Herr Tiessler, Head of the Reich Ring for National Socialist Propaganda and People's Enlightenment, explained this to us. He said, 'The role of membership and professional gatherings should not be underestimated as a way of organizing some parts of the population.'" She drew herself up to her full height and looked him straight in the eye. Once again, she was reminded that those glasses posed a glare issue, but she continued. "Herr Himmler, this is one of those professional gatherings, and it is a perfect opportunity for organization. I hadn't understood how to accomplish this, and then Herr Alfred Rosenberg, Special Representative of the Fuhrer for the Supervision of the Entire Spiritual and Worldview Education of the NSDAP told us that, 'Propaganda's task is to mobilize the forces, deal with current issues, and deepen the idea.' And that's why I feel it is important to showcase the Party's public appreciation of women as dutiful wives and mothers who should be protected by the men, and therefore should be on the middle riser with the men above and below, guarding them, deepening the idea." Her voice had been increasing in intensity, if not volume, as she reached the end of her closing argument. She waited, out of breath after the rushed outpouring of words, while he considered what she'd said. Finally, he agreed. She felt as if she'd just run and won a marathon. She accepted his decision with thanks and moved on to addressing an issue of lesser importance, the potential glare problem from his spectacles.

Finally, it was time for the actual photo session. There wasn't a cloud in the sky or any wind to speak of, but the billowing yards of red fabric, animated by the wind machine, swirled behind him, giving a romantic, emotional, and supernatural effect of forward movement as he stood, poised to lead the youth of Germany into the glorious Thousand Year Reich. The students had arrived, and she gave each of them a bouquet of native flowers before indicating where they were to stand on the risers. She was next on Himmler's schedule, after his 12:15 appointment with Herr Professor Kurt Kleinschmidt, Chair of the Faculty of Horticulture and faculty member in charge of carrying out Himmler's orders for the conference.

. . .

While Kristine was fighting her skirmish with Himmler on the steps outside, Professor Kleinschmidt had been engaged in full-blown warfare with his brother-in-law, Herr Professor Doktor August Erdmann Becker, in his third-floor office.

"For God's sake, Augie, shut the hell up and listen!"

Augie's face was now a deep magenta, having passed through a mottled red five minutes ago. "What?" he spat.

"I'm going to say this just once more. You *will* present your research at the conference. You *will* ensure that it conforms to the directive. And you *will* conduct yourself in a professional manner for the duration. Do I make myself clear?"

"No goose-stepping asshole is going to tell me what to research and what my findings will be before I even get started! Do *I* make myself clear?"

Kleinschmidt braced his hands on the edge of the desk and pushed. His chair, obeying Newton's Third Law of Motion, retreated, thus increasing the distance between him and Augie, if only by a meter. It was a marginal improvement. Marshalling his dwindling supply of patience, he tried reason. "Augie, try to see this from my perspective. This conference will make or break the department. That's your job, too, on the line, in case you'd forgotten. Herr Himmler is now

Reich Commissioner for the Strengthening of Germanism. Do you understand what that means? It means he's in charge."

"He's not in charge of me and he damn sure is not in charge of my research."

"God damn it, Augie! You're a fool. You're going to put us all in jeopardy. I can't allow that to happen."

"I don't give crap about you all."

"That much is obvious."

"What about you, then? What about your family?"

August Erdmann Becker, Professor of Horticulture and general pain in the ass, spun on his heel, ready to leave, but paused with his hand on the doorknob. "To hell with them. Let me explain it to you in terms *you* might understand. *They*, and you know who the hell I'm talking about. *They* take an idea, a theory, whatever, something with a germ of promise or a kernel of truth, and then they twist it ever so slightly." He twisted the doorknob just a fraction as he spoke. "They corrupt it just a little, so the idea still seems to hold merit. It's still plausible, and that's when they build their hellish creations. Their little *Frankensteins*." He glared at Kurt through slitted eyes. "Like this whole research concept they're ramming down our collective throats."

"Keep your voice down," Kurt said. "They can hear you all the way down the hall."

"The hall? How's this?" He increased his volume. "I want them to hear me all the way to the *Reichstag*!"

Kleinschmidt burst from his chair, knocking over his desk lamp and scattering papers to the floor. He covered the distance between them in two strides, grabbed Augie's shoulders, turned him around, and hissed into his face, "I'm warning you."

"Take your hands off me."

A soft knock on the door intruded. "Sir?"

"One moment, please, Fräulein Kunkler," he called. "Later, Augie. We'll finish this later."

"Anytime you're ready. You know where the lab is." Augie flung open the door with such force the doorknob impaled itself in the plaster wall. He stormed out of the office, nearly colliding with Fräulein Gertrude Kunkler waiting in the hall.

Kleinschmidt sagged against his desk, depleted, as was the very oxygen content of the room, Augie having sucked it dry. Fräulein Kunkler moved to close the door, but Kurt held up a hand to stop her. "Leave it open. The room needs a good airing out." He considered, not for the first time, that if there were a hell, it must surely be on earth, and his brother-in-law must be Satan's emissary. In the space of half an hour, he'd had to deal with both him and soon Himmler, neither of whom would ever suffer from hemorrhoids, being as they were both such perfect assholes. He gobbled a handful of antacid tablets from the ever-present container on his desk and sank into his chair. Gerda, ever-faithful and efficient, waited patiently, clipboard in hand and the conference folder under her arm while he calmed down. She frowned. Augie always upset him so much. It just wasn't right.

"The folder for the conference, sir," she finally announced, handing him a cumbersome file. "The schedule and agenda, as well as biographies on all the participants are inside. There are a few places where

I've noted you should look up from your reading and emphasize certain points. I've also left spaces in two sections where you will ask Herr Himmler for his advice." She used her pencil to indicate their locations. "Selection of music and order of introductions. That should please him."

Kurt gave her a grateful look. "Efficient enough to pass muster. Not so efficient as to pose a threat to his authority. Nicely done, Gerda. You're a student of psychology."

"No, Herr Professor. I am not, but I do know Herr Himmler, and there's no point in borrowing trouble. We want him comfortable during his visit. If he is comfortable, I believe we will be comfortable as well."

"Gerda, you're a rare jewel," he said, tapping the folder on his desk to straighten the papers inside. "What else?"

"I have arranged for each desk to have a different native German plant. Their placement will be unobtrusive, but they will create the desired effect. Even though Herr Himmler may not notice, notes will be taken by his staff." That remark caused her attention to turn to Kurt's desk, and she scowled. "The photograph, the one with you and Herr Himmler. It needs to be here." She indicated a spot that would be visible from the chair Himmler would be occupying. "Sir?"

"I'm thinking. I'm thinking. It's here, somewhere." He jerked every desk drawer open until he found the photo, stuffed at the back of the middle drawer, behind a sweater. "I wondered where that had gone to," he said, pulling out the sweater.

"The photograph?" she prompted.

"Yes. Got it." He produced the photo and handed it to Gerda, who placed it to the side of his desk lamp, making a symmetrical counterpoint to the photo of himself with Amelie and the children taken on their last ski holiday in Steiermark. He glanced at the picture. So much had changed since then. Everything had changed.

"Really, sir. This must stay out," she said, returning the room to order as she spoke.

He nodded, suddenly weary. "If only the man's head didn't look like a chicken's ass. If only..." He was interrupted by a cacophony of automobile horns, announcing the arrival of Herr Heinrich Himmler, Reich Commissioner for the Strengthening of Germanism. He reached for the antacid bottle one more time.

The office door was open, as per instructions, and he heard the footsteps before he saw the guards who preceded Himmler. They checked the room for threats and then, satisfied the area was secure, gave the signal for Himmler to enter, which he promptly did, pausing just long enough to give the required *Heil Hitler!* and waiting for Kleinschmidt to jump to his feet and respond in kind, before seating himself to the left of Kleinschmidt's desk in the upholstered chair, which conveniently, and not coincidentally, had recently been the focus of Gerda's interior decoration efforts. Himmler could not miss the desk photos of Kleinschmidt with Himmler, Kleinschmidt's wife and four children, and the essential wall photo of Der Führer,

Proof that Kleinschmidt was a good family man and devoted Party member.

"Report." Himmler wasted no time on pleasantries when dealing with underlings.

Kleinschmidt nodded, cleared his throat, and began to read from his notes. "We have received acceptances from all those invited. We excluded, of course, the English and the French, as their research did not meet our acceptance parameters. The Italians will present a paper that we have prepared for them. We are especially pleased that the Danish-American, Fräulein Professor Doktor Katrin Nissen, will be in attendance. Her commitment to the principles of Tüxen and Jensen gives us excellent leverage with the world press, and her study of the propagation of native, hardy perennials will segue quite nicely into the presentation on plant communication offered by two of our own eminent horticulturists, Herr Professor Doktor Jürgen Winkler from Bavaria and Herr Professor Doktor Stefan Bauer from the South Tyrol. These presentations are scheduled for the second day. This will give us a broad geographical perspective for our program."

Himmler responded with a curt nod of approval.

"We will begin the first day's program with a brief history of ecology," continued Kleinschmidt. "It is important to underscore for the world that the movement began here. Raise finger for emphasis." He raised his index finger and made a brief jabbing notion.

Himmler cocked his head, but Kleinschmidt, ignorant of his error in reading from his notes, continued. "I was thinking it would be beneficial to intersperse our own researchers with those from other universities throughout Europe on both the first and second days." Kleinschmidt delivered this line as a question to which Himmler merely nodded.

"I will deliver the keynote speech which I have entitled, *The Task Ahead—Ensuring the Purity of Native Species.* We will have students placed throughout the room who will ask questions, after I have concluded my remarks. I have these questions and answers prepared and have a copy for you." He tapped the folder.

"We will, of course, begin and end each day with inspirational music. What would be your preferences?" He waited patiently, pen and paper in hand.

Himmler considered the question and then rattled off his choices. "*Do you see Dawn in the East?* for the first day, and then, I think, yes, then *Heil Deutschland,* and finishing on the third day with *Germany Awake!* Yes, I believe those will fit well."

Kleinschmidt scribbled furiously. Finished with his notations, he continued. "The student group will hold banners and serve as honor guard. The third day will concern itself with the propaganda effort to disseminate our efforts towards achieving purity. The press will be allowed to interview the presenters. The questions and answers for this are also here." Kleinschmidt closed his notebook and waited for Himmler's response.

"Excellent work, Herr Professor Doktor Kleinschmidt. The conference will be a success. Your efforts are appreciated." He rose from the chair fifteen minutes from the time he had taken his seat. "Heil Hitler!"

"Heil Hitler!"

Himmler left the room, guards both preceding him and bringing up the rear. Kleinschmidt waited until the footsteps faded to nothing, closed the door, opened the bottom desk drawer, and poured himself a healthy measure of schnapps. At precisely 12:45, horns once again blaring, the motorcade left the campus. Kleinschmidt refreshed his drink.

Friday, June 14, 1940
German troops enter Paris

CHAPTER ELEVEN

Berlin, Kristine's Apartment

"Headache?" Ilsa looked up from her sketchpad, where she'd been roughing out backgrounds for the seven propaganda posters she'd been assigned to complete during the conference. This time she'd been told to take the sentences or slogans from the speeches given at the conference, which meant she'd have some control over the content. It was a welcome change from the scripted hatred.

Kristine had set her pencil down and was pressing her fingers against her tired eyes. "Yes. A beaut. The kind that starts out as a dull ache across the base of your skull and then spreads upward along every nerve ending until it shoots out of your scalp." She'd finally finished outlining every photo she needed to take to cover all three days of the conference. Each participant, speaker, and small group session was now accounted for, and she was currently working on the impromptu opportunities to fill out the contents of this assignment's portfolio. Impromptu didn't mean unplanned. She had to be everywhere anything might happen and be ready to capture it on film. Some of the best photographs couldn't be planned.

The saving grace for this project had been getting approval for Ilsa to use this opportunity as material for a series of propaganda posters aimed at university-aged youth, a vast recruiting ground for the Party and, as Kristine had explained to Herr Wassermann who had then explained to Herr Stottlemeyer, Ilsa's boss, what a windfall this vegetation conference would be for their respective departments and, not coincidentally, themselves. With both men seeing the potential for career advancement and Party approval, the request was granted, and Kristine and Ilsa were now up to their eyebrows in work.

Pushing her chair away from the desk, Kristine stood, stretched, and realized she was hungry. A glance at the kitchen clock told her they'd worked straight through lunch and it was now approaching supper time, but a further glance at the contents of the refrigerator didn't promise much in the way of sustenance. There was one lonely block of hard cheese on the middle shelf, surrounded by empty space. "I'm hungry," she announced to the cheese and sighed. Becoming a vegetarian was proving inconvenient, even if advantageous to advance in the Party. Her resolve was weakening with each passing day. She wanted meat.

"Anything in there?"

"Not unless you're a mouse. I am getting extremely tired of cheese. I want real food. I made a list, but I haven't had a spare minute to go to the market."

Ilsa got up and inspected the contents of the refrigerator. "This is pathetic. How do you function without food? Give me the list. I'll do the shopping. We can have a proper dinner, and then we'll see what else we need to do with all this afterwards." She made a sweeping motion with her arm at their work on the table. "I don't know about you, but I'm about played out. My brain needs a break and an evening without thinking about politics."

"Oh, and there's nothing in the house for breakfast, either," Kristine said. "We need eggs. Bacon. Good bread. Butter. You know, food."

Ilsa grabbed her handbag and the list. "I'll go. Wait a minute. This isn't a list, Kristine. You wrote *get food*."

"Yes, well, I wasn't sure what I needed, so I thought I'd see what they had when I got there. You can't count on finding anything anymore. Half the time, the shelves are empty."

"Take an aspirin for your headache and lie down until it goes away." Ilsa looked at the list again. "I should be back in about a week."

Kristine managed a weak grin. "Sorry."

"Just go." She gave her a hug and set off to replenish the larder.

▪ ▪ ▪

While considerably less than a week, it was nearly two hours before Ilsa returned from the market and the delicatessen with two shopping bags filled to the top with bacon, eggs, butter, sliced meats, potato salad, a nice bottle of red wine, and one luxury item. The bakery had been closing, but she'd managed to grab the last strawberry torte, along with a loaf of black bread. She set the bags down on the counter and began passing food to Kristine, who transferred everything connected with supper to the kitchen table and then cut a few slices from the lonely block of cheese in the refrigerator, adding them to the spread. Five minutes later, food on their plates, the wine poured, and the workday officially concluded, Kristine announced, "I am no longer a vegetarian."

"Kristine, nobody cares. They are all so full of themselves, they don't give you a second thought. Eat what makes you happy. Food is for the soul, not just the body." She pointed to the strawberry torte. "Let's make room for that on our plates."

Kristine grinned. "Good idea. I'll grab a couple of napkins. It's going to be messy." She had just reached the linen drawer, when something heavy fell against the back door. "Did you hear that?"

"I heard something."

Kristine walked to the door and tried to open it, but it wouldn't budge. It was jammed shut. An unseen weight was pushing inward from the other side. "There's something up against the door. I can't get it open."

Ilsa, now standing next to her, flipped on the porch light and peered out the window. "I don't see anything."

"Well, there's something there. That's for sure."

Pushing their shoulders against the door took all their strength, but they managed to create enough resistance to depress the latch, releasing the door, which now swung wide open, taking both of them with it, pushing them backwards. The door slammed against the wall, bringing with it a man who fell into the room and onto the floor at their feet.

Reflex caused her to step back, but instinct told Kristine to pull him the rest of the way inside the house. When she and Ilsa had finally gotten him far enough away from the door so they could shut it, Kristine groaned, for she recognized the still form now sprawled at her feet. His face was chalk, his hands were ice. He stirred and raised his head. "Hi Sis. Did you miss me?" And with that, his head fell back onto the floor. Dieter Weiss was out cold.

"Oh, Ilsa, what am I going to do?"

Ilsa, not usually at a loss for words, threw her hands up in the air and then let them fall to her sides. "Do you know him?" was all she could think of to say.

Kristine nodded. "He's my brother."

"Oh," she said, as if that explained everything. "I didn't know you had a brother."

"Neither did I." She looked up. "Until this week."

"All right," Ilsa said. "I understand. I don't actually, but some day when we have grown old together, if we should ever be permitted that, I must remember to ask you about all this; in the meantime, what the hell is he doing here, and what the hell are we going to do with him?" Her voice had taken on a note of desperation.

Oh, Dieter, what have you gotten yourself into? Kristine bent over the still form of her brother to assess the damage. His breathing was shallow. This wasn't good. She tried to recall her first aid training from years ago. He was so cold. His jacket seemed damp. Dieter needed to warm him, but first she had to get him into bed. She rolled him gently onto his right side and, as she did, his jacket fell away, revealing the makeshift blood-soaked bandage. Kristine inhaled sharply. With a shaking hand, she undid the ties until the bandage fell away, revealing a deep purple puncture wound that was seeping blood.

"Kristine. That is a bullet wound. Oh, this is bad. This is really, really bad. Why is he here? This is not good. Oh, dear God. We have got to do something." Ilsa knelt by his side. "We need to get him to hospital. He is hurt badly. He may die." She looked at Kristine. "And then what? What if he dies? Even if he lives, he has been shot. No, we cannot take him there. Let me think." She stood and paced the short length of the hallway, coming to a stop at the wall which was less than a meter from where she began, while Kristine went to the kitchen to get a pan of warm water, to the linen closet for clean cloths, and finally to the bathroom medicine chest for some bandage materials.

"The only ones with guns today are Gestapo and criminals. Either way, we are in serious trouble. If anyone saw him come here..." Ilsa was at a loss to continue.

Dieter hadn't stirred while Kristine was gone, a fact that worried her but made her task easier. She gently cleaned the wound and applied a fresh compress. Then, placing a pillow under his head and a blanket over him, she turned to Ilsa. "He is my brother. I have to help him."

Ilsa took a deep breath and exhaled slowly. This was just one more hurdle to overcome, and they would overcome it together. It was a bullet wound, that much was obvious. Whether the bullet was still inside or had passed through, they wouldn't know until they could get his jacket off, but that too might have to wait until he regained consciousness and could help them, if indeed he were able to. If the bullet hadn't hit any vital organs and had passed through, infection would be the biggest problem. If it had done serious internal damage and were still lodged inside, that would be a different story. Bullets didn't always travel neatly through a body. They could bounce around inside and create all kinds of problems, and in this case, not just for him. If he died, what would she do? Too much to think about all at once.

"We can get him into bed. He will, at least, be as comfortable as we can make him. In the morning, I will make some inquiries. I have a friend who is a nurse. I don't know if she will come here, but she may be our only hope. Kristine, I don't know what else we can do."

"Please do what you can. I am sorry you got caught up in this. I didn't know…"

"Let's just do what we have to do and then take it one step at a time after that. It is best that I leave as soon as we get him settled. We don't need any more complications." Ilsa went in search of her handbag. "You know, in spite of everything, I have the feeling we're doing the right thing, but I sure would have liked a piece of the torte."

"I'll cut you a piece to take with you. We need nourishment and it won't keep."

Twenty minutes later, Dieter was safely in bed. With his weight leaning full against them, they had negotiated the journey from the back hall to the bedroom. Now, propped into a semi-sitting position, they'd been able to remove his jacket. He was shirtless underneath. Kristine ran her hand over his back and finally located a second, bigger hole. The bullet had passed through. That was one question answered.

She helped him lie down and checked his bandage. The wound was still seeping. She arranged the bedcovers around him and he drifted off again. He wouldn't be answering any questions any time soon, that much was certain. They left him to his sleep. Hopefully, tomorrow, Ilsa would be able to convince the nurse to come by and attend to Dieter. Ilsa was hopeful, but Kristine wasn't convinced. These days, looking out for oneself was the most important aspect of any engagement, relationship, or appointment. So, with Ilsa now gone back to her own apartment, Kristine took a blanket and pillow from the closet and went to the sofa in the parlor to try to get a few hours of sleep before she had to leave for the university and another full day's work.

At 7:00 the next morning, having dozed only a little, she checked in on her brother. There was no change in his breathing or his position. She set a water glass on the nightstand by the bed in case he woke and was able to reach it. She'd have to leave him soon. So much depended on today, and she couldn't afford to let it pass her by. She'd give him one more hour, and then she'd have to go.

An hour later, she gently shook his arm. "Dieter. Dieter, I have to leave. There's water on the nightstand. Don't move around or you'll open yourself up again. There are towels under you, so use them if you have to. I'll be back late this afternoon."

A slight movement of his lips was the only response. She left him, closed the door quietly behind her, and set off for work.

CHAPTER TWELVE

Berlin

I was sitting on the edge of the featherbed, massaging my still-swollen ankles. Travel might have gotten faster, but it was still hard on the back and the feet and the posterior. There's not much opportunity to get up and stretch on an airplane, and, even if you try, it's not easy climbing over people to get to the aisle and then back to your seat. Also, in my case, my seatmate had made it clear that the less she had to do with me, the better. As a result, I had remained in my seat more than I normally would have and my body was letting me know it wasn't feeling all that great. Plus, I was still adjusting to the difference in time. I had conked out last night right after I'd finished with the briefcase paper tangle and hadn't awakened until the alarm clock blasted me out of the arms of Morpheus at 6:00 this morning.

I dressed quickly, choosing comfort over more professional, movement-restricting attire. The ivory blouse with the scoop neck was an ideal background for the ring on the chain, and the navy blue skirt with matching jacket completed my simple ensemble. The ring rested just at eye level for anyone of average height to see, and that meant it swung at bosom level. Since I was counting on Dieter's physicist to be male, the positioning should ensure at least a passing glance. One does what one can. I plaited my hair, dusted on some face powder, and I was ready to meet the day. Briefcase in hand, I ventured downstairs to breakfast, stepping aside to let Heidi, who was trudging up the stairs with an armful of freshly laundered sheets, pass by. She never looked up.

"Guten Morgen!" Marta was presiding over the breakfast table, coffee urn to her left and teapot to her right. "Coffee or tea?"

"Guten Morgen! Coffee, please." The dining table was set for five, and I hesitated.

"Sit down. Sit down. It doesn't matter where. Your colleagues will be down shortly, and Erich will join us as soon as he finds what he's looking for." She poured my coffee and handed me the cup as I took the seat on her left, by the coffee. Marta had beautiful hands with long, slender fingers. She had the hands of a musician or perhaps an artist. Talent doesn't always follow physiology, though, and she'd found her career in horticulture instead of the fine arts. "He's always looking for this paper or that paper, although lately he's been misplacing quite a few that he can't find. I just try to stay out of his way. Did you sleep well?"

"I did indeed. The bed reminded me of the bed I slept in as a child, so comfortable. My grandmother had a flock of geese, and when we butchered one for Sunday dinner, my job was to pluck the feathers and trim the quills. She kept a bag for me to fill and promised me that, when I married, she would make me a featherbed with them. Her featherbeds were so soft. I could burrow down and get lost in them." I smiled. "It's a happy memory." The coffee was strong, and I drank appreciatively. "I'm looking forward to meeting Herr Professor Doktor Kleinschmidt today. Preparations for the conference must be taking up most of his time."

"They are, but he has Gerda to help him. She keeps the department running."

"Gerda?"

"*Ja.* Fräulein Gertrude Kunkler. She's the Faculty's secretary, and she's its most valuable member. You'll meet her straight away." Marta consulted a small notepad by her plate. "No, that's wrong. First, you have the appointment with the photographer for your conference photo. After that, you'll tour the department and have a chance to meet your colleagues." She paused at the sound of approaching footsteps. "Ah, here he is. Erich, did you find what you were looking for?"

Von Reichstadt's concerned expression, as he joined us at the table, gave the answer. "I must have left it in my office. I was sure I'd brought it home. I distinctly remember setting it on top of the stack, just before Monika brought me the forms to sign for something." He looked up. "I don't remember what they were." He ran his fingers through his sparse, greying hair and seemed to see me for the first time. "I am so sorry. I am being quite rude." He stood and gave a curt bow and then reseated himself.

Erich von Reichstadt was the kind of person you instantly liked, one of those gentle souls you knew was going to be navigating through life with that strange combination of kindness and confusion.

"I hope your room is satisfactory." He made a sweeping motion with his hand as he was speaking, which Marta interpreted as a request for tea. She poured him a cup and dropped in a sugar cube.

"Herr Professor, please call me Katrin, and everything is quite lovely. It was kind of you both to allow me to stay here."

"It is certainly our pleasure." He drained the cup of tea in three swallows, stood, and bowed again. "I have an early appointment, so please excuse me. We will talk more this evening."

"Erich, before you go..." Marta held up a prescription bottle.

"Thank you, Marta." He took the bottle and went to the sideboard, where he poured a glass of apple juice for his pill. He bowed again before leaving.

Marta shook her head. "I expect he'll find that paper exactly where he left it, on his desk in his office. He's the most brilliant mind in the department, but everyday matters are beyond him." In answer to my unspoken question, she said, "Monika is Gerda's counterpart in the Physics Faculty." She buttered a roll. "We women keep everything organized. It's a pity the men don't always appreciate that fact. And he'd never remember to take his pill if I didn't remind him every day."

I nodded sympathetically.

"He had a heart attack last year," she said. "Not terribly bad, but enough to convince him he should follow the doctor's orders."

I nodded again. Digitalis was one of the miracles of the 20th century, and the field of research was offering hope where none had existed previously. There wasn't anything else to say, and I looked around. Marta's dining room was a comfortable place. She had already opened the bay windows to let in the fresh air, and the half curtains let in the light but kept the sun from making the room an oven. The furnishings went along with the age of the house. The china hutch behind Marta's chair had three leaded glass doors, and each door had a brass keyhole with its own key.

"My grandfather made that," she said, noticing I was studying it.

"It's beautiful," I said. "He was a master craftsman."

"Actually," Marta laughed, "he made cheese. The woodworking was just a pastime."

We ate our breakfast rolls, assorted meats, fresh fruit, one last cup of coffee and finished before the other two guests made an appearance. "I guess we shall see Professors Winkler and Bauer this evening," Marta said. "Shall we go? It's a beautiful day for a walk, and the university is only a short distance away."

"I never enjoy having my picture taken," I said, as we gathered our bags and set out. "I always seem to look as if I'm angry at something or someone. It's distressing. The camera doesn't like me."

"I understand completely," Marta said, patting her unruly mop of hair. "That's why I always wear a hat."

I patted the braid coiled around my own head, and Marta smiled. We had similar issues with our hair, but Marta had the kind of face that would photograph well. Her high cheekbones and elfin chin had just the right angles. My face was just too round, with nothing vaguely approaching an angle.

Marta set the tempo for our walk, and the leisurely pace gave us time for conversation. She was making a name for herself in the field of plant sociology, the study of natural associations of plants. Basically, plant sociologists looked at plants the way sociologists looked at people and studied why they lived where they lived and why they grew some places and made friends with some other plants while avoiding others. Kind of like why I avoided Cynthia Lawson at the university back home. I preferred to keep her out of my little sociological area.

"What is your area of interest as a plant sociologist?" I asked.

"Oh, yes," she said. "I am currently working in the ecology of plant sociology. We are looking at the general organization of these communities and the relationships of plants in these communities to each other and to the general environment. That means we are also interested in their life cycles—how they come into being, how they grow, and eventually how and why they decline. The Party is most interested in this research."

I'm sure they are, I thought. It fits right in with their plans. Start with something as seemingly innocuous as plants, establish a scientific validity for your research, and then use that authority to apply it to people. And from what I'd discerned from the references to Jews as *weeds,* they'd already begun the process. It was only a matter of time until the experiments in the lab turned a far more sinister corner.

"It has much potential for growth, and they are quite generous with funding my work. It's become my principal area of research and I expect it will increase in importance as time goes on," Martha continued, oblivious to my wandering attention.

"So essentially, you try to figure out what will grow where, why, and how," I said, reentering the conversation.

She stopped in mid-stride and looked at me. "Yes. That's it! I've been trying to find a more concise way of putting it. We do tend to overly complicate things, don't we? That is quite helpful. Thank you."

Indeed. We tend to complicate matters. I've always marveled at how we scientists can take a simple idea and turn it into the most convoluted mishmash of double-speak, and it seems the more tenuous the theory, the fancier we make it sound. And I'm just as guilty as the rest, on some occasions. I do enjoy listening to people talk about their passions, however, and while I couldn't expound on the joys of espionage, which I define as research conducted with the doors closed and the lights out, I did share that my interests were in exploring new methods for getting two or more plants out of one—the reproduction of hardy, native perennials—I inserted the word *native* to sound loyal to the cause. Reproduction is different in the plant kingdom, and studying it is essential work. Plants feed us, and the more of them there are and the healthier they are, the more food there is. That ended our conversation, as we had arrived at the university's front steps. "The Faculty is on the third floor," Marta said, as we entered the building. "I'll see you tonight at home."

The line of presenters was already forming just inside the door, where a long desk, manned by two students, had been set up. There was an array of folders, each with a name label, arranged in alphabetical order. Upon each folder perched a name badge, adorned with, of course, a swastika. There was a stack of walking maps of Berlin, information on hiring a car for those who wished to take a short jaunt into the countryside, a list of recommended restaurants, and some National Socialist propaganda. I gave my name and was handed my folder and badge. Inside the folder was the schedule for each day, brief biographies of the faculty, shorter biographies of the presenters, and a map of my path for today. The map began with a large **X** that indeed marked the exact spot where I stood.

I thanked the student who had already closed the small gap in the display of folders where mine had been. In a way, the action made me feel as if I were being eliminated. It was a strange sensation, and I made a mental note to keep my guard on full alert. Gene had been right. The university was a dangerous place to be these days, and it didn't matter that I was there by invitation. There was nothing to do but follow the path laid out for me on my map, and so I followed the hallway about halfway down until I found the second X taped on the floor in front of the third door on the left. This was the room where I was to have my photograph taken for my professional photo that would accompany the synopsis of my presentation for the conference folder. Folders here, folders there, folders everywhere.

The room had portable lights set up on either side of a stool that was positioned in front of a grey backdrop. Nothing fancy, here. This was your basic enter, sit, look professional, hold still, get up, and leave experience. The photographer, a tired-looking young woman with closely shorn brown hair, didn't know me from Adam's Eve, but I recognized her from the dossier. This was Kristine Trautmann, Dieter Weiss's sister. She waved me in and motioned for me to be seated on the stool.

"Name, please."

"Fräulein Professor Doktor Katrin Nissen." I gave her the whole shebang.

"You will please put on your name badge." She made a checkmark on a clipboard. "Here." She pointed to a spot on her chest, left of center, just slightly below her shoulder. I fumbled with the pin while she waited with noticeable impatience. She then spent a few seconds studying my face, before directing me to tilt my head slightly to the left. She shook her head. Too much. And would I please tuck the silver chain inside my blouse. It clashed with my hair and was too long, anyway. I smiled and said that I would be keeping the chain as it was. She walked to me and lifted the ring. For just a second, I was concerned that she was going to yank it off my neck.

"You will please do as instructed."

Again, I declined. I was afraid this situation was going to escalate, but, with her time at a premium, she released the ring, returned to her camera setup, took the photo without the fetchingly attractive head tilt, and motioned for me to leave. I obliged willingly and made for the door, but before I turned the knob, I gave her one last glance. She was bent over her camera, her hand raised to her forehead, and I sensed something was wrong. I was ready to ask if I could help. This could be a perfect opportunity to connect with her on a personal level, but the next person in line was knocking on the door, and I was forced to leave.

She seemed to be holding on to her professional manner by a thread, but why? Did it have something to do with Dieter? Trying to find a way to talk with her became my focus, but she'd be occupied all day long. If I could somehow position myself by the door when she'd finished up for the day, perhaps there'd be an opportunity for conversation. Then again, she hadn't reacted to the ring other than to regard it as a piece of intrusive jewelry, so perhaps her manner had nothing to do with Dieter, after all. Time would tell. By the time she got to the end of her schedule, our photographs would probably look like mug shots, but then perhaps her assistant, if she had one, hadn't shown up for work and she was doing double-duty. Best not to judge. I'd hoped I might have at least been able to break the ice with her, and I guess I had, but not the way I had planned. I had wanted her to remember me, so I had undoubtedly accomplished that much. I took two deep, cleansing breaths. I would need to talk with her, but it wouldn't be now. I needed every brain cell I had for today's tasks and couldn't afford to waste them on tomorrow's.

The third floor, home to the Department of Horticulture, or Faculty of Horticulture, to use the German terminology, was a beehive of organized chaos. There was a palpable energy in the air, and it was contagious. There was also a delightful fragrance, for each desk sported a beautiful specimen of a native flowering plant. All office doors were wide open and there was a steady stream of foot traffic in, out, and along the corridor. The office occupants were churning out pre-conference corrections, deletions, and additions to their presentations, and I could hear the rhythm of the constant ding of typewriter bells, signaling the typist had reached the page's margin and it was time to slap the carriage back to type another line.

Most academics are adequate typists, but it's the secretaries who are the professionals. I did a fairly respectable sixty words a minute, but I knew some department secretaries that easily did eighty and more, and that was without making a single error. The rest of us went through a drawerful of erasers trying to fix our mistakes. And carbon paper. What a mess, trying to fix a mistake on the original and also on the one or two copies behind it. Too often, the eraser just wore a hole in the paper and you had to start all over again, sort of like a Greek drama—when somebody flubbed a line, they went back to the beginning. Some of those productions could go on for a week.

Professional conferences were the lifeblood of an academic's career. We all published in the professional journals, of course. It was expected and necessary if you wanted to advance in your career and be tenured, but, to be honest, their primary function was to provide an opportunity for other researchers to add footnotes to their own research. If your research supported somebody else's, you were cited as an expert. If it didn't, you were cited as an idiot who didn't know your ass from a hole in the ground. It's how the game was played.

Conferences, though, are a whole different animal. For one thing, you can defend yourself if attacked. Everything is out in the open, and there's the opportunity to actively engage with others who share your perspective and expand your network. You can also get support and sympathy. Research is a lonely task, and affirmation is something we all crave. And so, just for an instant, I felt part of it, drawn into it, and it took a little effort to pull back and not get caught up in the excitement. I needed to keep on track. Time was at a premium. I wasn't here to promote my work, and while I might be temporarily promoting the Nazi agenda, I knew it was all a sham, a role I was playing. The end had to justify the means, but damage control at the end of all this could take the rest of my professional life. I took one more deep breath and consulted my map, which now directed me down the hallway to the last door on the right, the office of the Faculty secretary, Fräulein Gertrude Kunkler.

I paused at the entrance and knocked on the open door. As one of the supporting characters in my assignment, she hadn't rated a photo or a biography in my dossiers, and the mental image I had conjured up for her fell far short of the actuality. I had been thinking of Victoria, back in my own department at Yale. Victoria's impeccable business attire complemented her professional demeanor, so I was mentally expecting someone quite different from the woman at the typewriter. Fräulein Kunkler was wearing a housedress. There was no other way to describe the flowered frock with the short sleeves that was encasing her extremely corpulent body. She finished the sentence she was typing and placed a bookmark in the reference book she'd been using. I thought I recognized the book and craned my neck to check the title—*The Standard Cyclopedia of Horticulture.* Yes indeed, an essential tool of the trade. I had a copy on my desk back at the university.

Fräulein Kunkler removed her glasses, set them down on the desk blotter, and greeted me with a pleasant smile. She moved the reference book to the side, next to a pot that held an *Amaryllis hippeastrum* and a coffee cup with a broken handle that held paper clips. Interesting, and odd.

"*Guten Morgen!* You are Fräulein Professor Doktor Katrin Nissen. Welcome. You are right on time!"

The German obsession with punctuality is well known, and I had been careful not to have been a minute too late or a minute too early. First impressions can't be undone. "*Guten Morgen.* Yes, and you are Fräulein Kunkler." Stating the obvious always sounds so ridiculous, but formalities are formalities, and formality is as important as punctuality.

"You are here to meet Herr Professor Doktor Kleinschmidt."

We were slowly making our way through this regimen of foreplay, checking off each item on her admissions list of questions. I nodded, encouragingly. "Yes." Perhaps the less I said, the faster this would go.

And finally, Fräulein Kunkler rose from her chair. "You will please follow me." Finally. Victory. There was a reason people refer to senior secretaries as gatekeepers. They wielded the real power in any office, and if you didn't understand that from the beginning, you'd definitely have learned it by the time you'd left. I detected something more going on here, however. My highly honed powers of intuition were picking up some subtle signals. Fräulein Kunkler was more than a gatekeeper. She was a protectress. She was also an extremely short woman, under five feet tall, and nearly as wide, and we made a strange pair, as we left for Professor Kleinschmidt's—she out front, her tightly permed hair bouncing up and down with the rhythm of her steps, and me bringing up the rear of our little parade.

I am not excessively tall, as Danes and other northern Europeans go, but I *am* tall, and that had been a topic of initial concern for Gene in my early days with the Agency. Most operatives are middle. They're medium height, medium build, medium everything, and there's a good reason for that. If you blend in with the general population, you're not memorable. That always works to your advantage. I rarely blended, and Gene had finally decided the way to deal with this would be for me to just always be me or some form of me. Just as being unremarkable works to an agent's advantage, so can being obvious. If you're noticeable, you're often overlooked, just for that reason. You're too obvious to be anything suspicious. It had worked out well. At least, so far it had, and, case in point, here I was in Germany, as a version of myself. This version was unmarried and a Nazi sympathizer, but it fit the bill. I was right out there in the open. It was the best cover I could have invented. *I hoped.*

"Sir." Fräulein Kunkler's voice had softened and the gentle tone as she announced herself confirmed my suspicions. Yessiree. Fräulein Kunkler was in love with Kurt Kleinschmidt. It wasn't the first office romance I had encountered, although from past observations they frequently didn't end well, an impression that was reinforced when I saw the family portrait on Kleinschmidt's desk. Kunkler wasn't in the picture. Was this a one-sided, secret romance or just another ordinary office affair?

The office, apart from the desk which was covered with paperwork, a photo of Kleinschmidt with Himmler, the family shot, and a small potted plant—a *Helleborus niger,* commonly known as a Christmas Rose, was tidy as could be, and I immediately saw the reason for that. Fräulein Kunkler advanced on the only item out of place, a rumpled scrap of paper on the floor that had missed entry into the wastebasket by a good centimeter and a half.

Kleinschmidt's office held the pleasant aroma of a freshly smoked pipe and brought back a fleeting memory of my grandfather. Looking at the desk, raised my interest level. This was the second plant today that had intrigued me. It was the wrong season for a Christmas Rose to be blooming. Very interesting. I suspected there was some research underway here on this and that the Christmas rose was one of the specimens under study. If there were time, it would be useful to learn more about this. Findings in one area can have applications in another, and I might find this useful in my research. *If* there were time. Highly unlikely, unfortunately.

Kleinschmidt, as I saw when he rose to greet me, was as tall as Fräulein Kunkler was short. Clean-shaven and balding, he wore reading glasses, as I deduced when he removed them to greet me. He was also missing the entire pinky and half the ring finger on his left hand. Accident or birth defect? Could have been from some sort of accident. The greetings completed, Fräulein Kunkler removed herself and Kleinschmidt motioned me to have a seat, which I did. As soon as I'd taken my seat, he set the formalities aside and began a sincere and frank conversation, something I hadn't expected.

"Everything is in a bit of an uproar around here, I'm afraid," he said. "It's been a great boon for us, but I hadn't anticipated the amount of work this conference would be, or how stressful," he added. "The stakes are quite high, as you undoubtedly know. And I seem to spend most of my time putting out fires."

I gave him my best sympathetic look.

"Everybody wants to be the star. It's like working with…" he paused, searching for the right word. "Fifteen prima ballerinas who all want the starring role in the Bolshoi." He leaned back in his chair and laced his fingers across the back of his head. "I stroke this ego here, that ego there, and hope they don't kill each other when my back is turned." He released his head and sat upright. "Any different in America?"

"No, not at all," I said. "I think it goes with the territory. We're all terribly insecure and yet full of ego at the same time. We have enemies and choose allies. It's the sociology of human interaction. I guess if you stop to think about it, we're probably always at war. Perhaps that's our normal state and peace is the aberration."

"Indeed. I've thought of that on occasion. In any regard, thank you for accepting our invitation. Your work is of great interest to us. Please let me know if I can be of any help to you during your stay." He stood, indicating our meeting had come to an end. "I look forward to continuing our conversation."

Fräulein Kunkler reappeared almost instantly, having obviously been listening in, and she stood by the door as I made my exit.

The morning progressed in this fashion, in precisely measured fifteen-minute increments, and with the passing of each quarter hour, the ranks increased, as the presenters one by one, or two by two—if they were research partners—entered the department and began following their own maps, until precisely 11:45, when I opened the only lab door that was closed and promptly tripped over the body sprawled just inside the doorway. From the photograph in my welcome brochure, I could see that Herr Professor Doktor August Erdmann Becker, one of the last remaining holdouts against Nazi ideology, brother-in-law of Kleinschmidt, and general all-around pain in the ass, was quite dead. The body was sprawled as if Becker's last act had been trying to reach the door. His arm was outstretched, still reaching for the doorknob, and it appeared that he'd fallen to his knees just short of his goal. He lay on his side, his mouth contorted into a horrible grimace. I picked myself up, putting some welcome distance between his face and mine. I've seen more than my share of death, but when it comes suddenly and violently, it takes a moment to get beyond the moment.

"Well, he's mulch, and not any too soon."

The owner of this less than kind epitaph was Herr Professor Doktor Otto Crump, with whom I'd just spent my last quarter hour session, discussing the potential of ethnobotany—researching traditional folk remedies to find modern applications in medicine and his own work in discovering new species. Crump had been walking with me to my next appointment, and, while I'd enjoyed our professional conversation, I found his comment annoyingly out of place, given the circumstances.

"He doesn't look right," I said, as I studied the deceased's face, the mouth fixed in a godawful grimace.

"Of course he doesn't look right. He's dead." Crump delivered these comments in the same tone he'd use to shoot down a student who'd just failed an examination.

"Yes, thank you, Herr Professor." I hoped my voice dripped enough sarcasm to make my point clear.

Before the conversation could continue, another presenter stopped to see what was holding up the line, and I knew it wouldn't be long before the word spread and the unfortunate Herr Professor Doktor Becker's corpse became an unscheduled but popular new X on everyone's road map.

I stepped over Becker's body to take a quick look around the lab. It was like every other university horticultural laboratory with all the usual equipment. There were botanical charts on the wall, a chalkboard with some fairly detailed sketches on it, microscopes, jars of specimens on the counters, beakers, pipettes, and then the one odd thing-a half-drunk cup of coffee teetering on the edge of the counter behind him. I bent over the cup and inhaled. I frowned. There was something a bit off in the odor. "Come here," I beckoned to Crump. "Smell this."

He did and then shrugged. "I don't know. Probably nothing." He glanced back at Becker. "Looks like a heart attack to me."

It didn't look all that much like death by natural causes as far as I was concerned, but I wasn't about to argue. The less attention I brought to myself, the better. I shrugged as well.

"I'll stand guard here while you let Fräulein Kunkler know what has happened, if you don't mind," Crump said. "She can call the authorities."

I agreed and left him to his duty. I hadn't known Becker, except by reputation, but he was beyond caring about anything anymore. The person I felt for was Kleinschmidt. He'd had a lot on his plate already, and from what Crump had told me in our earlier conversation, Kleinschmidt had had a serious argument with Crump a few days ago. I was afraid the conference was going to be pushed way down on Kleinschmidt's list of concerns.

My errand took only a minute or so, as word had already traveled to Fräulein Kunkler. While we waited for the police, and against my better judgment that was reminding me not to get involved, I persisted with my observation that the coffee hadn't smelled right.

"Do you think it's possible Becker was poisoned?" I asked. "Suicide doesn't seem likely, given the circumstances of the body's location, but it's possible he changed his mind as the poison took effect and tried to summon help."

"Suicide? Not likely," Professor Crump shook his head. "Augie had too much ego for that. As for poisoning, I suppose anything's possible. He wouldn't have noticed anything off about his coffee."

My face reflected my puzzlement, and Crump laughed.

"Augie had no sense of smell or taste. He'd had some sort of childhood illness, and, when he recovered, no more smelling the roses. Strange affliction for someone in horticulture. I think that's why he settled on fungi and bacteria. If they smell at all, it's not pleasant."

The simplest answer is usually the right one. If this were indeed murder most foul, it had all the markings of an inside job. The only problem was that everyone seemed to have disliked Becker. Everyone knew about his medical issues, Crump said, and so that left approximately fourteen people, any one of whom could have and likely would have done the deed. Perhaps it was a committee decision, and they'd drawn lots to see who got the honor of getting rid of him. Stranger things have happened.

The police came and took our statements. The ambulance attendants took the body away, and that was that. The medical examiner would ultimately decide on the cause of death, but that wouldn't happen immediately, and probably not before I had left Berlin. In the meantime, the general consensus was death by heart attack.

Becker's unexpected, but not unwelcome, demise had caused just a minor and momentary blip in the morning's activities, as it set everything back about an hour. Once the not so dearly departed's body had departed the department, our activities resumed. Becker had been the last appointment for the day on my agenda of visits, and since his office was just down the hall, and since nobody else seemed at all interested in him, I decided it wouldn't hurt to just have a look around. I wasn't buying the heart attack as cause of death. I'd seen what victims of poison looked like, and it wasn't a gentle way to go.

Becker's office was fairly tidy, as academic offices go. I've been in some that look as if they were the permanent residences of cyclones, with no apparent sense of order at all. You'd be surprised, though. Usually those offices belong to the brightest minds, and those professors can usually put their fingers on whatever they're looking for in a snap. This office was somewhere in the middle on the mess index. Not as tidy as Kleinschmidt's but not in as much of an uproar as O'Reilly's back home. O'Reilly kept getting notices from the department higher-ups to clean up or else. The *or else* part was never explained; it just remained some sort of free-floating threat hanging in the air that he ignored, like smoke on an autumn day.

I closed the door behind me and sat down at Becker's desk. His native plant, courtesy of Gerda, was a small holly. I was picking up on a Christmas theme here, although both the Christmas Rose on Kleinschmidt's desk and this little specimen were poisonous. In the case of holly, it's the leaves and berries. I wondered what Gerda had been thinking. Perhaps she had a love/hate relationship with Christmas. Many people did. I hadn't checked out the other plants in the department and wouldn't be surprised if she'd continued her pattern, but for what reason she'd do that escaped me. Also, that amaryllis, while associated with Christmas, *wasn't* a native plant, and that puzzled me, as well. It didn't seem, judging from Gerda's well-thumbed *Cyclopedia*, that she'd have made that kind of mistake. Odd, indeed.

Becker's presentation, which would no longer be delivered, sat smack dab in the middle of the blotter, just begging for at least one person to read it, and that was what I intended to do-later. I wondered how Kleinschmidt would fill the now-empty time slot. One more problem for Kleinschmidt and Gerda the Guardian.

If Becker had been poisoned, and I was strongly leaning in that direction, what would be the motive beyond simple hatred? Seemed a bit foolish to put oneself at risk when the Nazis would take care of him soon enough because of his beliefs. No, there had to be something else. I got up and went to the filing cabinet. It was jammed with notes, correspondence, slides from the lab, everything one would expect to find. There weren't any obvious spaces where somebody had scooped up something of importance and made off with it. Everything seemed to still be where it belonged.

The bottom drawer of the cabinet yielded some intriguing information, though. A bottle of schnapps, not surprising. A diary, bound in leather and stuffed with odd scraps of papers. That was unusual. Personal information kept at work rather than at home. I wondered what that meant or if it meant anything at all. And then, I gave a low whistle. There was a gun, a Walther PPK. Nice firearm and a Gestapo favorite. Had Augie felt the need for some serious self-protection, or was he planning something on his own? I considered commandeering the pistol, but prudence cautioned against it. I left it where it lay. It was a pretty fair bet that it would be gone before too long. The Germans had had to surrender their firearms when the Nazis took over, but there were undoubtedly many weapons now in hiding throughout Berlin and greater Germany. This one was a promising candidate to join them.

I wondered what would happen to Becker's research and his presentation for the conference. It might be informative to read through what he'd planned on saying, if something there went counter to what was expected. As for the final disposition of the contents of the filing cabinet, my fellow houseguests

Bauer and Winkler might be interested. Nobody else in Kleinschmidt's department would touch it, I was sure of that, and Becker had mostly worked alone. That wasn't unusual. I enjoy the independence, myself. It would have been nice to have had a chance to compare notes with him. We would have shared some common ground.

With nothing else to see in the office and all dressed up with my little name badge, I had nowhere to go until the party tonight, where nobody would be mourning the late Herr Professor Doktor August Erdmann Becker. For now, as a parting gift, Becker's demise had given me a golden opportunity to visit the Physics Faculty, where I might have some luck tracking down my quarry. I gave the name badge, my entry ticket to just about anywhere in the university, a little pat of affection. *Herr Himmler, thank you very kindly for the passport.*

CHAPTER THIRTEEN

At Kristine's Apartment

Kristine Trautmann's day had been long. With worry eating away at her concentration, she'd been hard-pressed to keep her mind on her work. She'd loaded the wrong film into her Leica and had shot an entire sequence of candid shots before she realized the error. She was changing film and cursing her mental lapse when word of August Becker's death swept through the department. Curious, she walked to where a small crowd was gathering and caught a glimpse of the body on the floor. Her journalistic instincts taking over, she pushed her way through and snapped a few photos—a couple of head shots and a full length of the body. The man who appeared to be in control of the situation stepped aside for her. Nobody questioned her presence. It was one of the benefits of the job. These shots wouldn't go into the conference brochure, but a good photographer never misses an opportunity. A serendipitous occurrence might prove beneficial in the future. As a bonus, it got her mind off Dieter, if only for a little while. The body was face down on the floor of the botany laboratory, close to the door. The right arm was outstretched, as if it had been reaching for the door handle, when death intervened. It was the face that captured her attention, though. It had, without a doubt, the most horrible expression she had ever seen. She took a closeup.

Finally, the day wound to a close, and Kristine packed up her equipment. Ilsa would already be at the house. Hopefully, she had found the nurse and gotten some help for them. After two quick stops, first at the butcher shop, where she'd bought a chicken, and then the produce market, where she'd selected some fruit and reasonably fresh vegetables from the scant offerings, she pulled up to the curb and parked behind Ilsa's automobile. Kristine gave a sigh of relief. If Ilsa were already here, it must mean she had been successful. Gathering her bags, she went up the front walk, giving two quick raps, a pause, and then one more rap at the door to alert Ilsa she had arrived. She opened the door and set her handbag, groceries, and camera bag on the floor and went to the bedroom where Ilsa was setting up a first aid station for Dieter.

"How is he?" Kristine wriggled out of her jacket and tossed it on the chair. Ilsa had removed the old bandage and was studying a sheet of instructions.

"*Schatz,* I don't know. He seems to be the same as last night. Gudrun gave me some antiseptic, some saline solution, and some syringes to help in cleaning the wound. Keeping it clean and the bandage clean is the most we can do. She wasn't optimistic, but she can't do anything more for us. She wished us luck. She didn't ask for any details, and I didn't give her any. Just told her somebody I knew had a wound that might become infected and it could be serious. Gudrun took a risk just giving us this. So, here we are."

Dieter didn't respond to any of their ministrations, and that was worrisome, but they followed Gudrun's instructions to the letter. With the new bandage in place, they left him to rest. The act of cleaning the wound had caused his breathing to become more labored. For the first time, the possibility he wouldn't survive became a probability, and the ramifications of that would extend far beyond his death.

"What do you think?" Kristine asked.

"What I think doesn't matter. I hope we can help him and then get him out of here before we live to regret it."

Back in the kitchen, they unpacked the groceries. Added to what Ilsa had bought yesterday, the refrigerator now looked respectable, and the fruit bowl on the kitchen counter was no longer empty. It looked more like home now than a motel, although that's what it seemed to be at the present.

"As soon as he can travel, I am taking him back to our father's home in Rostock," Kristine said. "I've been thinking, Ilsa. It's the right thing to do. Papa abandoned him when he was a child. He owes Dieter, and he's going to repay part of that debt. It's long past time their differences were put to rest. He owes Dieter an explanation and an apology, and that's just skimming the surface of what he owes." Kristine's voice was firm.

"I hope your plan works," Ilsa said, "because I sure as hell don't have an alternate."

They ate their supper in companionable silence. The meal was essentially a rerun of last night's but with the most welcome addition of the torte that had been waiting patiently on the counter. Finally, the dishes done, and with nothing else they could do for the night, Ilsa returned to her own home, leaving Kristine with the rest of the torte, from which she was contemplating stealing one more slice, and her brother, for whom she could do nothing more except sit by him and talk to him of her childhood and her life. Perhaps it would help him to hear her voice. The evening had faded into night, and the sleepless night had dragged on endlessly. Kristine was approaching exhaustion, and still Dieter hadn't stirred. She sat by his bedside, moistening his lips with a wet cloth.

The fever began sometime after midnight, and there was nothing to be done except hope he had enough left in him to fight it. For now, it was just a process of waiting it out, and while she waited and hoped for the fever to break, she sat by the bed and talked to him about everything and anything she could think of. It didn't matter that he couldn't answer; perhaps, from some distant place, he could hear her and her voice would bring him back. She spoke of her own strained relationship with their father, of her struggles for independence, and finally, just before dawn, she told him about Ilsa.

▪ ▪ ▪

"Everything was going so well. Everything was working out just the way I'd planned." She sighed. "I thought nothing could happen to spoil my dream, but I was wrong, and now nothing will ever be the same again." She looked at Dieter's face. "Is that what happened, Dieter? Did you let your guard down?"

There was no response, so she continued. "I was at a propaganda training session a few weeks ago. They held it at the castle in Nurnburg in the Eifel, and that's where it all started." The night was turning cool. She took the blanket from the floor and wrapped it around her legs. "I had just received a promotion, and attendance at the propaganda session was a requirement," she continued. "I didn't mind. Others were complaining, but I was excited to have the opportunity. I was now part of something important. It was," she hesitated, "validation. I needed validation. It's been hard, always being careful. So there was that and then just being in the Eifel. It's a beautiful area, mountainous with lakes. It's a photographer's dream."

She paused and moistened the cloth to press against his lips, squeezing just a few drops into his mouth. Ilsa had said his body needed moisture. Almost by the clock, every minute, she pressed a bit more water between his lips, then she continued with her story. "So, on the second day, during our free time, I had taken my camera to see what I could photograph, and the light was perfect, and there was a woman sitting on a stone bench, reading. I walked up to her to ask permission to photograph her. She looked up from her book, and my world changed forever. It was Ilsa, and it was as if everything was perfect again. Suddenly, it was ten years ago, and we were once again young and in love, believing that nothing would ever hurt us." A sad smile punctuated Kristine's story.

"'One last photograph,' was all Ilsa said. But it wasn't the last; it was a new beginning for us. I've given up so much, but there doesn't seem to be an end to it, and if I say anything wrong, do anything suspect, it will all have been for nothing. I can't be careful enough. But I have to hope. Without hope, there is nothing."

And then she saw a few beads of perspiration appear on his forehead. She set the blanket back on the floor and remoistened the cloth. When she returned, he had opened his eyes. He took a ragged breath and accepted the drops of water she offered, closed his eyes again, and slept.

CHAPTER FOURTEEN

Cocktails, hors d'oeuvres, and murder

My afternoon trek to the physics building hadn't yielded anything of substance early on, although I made note of the placement of the entrances and exits, just in case. One never knows. Anything may turn out to be useful at some point. Seven scientists worked inside that building on a project of such importance that, if successful, could ensure Germany's victory in the war. Seven men, but I only needed to find one—the right one to make sure that Germany didn't come out the winner. Finding that right one wasn't turning out to be an easy task.

I found a bench and enjoyed watching the world go by for a while, and then, around three o'clock, my patience was rewarded, as von Reichstadt and Weber, the *Wunderkind,* emerged from the building deep in conversation. With his broad smile, Weber was easy to identify from my memory trick. He was the dwarf named Happy. I timed my approach to intersect their paths just before they reached the street.

"Guten Abend!" I called as I approached.

Von Reichstadt stopped and turned, seeking the origin of the greeting, and I waved at him. He seemed confused, and I realized he didn't remember me from breakfast and our conversation last night. I understood. When you've just met someone, it can be difficult to remember them when you see them again in a different setting. It's why these mnemonic devices can be lifesavers.

"*Guten Abend,*" I repeated, extending my hand. "I am Fräulein Professor Doktor Katrin Nissen, your house guest for the Vegetation Mapping Conference."

His face brightened as we shook hands. "Ah, of course, of course. *Guten Abend*. And this is Herr Professor Doktor Eric Weber." His words seemed to come with an effort I hadn't noticed before, no doubt the result of trying to keep up with a young colleague's pace.

Weber, breaking protocol, extended his hand, to the dismay of von Reichstadt. The woman is always the first to initiate any physical contact, at least in this regard, and to violate this rule of etiquette would no doubt have some verbal consequences from the head of the Faculty after we parted company. I didn't mind in the least. Weber had all the enthusiasm and appeal of a fat puppy, eager to meet new friends and blissfully unaware he had goofed. He was also eager to begin what had all the earmarks of a long and animated conversation, and that told me all I needed to know. He was not my man. The one I sought wouldn't be this careless. Being a chatterbox is never a good cover, as it's much too easy to get caught up in character and let something slip. Nope. Not him, and not von Reichstadt.

His absentmindedness would have betrayed him long ago, if he were my man. Also, no interest from either of them regarding the ring. Two down, five to go. We parted company halfway down the block, and I looked back to see von Reichstadt reading Weber the riot act. Weber was hanging his head just like a puppy who had had his first house training accident. He'd learn. All puppies did.

Without von Reichstadt to make any further introductions, my work with the physics lab was finished for the day, but I'd made some progress. In conducting experiments, even a negative result has value, and so it was with today's exercise. I had eliminated two men from my list. Hopefully, tomorrow would be the day I found the right one.

▪ ▪ ▪

The cocktail party at the von Reichstadt-Müller home that night was a get together for the horticulturists presenting at the conference, but Von Reichstadt had invited one of his cronies so he wouldn't be the odd man out. I didn't blame him. Listening to another department talk shop makes for a very long evening, but his friend was not one of the scientists working on the nuclear project. That was unfortunate for me, but von Reichstadt seemed relieved to have a kindred spirit around.

The evening was balmy, with starry skies and a gentle breeze that was just enough to keep the humidity at bay. Marta had opened the French doors onto the patio, and many of us had taken advantage of the space to spread out. The back and side yards were large by city standards but not for this older, established neighborhood, where one didn't have to close the shades to keep the neighbors from peering in while you were dressing or attending to other matters.

I ventured down a brick path lined with mosses that meandered from the edge of the patio through rhododendrons and ferns to Marta's greenhouse. It was a handsome structure, made of stone and glass with wooden timbers accenting the entrance, a glass door with flower boxes on either side. It looked like a miniature gingerbread cottage, although definitely more substantial. The roof had a steep pitch to help the snow slide off and six windows that operated with hand cranks positioned along the peak to help regulate the temperature inside. The floor was earth, covered with a substantial helping of small stones to keep the mud at bay, and there were potting tables along one side and shelving on the other. Illumination was provided by a row of lights suspended from a metal rod that ran the length of the roof.

There were bins of compost, potting soil, various fertilizers along the back wall, and stacks of pots under the shelves. The little greenhouse also had a chair and a small table in the corner for doing the bookwork. I was taking some mental pictures for a day when I might have a home with a backyard big enough for something like this. It was beautiful. I had just scooped up a handful of the compost and was squeezing it to check the moisture content when Otto Crump, also out for a stroll, made his entrance.

"It's a bit heavy on the peat," he said.

I turned from the bin. "Yes, it is. You're obviously familiar with the setup here. It's quite nice."

"Thank you. I built it. It's a little sideline of mine, when I'm not stumbling across dead bodies." He took a proprietary look around.

Crump was a powerfully built man, not tall, but well-proportioned. His dress was unconventional, I had noticed, for someone in academia. He always seemed ready to trek off into the hills, with his lederhosen and sturdy footwear.

"Well, it's beautiful, but only one body," I said.

"Actually, no." His usually cheerful face took on a serious expression, and I sensed that I might have opened Pandora's Box. "This makes five in the past year, all either accidents or natural causes, but I started wondering after the third incident."

He had my interest. "Five?" I was dubious. "Would you like to explain?"

"Of course. The third-that was Schneider," he began. "He was as healthy as an ox. The verdict was a stroke, but I'm not buying it, and it's got us all on edge, as you might expect."

Well, this was an unexpected turn of events, and I wasn't about to question his eagerness to share the dirt with somebody he'd just met. Crump was not only willing to talk, he was anxious to talk, and my face obviously showed my willingness to listen, as Crump did look over his shoulder before moving away from the door. He took the empty water barrel, turned it upside down, and made himself a perch. He was comfortably seated and ready to launch into what looked to be a lengthy account, although he hadn't taken note of that fact that I was left to stand.

Did I want to involve myself in a string of possible murders at the university? To be honest, I did, but I knew I couldn't and I wouldn't. Still, it wouldn't hurt to listen to Crump's theories. There was nothing I could do about identifying my physicist until morning anyway, and I intended to contact Dieter's sister tomorrow as well. That first encounter at the photo-taking session hadn't been the right time or place to dig for information, but with my search of Dieter's apartment having come up cold and rather bloody, she was my only logical shot at finding him. All that was for tomorrow.

Tonight, my evening was free, and the only other activity on the agenda was engaging in small talk with the guests. Hours of terminal boredom there. So, I walked to the little desk in the corner, took the chair, and set it down where Crump was waiting. I was glad to get off my feet, and I listened intently as he launched into a story that went from unusual to odd all the way to weird. By the time he had finished, I wished I had taken the gun from Augie's filing cabinet.

"It all began about a year ago," Crump said. "From all appearances, it was an accident—a hit and run, and the driver of the automobile was never found. This accident was the only one that didn't result in a death. Amelie Kleinschmidt, Kurt's wife, was the victim. She suffered a fractured spine and has been in and out of hospital ever since. She'd been run down just after they'd returned from a ski holiday in Austria. Kurt's never given up hope that someday she'll walk again.

He's always on the search for a new specialist who might be able to help her. Anyhow, Kurt just got brushed by the car and ended up with a fractured arm and wrist. He lost a couple of fingers, too."

"I'd noticed his hand," I said. "I thought it might have been some type of machinery."

"It was. A machine with four wheels," Crump said. "Probably the most dangerous piece of equipment there is. Anyhow, the second incident, the first death, was Steiner. It was ruled a suicide. He'd hung himself in the utility closet. He was a funny little guy, always cracking jokes. Everybody liked him; well, not everybody, if you discount the suicide verdict. The odd thing was that he was so excited about his upcoming move to full professor after his current study was published. He was on top of the world."

"Sometimes people who are depressed can appear happy," I said.

"No. Not Steiner. It wasn't a coverup for anything else. He was just a nice guy."

"So, that's two. They're pretty different in their *modus operandi*," I said. "You'd be hard pressed to make a murder case out of them."

"Just wait. Hear me out. Next came Schneider He was a health nut. Vegetarian, runner, in top physical condition, and he just up and died of a stroke out of the blue. Totally unexpected. The guy was as healthy as you can be. And he was young. I don't think he was thirty-five yet. No. No stroke. I'm not buying it."

That one gave me pause for thought. "All right. I get this one," I said.

"Then, Jung. He'd been electrocuted in the bathtub when the radio fell in. He'd apparently been trying to change the station and pulled the radio into the tub."

"Well, that *could* have been an accident," I said, although my tone was getting more uncertain as Crump went along and his face showed he knew it.

"And now, Augie. You were there. You saw what I saw. You're not accepting the heart attack, and neither am I. Too many coincidences to be random chance."

I had to agree with Crump. But why? And who? Means, motive, and opportunity. The means were all there, spelled out. The opportunities seemed random enough or easily arranged. That left motive. Why? What was the common denominator? I agreed. It was a puzzle.

"So, what are you planning on doing about this?" I asked.

"Me? Nothing. What can I do? Nobody believes me, but I'm not convinced we've reached the end of all this." He got up and stretched.

Story time was over. We'd run out of victims, and it was time to rejoin the party. I cautioned Crump to watch his back. I liked him. He was the field man, always taking students on treks into the countryside in search of the undiscovered. The students loved him, I'd been informed by Gerda, and with his round face and amiable smile, I could see why.

I had plans to watch my own back as well. It's never a bad idea to be cautious. When I got back to my room, I had plans to check on the research interests of the victims. There had to be something that tied them all together. Apart from Kleinschmidt's wife, they were all professors. What was the common denominator? I wondered, as I studied the sideboard laden with food, my plate in hand.

My interest shifted to food, and as I stood by the sausages, I struck up a conversation with Fräulein Professor Doktor Emma Strupp, who had literally written the book on mycology, although her research was currently under criticism, mostly because fungus doesn't operate according to correct Nazi principles. It isn't constrained by political borders, and this is not convenient for the native plant enthusiasts who wish Mother Nature would toe the Party line.

I found Strupp settled in by the sausages, methodically stabbing one after the other with a toothpick and then transferring them to her plate. She'd amassed a sizeable mound, and I was captivated by the violence she was inflicting on the helpless hors d'oeuvres.

"Guten Abend," I greeted her, as I attempted to snag a couple of sausages before she had cleared the plate. A fairly robust woman in her late fifties, she had the general appearance of an unmade bed. She'd worn what she'd been wearing to work, probably every day since the Kaiser had abdicated—navy blue suit jacket over a white blouse buttoned securely from her neck all the way down, and a navy blue skirt that ended about mid-calf. Her black leather shoes bore every scuff mark they'd ever earned and didn't appear to have ever made the acquaintance of a can of shoe polish. I wondered why she'd even come to the party, unless she was out of food at home and figured this was an easy and free meal.

I pride myself on my conversational skills, and I can usually talk to just about anybody, but this woman was a tough nut to crack. With her mouth now full, she waved the hand with the toothpick in my direction, an action I took for an acknowledgement of my greeting. This was going to be a challenge, and so I settled in for the long count. Strategy is important in these situations, so I positioned myself in front of the cheese plate, her next logical objective, as the sausages were just about gone.

"I am Fräulein Professor Doktor Katrin Nissen," I began, as I matched her stab for stab with the cheese cubes. Her forward, or rather sideways, progress impeded, she finally swallowed and looked at me. The same lack of care extended upwards to her face. She was not an unattractive woman, apart from the eyebrows that could have done with a bit of pruning. She wasn't wearing makeup, not even lipstick, and frankly, the overall impact of her physical appearance was less than impactful. Her voice, when she finally spoke, though, had an unexpected depth and resonance. It was the most powerful thing about her, apart from her well-known intelligence. Strupp had not been invited to present at the conference, but as a senior staff member, she'd been invited to the cocktail party as a courtesy.

"Guten Abend."

Obviously a woman of few words.

"I have your book," I began. "It is an honor to meet you." Strupp's seminal work with fungi bore the somewhat boring title, *Fungi.*

Blank stare.

I tried again. "I am interested in your research." That was the ticket. Sometimes it just takes a little persistence. I motioned to a quiet corner of the room, away from the string quartet that was sawing away at some piece by Mozart, where two guests had just vacated their chairs.

She nodded, her mouth so full that her cheeks pooched out like a chipmunk preparing to store food for a long winter. The truth of the analogy didn't escape me as we maneuvered our way through the crowd, snagging two glasses of wine on the way from a tray by the sideboard. We settled in, and I was afraid she'd resume her love affair with the sausages and the cheese, but she surprised me. She set her plate down and seemed to relax. I realized that Emma Strupp was a nervous eater, but having found a safe place and someone to talk with, was ready to unwind.

"Herr Professor Doktor Becker was a difficult man," she began. "It is not good to speak ill of the dead, but if a situation could be made easy or difficult, he chose the difficult path. If a request could be made in an easy or difficult way, be assured he made it as difficult as possible." She took a sip of wine and cradled the glass in her hands. "Mycology is a fascinating field of study and has much potential for other fields, but he couldn't, wouldn't, see that. His focus was so narrow." She shook her head. "That will make it all the more difficult for me and the others to continue."

I nodded encouragement. "You are working on mycelia." Mycelia were the underground tendrils of fungus that could extend for miles, linking plant roots together in a sort of network. It wasn't much of a leap from plant sociology to plant communications. After all, if you lived in the same neighborhood, why not strike up a conversation with your neighbors? And it seemed that's what plants did. The study of mycelia was the basis for one of the theories on plant communications and plant sociology and, although still in its infancy, promised to yield some interesting results in the future. The problem was, as plant sociologists, such as Marta knew, if a plant community of, say, sugar maple trees here turned out to be connected through this fungal network to a grove of sugar maple trees in Poland or Czechoslovakia or Romania, then what was native and what was foreign? Essentially, they were all part of the same family. It was a huge monkey wrench thrown into Himmler and Tüxen's rantings about eradicating all the non-native plants from the landscape.

"Our research, or rather *my* research now, is just one part of the whole. This is groundbreaking," she smiled. "Plants do live in communities. They communicate with each other. We know that now. They warn each other of danger. We believe they have the ability to share this information through various means – perhaps electrical impulses, release of certain chemicals, or through the mycelial network itself. We don't know, but we are beginning to ask these questions. Unfortunately, fungi operate beneath the surface of the soil and can't be easily seen and readily observed. They cannot recognize the artificial borders we set up when we create countries. Fungi have become politicized, and that may very well spell the end for my research." She replaced her wine glass on the table. "You are presenting at the conference. What is your particular area?"

I gave her a synopsis of my research with propagating hardy perennials and my interest in the applications of plant sociology to my work. Our conversation continued until we'd exhausted the more superficial aspects. I shortly excused myself, begging fatigue, to return to my room. Strupp remained in her chair, once again holding the plate of hors d'oeuvres, an isolated figure, soon to be an outcast. The writing was on the wall, and she knew it. I recalled something I had read by Voltaire: "It is dangerous to be right in matters on which the established authorities are wrong." Fräulein Professor Emma Strupp was in danger.

Halfway to the staircase, I came across my two fellow houseguests, who were not having a friendly conversation.

"What did you do with them?"

"I don't know what the hell you're talking about. I haven't been anywhere near your part of this presentation. You are most welcome to check my papers. I don't have yours. I haven't seen yours, and if you can't keep track of them, that's not my problem. Although, it *will be* my problem if you can't find them and ruin our turn at the podium on Tuesday. You sure as hell better find them." Winkler stormed off, leaving a confused Professor Bauer in his wake.

"Guten Abend," Bauer said, bowing slightly. "Just some pre-conference jitters, that's all. Everything is all right."

But his worried face contradicted his words.

▪ ▪ ▪

My assignment from Gene had been straightforward: Find Dieter Weiss. If I could not find him, I was to find the physicist with whom he'd been dealing. All I needed for that was access, time, and luck. Tonight's conversation with Crump, hadn't been anywhere near as straightforward. It was a puzzle, but I've always enjoyed puzzles. Crossword, jigsaw, any kind. This was a different kind of puzzle, though. I didn't know if I had all the pieces, I didn't know what it was supposed to look like when it was completed, and I wasn't sure the clues I did have were accurate.

Untangling the threads of one murder is challenging. Untangling the threads of four plus an accident that could have been and should have been fatal was more complicated. Strand by strand, I pulled them apart, trying to find the link. These were not random occurrences. There was some sort of design, however random it appeared to be on the surface.

I was back in my room with a notepad and pen and the biographies of the professors for the Faculty of Horticulture. I'd been filling the pages with everything I could remember from my conversation with Crump, and I was trying to connect the dots. People kill for a reason. The reason doesn't have to make sense to anyone else but the killer, but there's a reason all the same. So, how could the deaths of these people have benefitted someone? Who stood to gain?

Their ages ranged from 35 to 57.

There was one woman and there were four men.

All were connected to the Faculty of Horticulture in one capacity or another, with Amelie Kleinschmidt being the outlier, as her only connection was as Kleinschmidt's wife. And there I stopped. It was staring me in the face. Kleinschmidt had to be the catalyst around which all these murders revolved.

Could Amelie have been targeted simply because she was his wife? Possibly. Who was out to hurt him or even destroy him? Who were his enemies? Augie had been, if not an enemy, certainly not a friend. He was Kleinschmidt's brother-in-law, so there was the family connection again, but he wasn't the murderer. He was among the murdered. What had I found when I checked out his office? The obvious academic things, but the bottom drawer of the filing cabinet had yielded a variety of seemingly unrelated items. There was the schnapps, there was the gun, and then the diary. The schnapps didn't appear to be of any significance. I knew many of my colleagues who kept a bottle stashed in their offices. The gun was a different story. And the diary. I wish I'd taken a bit more time to see what was in it. Returning to the Kleinschmidt angle, two of the victims were related to him. What about the others?

Walther Steiner, age 42, who was supposed to have hung himself in the utility closet, was well-liked by everyone, well, almost everyone, as Crump had said, since somebody had killed him. But generally, he was popular, although had no close friends. He was, as Crump had noted, a *little guy*, and judging from his picture, he was short and quite thin, with a pencil-thin mustache that was a holdover from the late 1920s. His full head of slicked-back black hair and prominent nose seemed out of place on such a compact body. He had a piercing gaze. Steiner's area of research interest had been plant taxonomy, a field with similarities to bookkeeping, and indeed, he could have been a stereotype for the profession. He was, or had been, interested in documenting the discovery of new species and was a recognized world authority on that.

Louis Schneider, 42, had been the health enthusiast. A vegetarian, he neither smoked nor drank, had followed a strict regimen of exercise, and had run marathons. He had the trim build of a runner. Six feet tall, he was going bald, a fact that led him to shave his head. He had a current girlfriend. His professional interests focused on ethnobotany, a field that was looking to document the medicinal properties of plants from Asia and South America. Crump and I had briefly discussed that field during our scheduled meeting.

Georg Jung, 57, electrocuted in the bathtub by his radio, was possibly the least fit member of the group. He was a widower, overweight, balding, and a heavy smoker who would have been a more likely candidate for the stroke or heart attack. His research area was in plant communications, with a focus on the release of volatile chemicals to deter predators. He'd teamed up with researchers in Poland and in France, but that had ended when the Nazis had started rearranging Europe's borders.

And that was it, as far as their research interests were concerned. They would all have taught classes, attended meetings, and served on numerous committees as part of their academic responsibilities. That was the next thing to tackle, and the university biographies didn't offer a whole lot of help in that regard, but I made a list of each committee they had served on. If there was something linking the victims, I couldn't find it, but since December, four members of the Faculty of Horticulture, roughly one-third of the professors, had been permanently relieved of their duties. The link had to be there and Kleinschmidt had to be involved, but I couldn't see how.

It was 3 o'clock in the morning that the answer came to me. I'd been in that half-state between sleep and wakefulness when the lines of thought sometimes come together. The sheet that I had created flashed before me and I sat up in bed. I'd been in the right forest, but I'd been barking up the wrong tree. I didn't know who the killer was, but I was pretty sure I knew who the next victim was going to be.

Saturday, June 15, 1940
French troops abandon the Maginot Line

CHAPTER FIFTEEN

Interlude

Morning couldn't come soon enough. Crump had given me his business card, and I called him shortly before seven. His voice was a rather fuzzy. Either I'd gotten him out of bed or he'd gone heavy on the schnapps last night. Could have been a combination of both. I apologized for waking him and then told him what I was thinking and asked if he could make a phone call to Emma Strupp. If my theory was correct, she was the next victim on the list. The silence that greeted me, however, told me what I hadn't wanted to hear. Emma had been run down and killed on her way home from the party. It had happened sometime around midnight. A car had knocked her down as she crossed the street. The vehicle had then sped away, and the police were looking for witnesses.

I was too late, and the bad taste in my mouth had little to do with the quality of the wine I'd drunk last night. There were just two questions to be answered—who would be next, and who was the killer? Crump said he was leaving on his next field trip a week from Wednesday and was toying with the idea of not returning. It seemed like a reasonable plan. Without knowing anything more about department politics, I couldn't venture a guess as to who was behind this. As hard as it was, I had to let it go, get my job done, and get out in one piece.

I intended to let it go, but it was still on my mind. It's just not that easy to drop something in the middle, especially murder, because if I'd had any doubts at all, Emma's death was the clincher. If I just had a little more time, but regardless, it wouldn't hurt to let it simmer on the back burner while I attended to business. I'd just keep my eyes and ears open, but today was the start of the weekend. With two days before my next opportunity to connect with the Physics professors, I was on the train to a town just outside Prague in Czechoslovakia, one of last year's Nazi acquisitions, on my own botanical field trip. It might sound like a long journey, but takes just about the same amount of time to go from Berlin to Prague as it does from New Haven to Washington, D.C., roughly four hours. Europe is a compact continent, unlike my adopted homeland.

It was an opportunity I couldn't pass up, because I knew that, even with my impeccable credentials, it wouldn't be long until no travel would be permitted for Americans, regardless of their political sympathies. And so, I'd left early in the morning to arrive in Prague by lunchtime. My plan was to check out the location where Heinz Hagemann, Carl Förster's chief gardener, had discovered some low-growing *rudbeckia* back in 1937, study the soil, take a few samples, photograph the general terrain, and then catch the evening train back to Berlin. That was my plan. Nothing complicated. Nothing dangerous. The university was expecting us to take day trips during our free time. That's why they had the cars for hire. I kept telling myself that, even as I knew that my little side trip was well outside their suggested geography. Still, nobody had specifically said we needed to stay within Germany, and I was only going a short distance from the border to the Bohemia region of Czechoslovakia. It was practically almost Germany. *Practically*. Almost, but not quite.

I've always had a soft spot in my heart for *rudbeckia,* commonly known as black-eyed Susans. They're tough, resilient, drought-resistant, and pretty. They aren't terribly concerned about where they live, and they serve as one of the clinical specimens in my studies on the propagation of hardy perennials. I was hoping to photograph the location where Hagemann had located them, so I could research why and how they adapt to their environment, how they spread, what difficulties they encounter, how they overcome them, and so forth. Basically, I wanted to learn everything I could about them while I still had the opportunity to do so. So far, this was allowed by Nazi ideology, but only because they hadn't thought much about black-eyed Susans. Yet. Give them time.

And everything had been going so well. That should have been my first clue. Whenever things are humming along smoothly, it's because the monkey wrench that's just about to be thrown into the mechanical works hasn't made contact yet. When things are going well, however, one doesn't always stop and consider contingency planning. It's not the time for the *what ifs,* and that's usually when everything falls apart. I should have listened to that *little voice* that kept nagging at me. I was depending on people I didn't know. My driver, for instance. I had hired him at the railway station. He had the run-of-the-mill car, and his rates were reasonable, but something was just a bit off. I couldn't put my finger on it, and since time was short, I chalked it up to fatigue, worry about who the killer was at the university, how John was faring in England – a whole host of things, but the bottom line was, I didn't listen to my gut instinct, and, as a result, this day had serious potential for becoming my last. If I couldn't get out of this mess that I'd gotten myself into, they'd be putting the *rudbeckias* on my grave.

The roadblock had been set up about five kilometers from the train station and should have been just a routine check of papers. It's an everyday occurrence. Everybody with a badge and a uniform wants to see your papers. It doesn't matter if they've stopped you on your way to the butcher's or the airport. Anyplace, anytime, anywhere. It's the control factor, reminding you they're in charge, and you're not. And this would have been just one of those annoying, yet predictable stops as well, if my skittish driver hadn't panicked and bolted from the car and hotfooted it into the woods, leaving me high and dry. I didn't know why. Stolen car? Forged passport? It didn't matter. What did matter was that this made the SS suspicious, of course, and they dispatched a motorcycle to run him down. And that's exactly what they did. He lay in the road as flat as a sausage waiting for a bun. And now, his problems were over, but mine were just beginning.

My crime was guilt by association, even though I didn't know this guy from Adam. He was just a taxi driver, but it was enough. When the SS yanked open the passenger door and hauled me out, they weren't terribly polite about it, as attested to by the resulting large bruise on my left cheekbone and my split lip. They practically threw me to the side of the road, where a young man kindly caught me before I took a nosedive into the drainage ditch. Now, I was just one more of the unfortunates lined up by the side of the road waiting to be trucked into town to be dealt with.

I didn't have to wait long, as it seemed I was the last person needed to fill some quota, and so, the quota met, we were loaded into a truck, transported to town, and marched to the city hall. Inside, we were ordered to take our seats in the wooden pews confiscated from the church and have our passports ready for inspection. Judging by the potential for occupancy, the SS was planning on turning this place into a major processing center, and they'd raided the local church to fill their seating requirements. The pews were positioned in three neat rows that ran the entire length of the wall opposite the front door. The hymnals were gone and so was hope, it would seem, but hope springs eternal, and I'd be damned if I'd let some lily-livered taxi driver be the reason I departed this earth. I had flower seeds in my pocket. They were possibly *rudbeckia*. I had every intention of taking them home, analyzing them, and planting them, whatever they turned out to be, and that wouldn't happen if I bit the dust here.

So, what to do? It was a doozy of a problem, and I couldn't let fear or wishing I'd done something different take control. In spy school, we were taught to isolate each hostile situation, identify its characteristics, and then develop appropriate strategies for turning the situation to our advantage. It had all seemed so simple then. At the present moment, with the fear factor trying to intrude on my thinking, I was having a little problem with the isolating step. I did finally get my thoughts organized. I knew what I had done wrong. I had assumed the driver of my rental car was licensed by the state. I hadn't considered the possibility that he was a freelancer. Point against me.

The Gestapo's first mistake, however, was not shooting me when they'd had their chance. Point against them. Their second mistake was what would ultimately, if it could, get me out of here. It was assuming I would just sit like a lump on this hard wooden pew while they took their sweet time getting around to dealing with me. It's the arrogance of those in authority. They assume everyone is cowed by their presence. I wasn't the least bit cowed. I was furious and I was also uncomfortable. My move would have to come soon, as I didn't want to press my luck, hoping they'd go for a third mistake which would somehow be forgetting all about me until closing, when the desk clerk finally would look up from his paperwork and see that they'd somehow overlooked someone and just tell me to go home.

No. That wasn't likely to happen, not even in the movies, so, how to get myself out of here before they called my name became my obsession, along with the entrance door. I'd memorized its every splinter and knothole. A strip of rubber tacked onto the bottom kept the rain from seeping underneath. Work schedules and official notices were tacked to the panels above the dented brass doorknob. A pneumatic device by the top hinge sighed gently as the door opened and closed. Four centimeters thick. Four centimeters that were the barrier between life and certain death. I wasn't all that enamored of the *certain* aspect of that outcome.

Thinking and planning are all well and good, but without any opportunity to put the plans generated from that thinking and planning into action, it's just passing time. I'd been sitting still as a stone for at least three hours and every muscle was screaming with fatigue. A trip to the bathroom would have been welcome, but I didn't think the Gestapo would oblige my request. I shifted in my seat. The misery around me was palpable, and there was nothing I could do about it. The heavy-set woman to my right was sobbing softly into her handkerchief. Every so often, she'd twist the cloth into a coil and pull on the ends, as if fashioning her own noose. She had given up. She was too old for the slave labor battalion, and her fate was sealed. The boy on my right was rail thin with a pimpled face. About sixteen, he'd been cracking his knuckles, his neck, and his back for the past hour. He had a limited future ahead of him, even if he turned out to be a productive worker. I understood his terror, but he was making it difficult to concentrate. If I could think of something, maybe there'd be hope for all of us.

There had been eleven of us to start, but our numbers had now dwindled to five, as each detainee was processed and removed by an armed guard. Some went down the hall to the right, and others were escorted out to the left. I didn't know what the distinction was, but neither one was going to end well, and I had no intention of joining either of the ranks. My thoughts raced. There had to be a way out, but damned if I could find it. Once again, I studied the room, looking for something, anything that could help me. At the rate we were being shunted through reception, if that term even applied, I had ten, maybe fifteen minutes of maneuvering time left.

A year ago, this wouldn't have been happening, and what the Nazis had done to Prague since overrunning Czechoslovakia last September was a crime, but then they excelled at that sort of thing. The building, my current prison, had been the former city hall. It had been gutted and turned into a recruitment center for forced labor. The art that had once decorated the walls had been spirited away to some secret Berlin vault, no doubt. The dominant color was now grey, and the atmosphere stank of fear, stale sweat, and despair.

The room itself, where I waited, was jammed with filing cabinets, desks, and harried office staff. A portrait of *Der Führer* positioned at midpoint on the far wall supervised the room's activities. Beneath Adolph's chin, a door opened onto a hallway. This didn't look promising as an escape route. Going deeper into the bowels of the building would not achieve my objective. Two floor-to-ceiling windows looked out onto the street, and I briefly considered the possibility of running full tilt at them and crashing through. Odds of surviving that option were not good. If the glass didn't sever an artery, my back would make an excellent target. Nope. It would have to be the main entrance or nothing. So, I waited for my chance and figured that since I was already in a church pew, I might as well send a request to heaven for a little help.

Things must have been a little slow in the request department up above today, because I had no longer breathed an *amen* when a diversion came. I have found that recognizing opportunity when it presents itself can be difficult, and so I wasn't sure this was it, but waiting any longer wasn't going to improve my chances. I had to recognize this was all I was likely to get.

"*Herr Kopchak.*" The intake official, working down his list, barked out the name. A stooped man, in his late seventies, gripped his walking stick and rose with difficulty and then shuffled to the desk to take the designated spot before the clerk. Instead of meekly answering questions, however, the old man lifted his cane as high as his arms would let him and then brought it down on the official's head, not once but twice, before the guards could draw their weapons. It seemed that once they'd started firing, they would never stop, and they pumped round after round into him, continuing long after Herr Kopchak, resistance fighter, had escaped this world.

Then, amidst the din and the confusion, and with a quick prayer for the old man's soul, I rose, made a quick gesture with my eyes to the old woman and the boy to give them a chance, turned, and walked deliberately to the front door, which two entering SS officers politely held open for me. I favored them with a confident smile, and with just three steps down to the street, was thinking this might just work.

"Keep walking, Fräulein." A uniformed arm slipped through mine and propelled me down the stairs, where we made a left turn and proceeded down the sidewalk. "Don't turn around," the voice commanded, and I saw no reason to argue. We moved away from the building at a steady pace and, as my heart rate slowed, training took control. My companion, whose face I had yet to see, walked with a pronounced limp. From the few words of our one-sided conversation, I detected a faint accent, but from where I couldn't decipher. Two very long blocks later, we turned off the main drag and finally stopped at a sidewalk café. Seated, facing the street, our coffees having arrived, I remember breathing for the first time since I had left the city hall. I knew I had to have been doing that all along, but breath, a reminder of life, somehow hit me hard.

"And so we meet again," my companion laughed, although it wasn't a pleasant sound.

Now, I can think of a million or maybe just a thousand things this man could have said, but laughing was not part of the equation, because then I knew. I remembered that voice. I also cast a quick glance heavenward and wondered if the *Powers that*

Be were enjoying this little farce, for farce it was fast becoming. The man's visage was slightly different, thinner. There was that disgusting little mustache below his rather nicely shaped nose. But it was the eyes that struck me. How cold and empty they were, even while he laughed. I felt that I might have escaped one terror only to be thrust into another. I knew who he was, what he was capable of, and that I was at his mercy. That his uniform bespoke an officer in the *Schutzstaffel* didn't help matters one whit.

"What do you want, Ronin?" I asked, trying to suppress the upwelling of terror trying to overcome me.

"Oh, so many things."

I wasn't enjoying this, not one iota. I tried again. "Whose side are you on, *this time*?"

"I am on my way, or rather I *was* on my way to Berlin, when our paths chanced to cross. My presence is requested at the highest levels." His tone mocked his words. "This could be quite a coup."

My heart sank.

"But they weren't the highest bidder, and that's all that matters." He drank some coffee, but his eyes were watching the street.

I do not believe in coincidences. Events simply intersect in time in the grand scheme. It's all part of the *small world* syndrome. We tend to meet the same people or the same kinds of people as we go through life, just because that's the way it is. We move in the same social or economic or political or religious circles as our peers and so we have a higher degree of probability of meeting others occupying similar notches in the world than those who don't. Take, for example, the world of espionage. How many of us are there, actually? Exactly. Not all that many. So, it's not unusual for our paths to cross from time to time, as ours just did. This can be good or bad, and in this particular situation, I wasn't sure which. I wondered where his sister was these days. She was working on our side, but my companion's allegiance was only to his bank account. Still, engaging him in conversation might be beneficial.

"I met Margo a few months back," I said. "She warned me about you." I realized I had a death grip on my coffee cup and my fingers had turned white.

"Yes, well, she has her own problems. Are you finished?" He glanced at my drink, and without waiting for a reply, stood. "You can take your chances here, if you like, or you can accompany me to Berlin. I assume that was your next stop before all this happened. If you're coming, come now. I won't ask again."

"Why? Why are you doing this?"

He hesitated only a brief second. "I had a bad fall a few months ago, as you may recall."

"You didn't need to jump out the second-floor window. That was your choice, and judging from the way you're walking, not the best one."

"And the alternative? I believe you had other plans for me. Anyhow, fractures take a while to heal. One of your countrymen without political scruples took me in and asked no questions. Let's just say I'm evening the score, but when you get out of the car in Berlin, don't look back. The debt is repaid. Don't expect anything else from me, and pray, if that's what you do, that our paths never cross again." Three hours later, approaching the border, he broke the silence. "Your passport, please."

For me to retrieve it from the money belt where it was residing next to my little camera required some physical maneuvering, and he shot a questioning glance at my handbag.

"It's best that Tereza Novak remains somewhere in Prague." I handed him Astrid Andersson's passport, which he accepted without comment. We all know how the game is played, and I had decided to use one of the passports Gene had given me on my little day trip to Czechoslovakia. I hadn't been all that sure that Katrin Nissen would have been allowed across the border. It was just a feeling, and so I had made other arrangements. I would only resurface once we had safely crossed the border back into Germany. After today's little adventure, the less association I had with Czechoslovakia right now, the better.

Given Ronin's uniform and the official car, the passports were just a formality, and when finally we pulled up in front of Marta's home, he spoke one last time. "Kiss me."

"I don't think so." I was appropriately indignant.

"It's not a request, damn it. Do it. We are being watched."

Well, of course, in that case, safety first. After an appropriate length of time, he released me, I got out, and he drove away. And sure enough, Marta was waiting by the door, holding it open for me.

"You don't waste much time," she said, smiling.

I returned the smile, my hand ostensibly smoothing my hair but in reality covering the bruise. I needed a patch job with some Coty face powder pronto. It had been one hell of a long day, but one thought kept replaying itself in my mind. We would meet again, Ronin and I. I was almost certain of it. But when? All paths converged in this game, and today had been a chance or perhaps a not so chance encounter. I wondered what his assignment was that had taken him first to Prague and then to Berlin. He was working on our side right now, but he couldn't be trusted. He'd even told me as much, and his warning was clear. The next time our paths crossed, he might very well kill me, and he'd do so without guilt or remorse. Contrary to what some may believe, the enemy you know is far more dangerous than the one you don't. And I knew Ronin.

CHAPTER SIXTEEN

Kristine's home

"This seemed like a good idea at the time," Kristine said, "but circumstances have most assuredly changed." The publicity dividends she would reap from hosting the press reception could help her move up in the ranks of the Party, but with the complication of a gunshot victim who just happened to be her long-lost brother and who was now sleeping in her bedroom, publicity was the last thing she wanted.

"And this is probably also not the best time to tell you that a black cat crossed my path on the way here," Ilsa said.

"Right to left or left to right? It makes a difference."

"Coming from the left."

"Damn, Ilsa. When things start to go downhill, they just seem to accelerate. We are *not* going to be superstitious. It was just a cat. They don't bring bad luck. They go all different directions. All the time."

"Right. I shouldn't even have mentioned it."

"Anyhow, it doesn't matter. It will be what it will be. All we have to do is get through the evening without anyone finding out about Dieter. How hard can that be?" Kristine looked at Ilsa, defeat in her face. "It's going to be impossible."

Ilsa took a deep breath and exhaled with little puffs. "Enough of the gloom and doom. We can handle this. First things first. We need to find someplace for Dieter. He can't stay in the bedroom. It's too close to the parlor and the kitchen. Somebody is bound to open the door, looking for the bathroom or just being nosy. This is the press we're talking about. They get paid to be nosy."

"There's just one other place," Kristine said. "The dark room. It's the only place that has a chance of working. We can make up a bed for him there and put a sign on the door or something." She opened the door to her darkroom and switched on the overhead light. The darkroom was a converted spare bedroom just off the parlor where the party would take place. There had been one window on the street side that she'd had boarded up, sealed, plastered, and painted, so that light couldn't intrude. She'd removed the closet door and installed shelves for her dry supplies—the film and photographic paper, enlarger and cutter, and had had a counter installed with cupboards beneath on the long wall opposite for the developing, stop, and fixing tanks, and chemicals—the wet supplies used to develop the film. All her cameras and lenses were housed in a separate set of cupboards just inside the door. It was a neat and tidy setup and she'd put every centimeter available to use, which was what was creating the problem now.

"It's going to have to be here," Kristine said, "right where I'm standing. Smack dab in the middle of the room. There's no place to hide him, and anybody who opens the door and turns on the light will see him."

"What about the basement then? No, scratch that idea. We'd never get him down there. It'd be too hard on him and we'd have to go outside to do it, anyway." Ilsa rested her hands on her hips and looked once more around the room. "We can make it work. You're right. It's not ideal, but it's all we have. Do you have a cot or a sleeping bag? If you've got both, that would be good."

Kristine shook her head. "All my camping equipment is back in Rostock. I didn't think there'd be much use for it here. Boy, was I wrong on that one. I've got about three blankets and that's it. It's not enough."

"All right. I'll go back to my place and see what I can scare up. I won't be long. That floor is going to be too hard without some cushioning."

While Ilsa went for more bedding, Kristine went to check on Dieter. He was still running a fever and hadn't shown any interest in the chicken soup she'd made for him. She had coaxed some water down his throat, but even that had been a struggle, and now they needed to get him out of the bedroom and into the darkroom, when he should be left alone to rest. She counted off eighteen steps from the edge of the bed where he now was to his new temporary quarters. Getting him there wasn't going to be easy, but it was the fever that worried her the most. After they'd gotten him resettled, if he suddenly cried out or started hallucinating, it would all have been for nothing.

She taped a hand-lettered sign on the door that said *Darkroom—Do Not Enter,* then stood back and examined her handiwork. It didn't look in the least bit professional. Somebody would think that she was hiding her dirty laundry in there and would open the door just because of it. This was becoming more and more worrisome. Still concerned about the possibility of Dieter giving himself away in his fevered state, she took the radio from her nightstand and moved it to a table close to the darkroom door. She'd have it on when the party was in full swing and hoped that any sounds coming from inside the darkroom would be covered by the noise of conversation and the music from the radio.

"I saw the cat again," Ilsa said upon her return. "This time he was going the other direction, so I think he canceled himself out. I hope. He's sitting on your porch with a dead mouse." She had brought an armful of blankets and was stacking them on the darkroom floor. Added to Kristine's three, the new bed wasn't anywhere near as soft as the real bed, but at least it offered some comfort. "It's not terrific, but it's not horrible, either," Ilsa said. "Let's go get your brother."

. . .

"Dieter, wake up. I need you to wake up. It's time to move." Kristine rested her hand on his forehead. He wasn't getting any better. If his fever didn't break soon, he wouldn't make it. "Dieter. Please wake up. You can go back to sleep as soon as we get you in the darkroom."

Finally, his eyelids fluttered and he made a small sound.

"If we help you, do you think you can stand? Once we get you on your feet, it's not far. We can take our time."

This time he opened his eyes, and she took that as a sign he was ready.

She waited as he struggled to pivot on his good side and swing his legs over the side of the bed. "Don't rush. We've got all afternoon."

He managed to get one leg in position and grimaced.

"What does the pain feel like? Is it an ache? Is it sharp?"

"It hurts." Dieter got the words out with effort as his second leg joined its partner. She bent and took his arm, positioning it across her shoulders, and guided him to his feet, where Ilsa took his other arm.

"Dieter! Look at me. We won't let you fall. We can hold you." She felt the weight of his body leaning into her. "Here we go." She took a deep breath, pushed off, and they half dragged, half carried him, stopping to rest after each step. "We're almost there. Just a few more steps and you can lie down again." She gritted her teeth as they lowered him onto the floor. His lips moved and Kristine leaned closer.

"I liked the bed better," he said, and she patted his shoulder.

The effort of moving him had taken its toll on all of them. The lack of sleep and the constant worry were making it difficult to concentrate, and Kristine collapsed on the floor next to Dieter. She took his hand and her eyes traveled to his ring. "Remember. You must be quiet, and you must be still. I will come in when everyone has gone."

Dieter took a shallow breath. He moved his lips, but no sound came. She checked the bandage and was relieved when she found the wound hadn't opened up again. She tucked her duvet around him and looked once again at his ring. It was ebony, with a griffin made from gold about to leap, as if on some unsuspecting prey. She'd seen that ring before.

"I know this ring," she said to Ilsa. "I've seen one just like it, but I can't remember where." Her mind was clouded with fatigue and stress, but she'd remember in a minute. Then, her thoughts cleared. "Yes. It was at the university. One of the women I photographed had the same ring on a chain around her neck." What was her name? She couldn't remember. It had been early in the day, though. Easy enough to find out. She had the negatives from the day's shoot. There had to be a connection, but what was it? Had she shot Dieter? Without any answers, each question just built on the previous one, in an ever-lengthening chain of fear.

She raised his right hand. "Dieter? What is this ring?"

But Dieter had fallen back asleep.

"Be careful, Kristine. You are going somewhere you maybe shouldn't be going." The concern in Ilsa's voice matched the concern on her face.

"I have to find out. I have to find out what this all means, what it's all about."

"You need to stop and think. You're all caught up in this because he's your brother, but think, and not just about where you've seen the ring and who was wearing it. What do you know about him, really? Why has he come here now to find you?"

"I know what you're saying, Ilsa, but he is my brother. I read the letter from my father. I saw my picture." She stood. "I know there is more to his story than he told me, but he came here because he trusted me. He came here because I am his sister. I have to trust him, too."

"Just be careful, please."

"One more thing." Kristine dragged the chair over and stood on it while she loosened the light bulb in the ceiling fixture so it wouldn't come on if somebody tried to turn on the switch by the door. "You'd better go now," she said to Ilsa. "The caterers will be here soon. I can clean up the bedroom. Tomorrow morning, if he's better, we can put him in my car and I'll take him home. It's too risky for both of us if he stays here much longer."

"You sure you'll be all right?"

"I'll be fine. Don't worry."

"Easy thing to say. Hold on, here's one more thing we can do." Ilsa moved the small table with the radio from the wall and centered it in front of the darkroom door. "Just a little extra insurance," she said. "I'll be back tomorrow after the caterers have cleaned up."

. . .

Half an hour later, everything was put back in order. Kristine had opened the windows to air out the bedroom and had stuffed all the bedding down the laundry chute, but the bed was lacking a duvet, which would be odd, if someone looked, but there was nothing to be done about it. She only had one, and Dieter had it. She tidied up the rest of the house in preparation for the arrival of the caterers, due in an hour with the hors d'oeuvres and the drinks. They were scheduled to return in the morning. She'd specifically requested an early time slot, so they'd be done with the cleaning and be gone by 9 o'clock. Only after they left, would it be safe to move Dieter back to the bedroom.

Kristine returned to Dieter with the water pitcher and a glass and some soup for when his fever had passed. She filled the glass and put it on the floor within arm's reach. Then, she fetched the chair and sat next to him, waiting for him to awaken. He looked comfortable enough, or maybe it was just wishful thinking, but he had spoken to her and had tried to help as they struggled to the darkroom, even though it was just a few words. He was young. That should help him recover. With bullet wounds, though, there was no way of knowing what havoc the bullet had caused inside. If the damage hadn't been too severe, he should be getting better soon, but it couldn't be rushed. He needed time.

And then the big question. What was the significance of the ring? When they had first met, Dieter had said he had to leave. Where had he gone? Had the woman she'd photographed at the university been involved? It seemed the longer she knew him, the less she knew about him. She got up and went to the stack of negatives from the university assignment and shuffled through them until she found the one she was looking for. She closed the door and turned on the safe light and developed the negative in the red glow. The process couldn't be rushed. Everything was taking time, too much time. Finally, the sequence from the developing solution to the stop solution and finally to the fix was completed, and she clipped the photograph to the wire suspended above the tanks to dry. She stared at the face and read the name badge. Fräulein Professor Doktor Katrin Nissen stared back at her. Kristine remembered her now. She was the woman who wouldn't follow directions. She wouldn't tuck the ring into her blouse. She wanted it to be seen. Why? What did the ring mean? What was her connection to Dieter? Why had Dieter been shot? Dear God, would the questions never end? There were too many questions, and she didn't know what to do to get answers. She went back to the chair and sat once again.

"Dieter, please wake up. We must talk," she pleaded. "You must tell me what this is all about. I'm frightened, but I have to get ready for the party now. I will have to leave you for a little while. It will only be for a few hours. Please talk to me, Dieter. Tell me what to do." If he would just answer one question... but Dieter slept on. She rose from the chair, looked at his pale face and felt totally helpless. What more could she do? Right now, nothing. If he were better in the morning, she would take them to their father. If there was no improvement, she'd have to risk calling for an ambulance. She could get him back outside somehow, so they wouldn't know he'd been here. But he'd be better in the morning. Yes. He would. He had to be. Something had brought him here, and whatever it was, it waited just outside the door. It was something foreign, something evil from which there might be no escape. She turned off the safe light and went to dress for the party.

Sunday, June 16, 1940
French Prime Minister Paul Reynaud resigns and is replaced by Marshal Philippe Pétain

CHAPTER SEVENTEEN

University of Berlin

Any other Sunday would have been a quiet day at the university, but this was no ordinary Sunday. With the conference scheduled to begin in less than twenty-four hours, the stress was taking its toll. Tempers were short and nerves were frayed. Kurt Kleinschmidt was trying to keep the lid on, but he was just as wound up as the presenters, if not more so. While reaching for the schedule, he knocked over a cup of coffee on his desk, soaking his speech papers. He picked up the sodden mess and tossed it into the wastebasket by his feet.

"Gerda!"

"Yes, sir." Gerda, covering the short distance from her desk to his office almost instantly, took one look at the damage. "I'll clean this up. And I have more copies of your speech. I've already typed the corrections you made yesterday, so just give me a few minutes here." Her voice had taken on a motherly tone and had the intended effect.

Kleinschmidt leaned back in his chair and exhaled audibly. He rubbed the tight muscles in his neck and then stood. "Thank you, Gerda. I'll just go make the rounds again."

Gerda smiled as she watched him make his way through the main office. She hummed as she dried off the desk blotter, straightened the stacks of papers, and trimmed a leaf and a wilted petal from the Christmas Rose. She retrieved a clean copy of Kleinschmidt's speech from her file and set it on the desk, placing a fountain pen alongside for him to use for corrections. One last look around and she was satisfied. Everything was perfect.

. . .

Everything wasn't perfect, though. As Kleinschmidt walked down the hall, he passed two offices where the lights were off and the doors were closed. He'd lost two staff in the past forty-eight hours: one, his brother-in-law and the other, a woman he'd known and respected for a good many years. Augie's wife-widow, he reminded himself—was now staying with family while she sorted out his affairs, but Emma Strupp had nobody to handle hers. He'd have to get the university attorney involved on Monday. As far as he knew, Emma had no living relatives. He paused by Emma's door and then let himself in.

He wasn't prepared to find that the room had been stripped of everything that had been Emma's. There was nothing left. Her desk was bare. He pulled open the drawers. Empty. He opened the filing cabinet. The drawers were empty. All her research was gone. All her personal items were gone, as well. It was as if her ghost had come in the middle of the night and removed every trace of her.

Bewildered, he turned to look across the hall at Augie's office. The same emptiness greeted him when he opened the door. It was as if Emma and Augie had never existed.

They had been erased, and more importantly, for the department, regardless of their political beliefs, their research had also been erased. Not even forty-eight hours after their deaths, they'd been cleaned out. This was an outrage. Where was the common decency? The funerals were still being planned. It was not right. Who could have done such a hateful thing? Was it Gestapo? Surely, he would have been informed before they removed valuable documents. And why would they? The Gestapo did nothing quietly. There would have been a dramatic entrance, crashing about, and general disruption. No. Not Gestapo.

Then who? And why?

He left Augie's office and, heading back towards his own, noticed for the first time the two additional plants on his secretary's desk. And then the realization of what this meant hit him. His face was a mask of barely controlled rage as he strode to Gerda, who greeted him with a pleasant smile.

"What have you done?" his voice thundered throughout the department, and Gerda's smile vanished in the instant. "Answer me! Where is the research?"

Gerda's voice quavered under the assault. "I did what I always do. What I am supposed to do, of course. I cleaned up. I threw away the trash. Their work was trash. You know it, I know it, everyone knows it." She straightened in her chair, meeting his gaze straight on. "I did what I had to do. It's dead. I buried it. It's gone." The smile never left her face.

"Where is the research?" His voice had become dangerously even, and he reached around the desk and pulled her to her feet. "Tell me. Now." He twisted her arm, pulling her towards him.

"I just told you. You weren't listening. With the rest of the trash, of course." Her voice had taken on an air of righteous anger. "I took it to the basement for the janitor to dispose of. Really, sir. You don't need to worry. It's all gone. It can't hurt us anymore."

"When? When?" he repeated, his voice growing more and more agitated.

"This morning, of course. I arrived early to clean up." Her voice had taken on a tone of patient exasperation, much as one would use in trying to explain something complicated to a child.

Kleinschmidt released his grip on her arm and spun away, breaking into a dead run down the corridor to the stairs and down the four flights to the basement and the furnace room, leaving Gerda massaging her bruised arm and staring after him, hurt and some nameless, darker emotion in her narrowed eyes.

Kleinschmidt's thoughts were coming in staccato bursts as he tore down the stairs. What would he find? What had she done? It was Sunday. The janitors would not be there. It was June. The furnace would not be in use, so Gerda couldn't have burned it. Still, what could have possessed her to do this? So much paper to sift through in so short a time. He opened the door to the furnace room and was greeted with a veritable mountain of trash. Gerda hadn't used the refuse bins. No. She'd opened the door and flung everything into one enormous pile and then emptied the trash bins from the entire office on top of them. What she had said had been accurate. She had literally buried Augie and Emma's files. The entire building's refuse ended up here, awaiting the Monday collection, and when the janitors arrived in the morning, they'd have no choice but to shovel everything back into the bins and wheel them away. There was no rhyme or reason to it. It was pure insanity.

To find what he was looking for meant he would have to check every piece of paper. It was a staggering task, and he needed time, but time wasn't on his side. Kleinschmidt removed his jacket, tossed it aside, and rolled up his shirtsleeves. He was looking for manila folders and cardboard boxes and all the slides and all the lab reports and God knew what else. He groaned. How would he know when or if he'd found everything? The filing cabinets had been jammed, but if he could just find something to get him started. He righted one of the empty bins, wheeled it over, and picked up the first piece of paper.

CHAPTER EIGHTEEN

Homeward Bound

From the instant Dieter had shown up on her doorstep, Kristine had not slept more than a few hours, and the fatigue was threatening to overwhelm her. There had been no time to sleep today, and the Press Reception had gone by in a blur. The caterers were on time to set up, and the servers and food had arrived at 6:00, along with the wine. She'd foregone adding music to the soiree, apart from her radio. From past experience, she knew that all the press wanted to do was consume as much free alcohol as possible, get loud and obnoxious, and stumble off into the night. Tonight's event had only reinforced her opinion, and when she'd finally shut the door behind the last of the stragglers, it was nearly midnight. She leaned against the door, took a calming breath, turned the lock, and went to check on Dieter. No one had moved the table blocking the door or breached her *Darkroom—Do not Enter* sign. There'd been no problem with the wait staff or the caterers. She had to give them credit for that. There had been no ugly scene, no hotheaded arguments, just the interminable, predictable cocktail chatter. Now, with the quiet finally descending, she could relax and hopefully get some sleep after she'd attended to her brother.

"Dieter," she called softly as she opened the darkroom door. "I'm here." She reached for the chair so she could stand on it to tighten the lightbulb in the fixture and then hesitated. The sudden burst of light might be too much for his eyes. Instead, she made her way in the dim light to his bed and spoke again. "Dieter, they're gone. You're safe."

The water pitcher and glass were just as she had left them. The bowl of soup, cold now, sat untouched by the bedside. Everything was the same, but it wasn't. She touched his hand. It was now cool. The fever had been banished. She touched his face, but there was no response, no flicker of the eyelids. She felt for his pulse, but there was no reassuring rhythm of beats. Then she knew. Sometime during the evening, Dieter had lost the fight. She sank back on her heels. So many questions that would never be answered. So much time that would never be made up. It seemed so cruel, so unfair. In the dark stillness, she stroked his cheek and wept.

Later, she had no idea how much later, she wiped her eyes and stood. *Kristine, you have a problem.* Dieter's problems were over and done with, but unfortunately, lately, hers just seemed to go on and on. She could telephone Ilsa, but what could Ilsa do? She needed her rest, and there was really only one thing to be done. Dieter had passed from her life, and the cold reality threatened to consume her. She couldn't let it. She wouldn't let it. She'd been alone before, and she would get through this on her own.

Priorities. Self-preservation was priority number one. She could do nothing more for Dieter. She had done what she could, and anyway, this was no time for recriminations, for *what ifs.* A week ago, she hadn't even known he'd existed. That might sound cruel and uncaring, but she couldn't let a stroll down the memory lane of what might have been distract her from the here and now. Dieter was dead. She was alive, and if she wanted to stay alive, she had to find a place for him. That place wasn't here, but she had to find it, and find it now. She touched his hand, noticing once again the ring. She removed it from his finger. It was one thing, at least, she could keep to remind her he had lived. The more she tried to think of other options, the more she realized there weren't any. It was the middle of the night. Traffic, what there was of it had slowed to a trickle and her street was quiet. Every house on her street was dark. Morning was hours away. She looked at his face, so still. "Dieter, it's time to go home."

Rolling Dieter up in the duvet wasn't as difficult as she thought it would be, but literally lifting a dead weight was not easy. She grabbed the corner of the duvet and pulled it behind her through the house and outside to her car, where she braced his body against it and then half-rolled, half hoisted him into the trunk, positioning him as best she could. Back in the house, she gathered up his makeshift bedding and shoved everything down the laundry chute, where it joined the rest of the bedding. She returned the pitcher, glass, and soup to the kitchen, which was a mess from last night. Glasses and dishes everywhere. She'd need to call the caterers to change the time for them to come and clean up. She took one last look around the darkroom and shut the door. It was just an empty room. It was as if he'd never been there.

Half an hour later, she was well outside Berlin, en route to the only safe haven she had. Somehow, just the motion of driving helped. She was at least doing something. It was a good four-hour drive to Rostock, and she'd be pulling up to the house just as breakfast was being laid out in the dining room. Her father had always been an early riser. He'd already have been outside working with his roses. She hadn't figured out yet what she'd say when she showed up, but she'd think of something. He'd always wanted her to come visit. *Not like this, papa, I'm sure. Not like this.*

CHAPTER NINETEEN

Forging Alliances

In the movies, heroines are invincible. When wounded, they snap back to their strong, perky selves soon after the intermission. If they fall from a cliff, their injuries are negligible. If thrown from a galloping horse, they spring back to their feet, run down the animal, remount, and continue the chase. In real life, the body doesn't heal instantaneously. It's a process that can't be rushed, and bruises don't disappear overnight. They can take a couple of weeks, if they're the industrial strength variety, as mine was, and they pass through an ugly color progression of black, blue, green, and yellow along the way. The mirror on the wall above the dresser didn't lie. I could do a passable job of covering the damage with face powder and hope it would hold up in daylight under close scrutiny. If I were going to finish the task at hand, I didn't have the luxury of time to hide out and avoid inquisitive glances until my face returned to normal. Even after a decent night's sleep, I was still bone-tired. Almost being executed is draining, and, even for experienced agents, takes a little time to work through.

This morning, I wanted time for a heart to heart with Marta. She was a professor in the Faculty of Death, and I needed to find out what her opinions were on the body count. With the exception of Kleinschmidt's wife, each of the victims had been involved in research that didn't go along with Nazi thinking. The key to all this had to be the native plant angle. It just made sense. Professor Steiner had been interested in discovering new species, and that quest had taken him beyond the political borders of Germany. Professor Schneider had been investigating plants in Asia and South America, looking for a natural resource for developing new medicines. Same story. He'd been working outside Germany. Professor Jung had had research partners in Poland and France. Again, not working within the confines of what would have been officially approved. Emma Strupp and Augie's work with mycelia had also covered broad territory, extending for miles beyond the German border. Augie had been the only vocal resister; the rest had just methodically tried to continue with their work without engaging in political arguments. It hadn't been enough, however, and they'd been eliminated. That was one motive. They'd all served on committees, some had served on the same committees. The means by which death had been inflicted had been varied. Opportunity was the last variable. Someone with access to the Faculty of Horticulture would only have to wait for the right time. That left only *who*.

Logically, if my theory were correct, anyone in the Faculty who was faithful to the Party would not only be spared but would also be a suspect. This was not about professional rivalry. This could be a Nazi hit job, perhaps not by a Gestapo agent, but definitely by someone in the Party. The alternative was that it had been made to look like one. But then, what about Amelie? She was the one victim that just didn't fit. No, there had to be something I wasn't seeing. If I didn't see that something today, my amateur investigation would be history. Come Monday morning, it was back to official business.

I spent more time on my face than my attire this morning, settling for the same polka dot outfit I'd worn before. My cheek looked pretty good for looking pretty bad. After fastening the clasp of the necklace, I set off downstairs for breakfast and a few words with my hostess. I had a slight advantage, with Marta having seen me arrive in an automobile with obvious connections to the Party, and the amorous interlude with my travel companion wouldn't hurt my cause in the least. I was curious as to what her comments would be.

An apple pancake with a small side dish of apple cinnamon compote and a cup of strong coffee were my selections after I checked out the food on the sideboard in the dining room. With the addition of a vase of blue Forget-me-nots set to one side of the spread, Marta's current perennial in bloom, breakfast was almost too pretty to eat. Almost. It tasted as good as it looked and smelled, and I savored every delicious mouthful, because frankly, I can't cook. Oh, I try, but nothing I make ever comes out as good as this. Someday, when we have that home in the country, I'll learn to cook. Or maybe I'll hire a cook. That sounded better.

"*Guten Morgen, Marta,*" I said, taking my accustomed seat at the table, which allowed me an added bonus today, since my damaged cheek would not be directly in her line of vision.

Having just taken a sip of coffee, Marta gave a little flutter with her fingers in reply.

"I am so sorry to hear about Frau Professor Doktor Strupp's accident," I began. "Do the police have any idea who might have done it?"

"No, there were no witnesses. It's not likely the driver will be found." Her reply was curt and her tone dismissive.

"It's a shame. We had a congenial conversation at the cocktail party. I understand she'd been working on expanding her area of research into Poland and other areas of eastern Europe. Who will take over for her now?" I hoped that would be enough to get Marta motivated to join in. Meanwhile, I took another forkful of apple pancake. It was then that Erich made his appearance at the door.

"Coffee?" Marta asked.

"I don't think so. I'm not terribly hungry this morning. I'll get coffee at the office." He bowed in my general direction, and I soon heard the front door shut.

Marta sighed. It was the sigh of a long-suffering spouse. "He's forgotten his heart medication again. I'll have to drop it off at his office on my way to mine. It's not that close, either." She looked hopefully in my direction and then at her cane propped against the counter.

"Yes," I said, reading her look. "I'd be happy to deliver it for you."

"I'd appreciate that. Thank you. Where were we?"

"Emma Strupp," I said. "We were discussing the future of her research."

"Yes, it is a shame, but I don't believe there is any real interest in continuing her line of inquiry. The field has been exhausted, and there's not much else that can be done there, especially when there is so much fertile ground for study in Germany." She took another sip of coffee. "*That's* the future for our work, isn't it?" She gave me a broad smile.

"Most definitely. The entire field of native plant study is all-encompassing." Here I was again, cheerleader for Hitler. "I don't understand the need to look beyond one's own borders. It's the same for America. There's a great deal of discussion in my own department now, and it seems as if everyone is choosing sides. It's going to get worse before it gets better, I'm afraid. Regardless, you have certainly had more than your share of deaths this past year. It must be quite a strain on the rest of you." Not the most original segue into what I wanted to find out, but it worked.

"It has reduced the number of staff in the Faculty, that's for certain, but fortunately, those involved in critical research have been all right. I believe that will continue. Sometimes accidents happen, and some people are weak."

Cold and rather heartless comments. Marta was one cold lady. I tried one more question. "What about Herr Professor Doktor Crump? I haven't had much of an opportunity to discuss his work with him. He seems to always be setting out or just returning from a field trip to the hinterlands with his students."

"Oh yes," she said, her voice now warm and thoughtful. "Otto is always working with the students. His work mostly takes him out into the countryside, although on this last trip, they ventured to the Eifel to study a fairly old stand of edelweiss."

"That's a beautiful flower," I said. "And native." I swore that if I had to say *native* one more time, I was going to go wild.

"Yes. His research will prove most valuable." She set down her cup and pushed back from the table. "I've been noticing your ring. It's quite distinctive."

My hand went to the necklace in a gesture of ownership, something I had practiced in the mirror. "Yes, it was my fiancé's."

"Was?" There was concern in her voice.

I gave a sad smile. "He's gone now." And I also pushed back from the table before I was dragged into a lengthy tale of love lost.

"Well, you've got a new friend, or so I surmised after your outing. And judging by the automobile and his uniform… Yes, yes, I was spying!" Marta giggled with excitement. "Your taste in men is excellent!" She picked up her plate and put the cup on it for the trip to the kitchen.

I considered this and remembered Ronin's warning. "Oh, no. No. He's not new. We go back a ways. Quite a ways." And I left her pondering that titillating piece of information, as I excused myself and left for the university with von Reichstadt's medication.

. . .

With only three days left to find my man or men, if somehow I could find Dieter, my level of concern was increasing. Monday was looking like my best chance to make contact with the remaining five physicists, although there was an outside chance one of them might decide to drop by work today. Scientists, especially those working on critical projects, tended to keep irregular hours. At any rate, I wouldn't make any progress here at the house. There was no way at breakfast, though, I could have predicted that, instead of casing the Faculty of Physics, I'd be sifting through trash with Kurt Kleinschmidt in the bowels of the building that housed the Department of Horticulture. Plans change.

Good people will suffer fools and evil just so long, and I had a gut feeling that Kurt Kleinschmidt was a good person caught up in some bad circumstances. There comes a tipping point, however, when a decision has to be made as to which direction one will go. The decision has to do with ethics, morals, and the essential nature of goodness. If the decision is postponed too long, sometimes it isn't possible to get things back on track. The difficulty is in knowing when *too long* is. For purposes of the conference, Herr Professor Doktor Kleinschmidt had chosen the path of political expedience, but four members of his staff with opposing political views were now dead. My curiosity was piqued, and I figured a little digging around couldn't hurt. Little did I know. So, my plan was to first stop by the Physics Faculty for my drug delivery and see what was going on there before I tackled Horticulture.

Nothing was going on there. At least nothing that I could use to any advantage. Everyone was attending a meeting organized by a member of Himmler's staff. No doubt they were being instructed on proper behavior during the Conference. It appeared they were going to be occupied most of the morning, so with nothing to see, nobody to talk with, and nothing to do there, I left the pills with Monika, the Faculty Secretary, and headed back to Horticulture.

Not surprisingly, most of the botanists were hunkered down in their offices and Gerda the Gatekeeper was at her station, guarding Kleinschmidt's office. It seemed almost medieval. All she needed was a moat and a pet dragon.

"*Guten Morgen Fräulein Kunkler,*" I began, but my greeting wasn't acknowledged. She didn't look up from her paperwork. I tried again, and with an audible sigh aimed in my direction, she finally looked up.

"*Ja?*"

How one word, a simple *yes*, can convey so much information never ceases to amaze me. I ignored the lapse of protocol and good manners. "Is Herr Professor Doktor Kleinschmidt in?"

"He's in the basement." She lowered her gaze back to her papers, picked up a rubber stamp, and slammed it savagely onto an innocent requisition form.

I had been acknowledged and dismissed. No pleasant smile today. All right, then. I turned and retraced my path, all the time feeling as if Gerda were watching me leave, and it was not a pleasant sensation. She was furious. That much was obvious. Whatever had happened, I was quite glad I had had nothing to do with it.

A strange place to be, the basement, but if that's where Kleinschmidt was, then to the basement I would go. It wasn't hard to find. It was where all basements were, so I went back down the stairs and kept going after the ground level to where the flight of stairs ended at an open door marked *Furnace Room*. Sure enough, there was the professor, ascending a pile of trash like a mountain climber tackling Everest. When his footing appeared as secure as it was likely to get, I offered a greeting.

"Guten Morgen!"

Kleinschmidt turned slightly and raised his left hand in response, his right one clutching a sheaf of papers.

"Can I help you find whatever you're looking for?" It was obvious he was on the hunt for something he'd thrown out by accident, and after a quick look at the challenge ahead of him, he nodded.

"I need to find two years' worth of research notes."

Hmmm. Two years? That's not an accident. That's a catastrophic event.

"They're here somewhere. I've just located one folder, but it's empty. And, ah! Hold on." He bent to retrieve a short stack of papers, which he stuck inside the folder, then stepped to the side and snagged another sheet.

"I'll be happy to help. What am I looking for?"

"The mycelia research of Professors Strupp and Becker."

If raising an eyebrow wouldn't have caused my cheek to hurt, I would have raised it, but hopefully, there would be time for answers down the road. I put my questions on hold, and, for the next few hours we worked our way up and down, sideways and across, and back and forth, crisscrossing each other's paths until we had covered every inch and created our own miniature version of Everest at the base of the mother mountain.

"I can't be sure we've found everything, but it looks good. I don't see any lapses in pagination." Kleinschmidt was seated on the floor, putting numbered pages from a loose-leaf notebook back in order. "No, there's a page missing here." He looked back at the heap and shook his head. "I don't think it's critical."

"So," I began, seizing the moment. "What happened?" And, as if someone had opened the floodgates to the Johnstown Dam, the story unfolded.

"Gerda threw it all away in one of her cleaning frenzies. She spends her life trying to make mine easier, and she thought by getting rid of this," he motioned to Everest, "she'd simplify my life. But what she didn't understand was that most of my anger at

Augie was because, in my heart, I knew he was right. Not about his research, I don't know enough about that to offer an opinion, but about his point that silencing the opposition never leads to anything good. Without dissent, the silence grows until silence is all that is left." He paused for breath and looked at me. "We are almost at that point. I am trying to keep the Faculty together, but it's futile. We all want to survive, but survival isn't guaranteed, even if you keep your silence. Augie's death was convenient. I can't argue with that, but Emma's? Research is about discovering facts, not promoting ideology. At least it shouldn't be. Emma wasn't political. She was a scientist." He shook his head at the incomprehensibility of it all.

"Herr Professor," I searched for the right words. "My research focus is life. I study how plants multiply and divide to ensure survival, but that's just the baseline. I study how they adapt as their environments change over time, and while there are points my fellow Dane, Jens Jensen, and I agree on—invasive species that displace native ones must be managed or not allowed to propagate—we don't share the same perspective on noninvasive species. If his view silenced mine and prevailed, if that were so, there would be no roses outside of central Asia, no orange trees outside of China. Our lives wouldn't be richer, they'd be poorer."

Kleinschmidt nodded. It seemed as if he'd been waiting, hoping someone would affirm his thinking. "We're living and working in a world where insanity is supposedly sane, and nonsense is supposedly reasonable. We've already lost all of our Jewish colleagues, and there are plans to keep reducing the number of female students and female staff, as well. A university is about increasing knowledge, expanding our mindset. This is not healthy, and it's not moral, but it is going to continue, and there's no way of knowing who will be next." Our conversation continued in this fashion, and for a little while, at least, we kept the silence at bay.

"What's going to happen to all this work?" I asked. "This was their research focus. Strupp and Becker devoted their careers to this line of investigation." We had placed Augie's research in one of the wheeled containers and Emma's in another. Just going through it, reading it, looking at the slides, would take weeks, if not longer.

Kleinschmidt shrugged. "I don't know what will become of it. Perhaps, after all, it will end up back down here, but not if I have any say in the matter." He scowled, a foreign expression for his usually pleasant face. "I suppose there will have to be some sort of disciplinary action. Gerda means well, but this time she's gone too far. She's always trying to help. After my wife's accident, Gerda was like a rock. She helped care for Amelie. Whenever I've needed help, she's always been there."

This time, the eyebrow ignored the bruise. A pattern had emerged, one that Kleinschmidt hadn't recognized. I'm not always a quick study, but I am persistent, and I'm pretty good at putting the pieces together when they're all there or mostly all there. Kleinschmidt had just given me the last piece of the puzzle. Everything fit. I just needed Kleinschmidt to see it too. "Your wife's accident?" I asked.

"Just like Emma's." There was visible pain in his eyes. "It was late last year. We had just returned from a skiing holiday in Austria. A car came out of nowhere and disappeared just as quickly. Johanna's spine was fractured, and she's been in and out of hospital ever since. She doesn't complain, but..." his voice drifted off and he suddenly looked incredibly tired.

I had to ask the next question, although I figured I already knew the answer. "When did Fräulein Kunkler start work in the Faculty?"

Kleinschmidt rubbed his forehead, thinking. "Oh, just before Christmas. She was a godsend, the way she just moved right in as if she'd always been there and knew exactly what to do. Why, she even…" he stopped mid-sentence. "What are you saying?"

"Herr Professor, I think you know what I'm saying."

"No. That cannot be. That's ridiculous. That's…that's…" but the more he protested, the less convincing his words sounded, until finally it was obvious even he didn't believe them any longer. "Oh, dear God." Kleinschmidt's face was ashen.

The sound of the door closing caused us both to turn in its direction.

"Oh, sir, you should have just let me take care of everything. I always have, you know."

Damn. I *knew* I should have picked up Augie's gun. Gerda stood just inside the door, the weapon in her right hand. It was the final touch to the most surreal setting I have ever had the misfortune to find myself mixed up in.

Gerda's voice was soft, gentle, but it didn't match the look in her eyes that blazed fire. It didn't take any spy school training to tell me this was not a good situation. Nope. Not good at all. Whackos are the toughest to deal with. At least with another agent, training kicks in and you know what to expect. It's like a chess game played by masters. Move, countermove. Strategy is key, but this was no chess game. This was a street fight, and this lunatic might do anything and undoubtedly would, unless I could find a way to stop her. Silence was the enemy here. Nature abhors a vacuum, as they say, and she'd be likely to fill the void with a gunshot that would be headed in our direction. I had to get her to keep talking until she relaxed long enough to let down her guard for just a second to give me a chance at her.

"That's right," I said, nodding thoughtfully. "You always have taken good care of Professor Kleinschmidt, Gerda. Nobody could ever say you haven't. You've done more than anyone else ever has." Nothing like stating the obvious.

"Of course, I have. Don't be foolish. I know how important I am." Her gaze slipped towards Kleinschmidt. "But sir, why did you have to tell her? Now everything is spoiled. It was our little secret. Nobody else is supposed to know. Just us. It's *our* little secret." Gerda's mood was going up and down faster than a roller coaster with a stuck throttle, but I needn't have worried about keeping her talking. The woman wouldn't shut up.

Kleinschmidt couldn't hold back any longer. "Gerda, what are you talking about? What secret?" The fear in his voice was gut wrenching.

"Oh sir, you know. You're just teasing me." She gave a delicate laugh. "Your wife, of course. I'm sorry I didn't do it right, but sometimes things don't work out exactly as you plan. Still, it was good enough. She wasn't a bother to you anymore, and you had me to take care of her. I didn't mind at all." She sighed, and a radiant smile spread across her face. "And I got better as I went along. It got easier, you see." She leaned forward, confidingly.

"Gerda," I had been able to rotate slightly during her monologue. Just a little more maneuvering room was all I needed. She redirected her gaze in my direction. Good. Keeping her concentration broken up was the plan. "But what about Augie? Why did he have to die?"

Kleinschmidt shot me a look of horror. He'd gotten as far as Gerda stealing the research notes and attempting to murder his wife. He hadn't considered the scope of her madness.

"What about Augie, Gerda?" I persisted. "He wasn't nice to Professor Kleinschmidt, that's it, isn't it? You were helping again."

"No, he wasn't *nice*." She made a face as if tasting something bitter. "He wouldn't do what he was supposed to do, and he wouldn't stop making trouble. He was writing everything down in that diary. All his suspicions. He didn't trust me, you see. I don't know why, but I had to end it. I took that vile book home and burned it." She turned to Kleinschmidt. Her voice was reassuring. "It can't hurt you anymore, sir." Then she swiveled back to me, her eyes, still unnaturally bright, squinted at me, a dark cloud of suspicion across her face. "How did you know that? How did you know about him?" She turned the gun in my direction.

"Professor Kleinschmidt told me. He told me everything, Gerda. He told me how much you help." I had my answer. Now, I needed to get her looking at Kleinschmidt again, not me, if this was going to work.

"Tell Gerda, Professor Kleinschmidt," I said. "Tell her what you said to me and that everything is all right." I hoped he had recovered enough to join in. I needed a little help here. My mouth was dry and my heart was racing. *Slow down, Katrin. Easy does it.*

"Oh Gerda," Kleinschmidt began, picking up on my prompt to take her attention from me. "No, of course you don't have to worry. Really. Fräulein Professor Doktor Nissen is a friend. She won't hurt me. We're all going to be just fine." He managed a weak smile that wouldn't have convinced any sane person, but then Gerda wasn't a sane person, so it bought another brief respite.

Gerda gave a quick nod—more of a jerk than a nod—and continued. "Yes. He was easy. He couldn't taste anything." She laughed again. It was a piercing, unnatural sound. "Every part of the plant is poisonous, you know. I just made an extract from the leaves of the Christmas Rose and put it in his coffee. It couldn't have been any easier." She straightened. "Oh, sir. You see, this isn't going to work anymore. You are telling everyone about our secrets. Did you tell her about Emma, too?"

She shook her head in disapproval and disappointment. This was a lull in the conversation, and lulls weren't good in this type of situation. During the headshake, I managed one more sidestep and was now positioned to lunge, if she'd just cooperate a little and stay exactly where she was. No, not this time. She pivoted and turned towards me, now waving the gun in a slow, deliberate, exaggerated circle, until it came to a stop pointed directly at me. It would be a body shot, probably get me right in the midsection if she discharged the weapon now. Not a good situation. She couldn't miss from that distance, and I'd be a goner.

I kept my eye on her, but my words were aimed at Kleinschmidt. "This would be the time if there ever was one," I said, and with the shock finally wearing off, he got my message and took a step towards her, the perfect distraction. "Gerda, my dear," he called out, and the effect was instantaneous. Finally, the words she had been longing to hear caused her to relax just enough so that the gun was now pointed at the floor.

I lunged. It wasn't graceful, but I rammed her in the gut, and even though she went down hard, she still held onto the gun. In the movies, she would have fallen on the gun and died by her own hand. No such luck here. Even flat on her back, she was still as dangerous as before. I swatted at her hand, driving it backwards and heard her wrist snap as it contacted the water pipe. The gun fell, I grabbed it, and Kleinschmidt grabbed her. Wasting no time, we hauled her upstairs, where I said the words I never thought I would say, "I'll call the Gestapo."

While we waited, I filled in the rest of the blanks. "They'll find some significant body damage on her car, and I expect some of it will be older damage from when she struck your wife."

"She would have killed again," he said. "Dear God, she's killed a third of my faculty."

"Well, she would have killed me, that's for sure. And you'd have been on probation, while she made sure she could trust you again. No telling what would have happened next. But I wouldn't be too quick to let my guard down."

"What do you mean? She's confessed. It's finished."

I shook my head. "No, I don't think so. I think there is somebody encouraging Gerda, manipulating her. There's someone operating in the shadows who is the real maniac behind this. I don't believe Gerda acted alone. The problem is, it could be anyone." I looked at the gun, now on the table in the hall, out of everyone's reach, especially Gerda's. There is nothing that can cause a situation to deteriorate quite as rapidly as having the police respond to a call and find someone holding a firearm. Questions are not the first thing that will happen, and I wanted plenty of distance between us and it to ensure our safety.

"Why did Augie have a gun?" I asked and saw his quizzical expression. "I was walking through the department and saw Augie's office," I explained. "There was something not natural about his death, and it had been bothering me. The horrible expression on his face didn't seem consistent with a heart attack, and I suspected foul play. The door to his office was closed, and I was curious, so I went inside. I saw his presentation on the desk, all ready for delivery, and then I did a little looking around. I saw the gun in the drawer in the filing cabinet. Unusual to find one these days."

"Oh, there's a lot of them still out there, hidden now, of course. Augie had this idea of joining some kind of a posse and working against the Nazis. I think he had a fantasy of dying in a shootout like in one of your Western films. He was hoping to get to America before it was too late." Kleinschmidt gave Gerda a quick glance. "He waited too long."

"It would have been easier and quicker than being poisoned, that's for sure," I said. "So, now, this gun has to be surrendered to the Gestapo, thanks to Gerda."

Kleinschmidt nodded. "One less weapon to fight them with." He had made his decision and chosen his side. I hoped the mastermind behind these killings wouldn't find out before he or she could be unmasked.

Gerda had spent all of her manic energy and now sat on the bench in the hall, cradling her broken wrist, and crooning a lullaby. Prison was not in her future. She had been controlled and programmed to kill out of some twisted kind of love. We'd taken her out of the picture, but the artist was still out there, someone far more dangerous than Gerda. Even stranger, though, was that Gerda and our mastermind had done what the Nazis would have done sooner or later, anyway. Our killers would be branded criminals; the Nazis would have given themselves medals.

CHAPTER TWENTY

Rostock

Rostock is a charming, old seaport town on the Baltic. It's home to the oldest university in Europe, churches dating back to medieval times, and the New Rostock Brewery, of which Gerhardt Trautmann was the brewmaster. Trautmann was a short, stocky man, well into his fifties, with jet black hair, a ruddy complexion, broad shoulders, the hands of a working man, and a stomach that attested to his love for beer. He had a literal mind and lacked imagination, but his real weaknesses were women, especially his daughter, Kristine, and roses.

Regarding the latter, he'd been tending the flower gardens along the driveway since before breakfast, just as Kristine had known he would be, when the sound of an automobile engine caused him to look up from his labors. The car passed him and stopped at the front steps to the house. Kristine finally opened the door but didn't get out. Strange. He dropped the trowel into the bucket with the rest of the garden tools and walked to the car. And of a hundred things his daughter could have greeted him with, he could never have thought, "*Your son is dead*," would be her words.

"Papa, I didn't know what else to do, so I brought him home." She took the keys out of the ignition and the letter from her handbag and handed both to her father. "He found me last week. He showed me the letter. He was shot. I tried to take care of him. He died last night. The trunk." She told the story in its simplest, most painful form. She slumped over the steering wheel and sobbed, deep heart-wrenching sobs, as exhaustion finally overcame her.

Gerhardt was not a quick-thinking man. He was deliberate in his actions and in his speech, and so, while Kristine bawled, he mentally reconstructed the last three minutes and reviewed his findings until he came to the only conclusion he could. This was really happening.

"Kristine. Kristine. You must stop this." He was patting her shoulder with no effect. Kristine couldn't stop crying, and so Gerhardt, ignition key in hand, opened the trunk, unwrapped part of the duvet, looked inside, and slammed the trunk closed again all in the space of half a minute and returned to Kristine, who was finally winding down. He took her by the hand and led her from the car into the house and to the parlor, where she fell onto the sofa. He left her there while he got her a cup of coffee and then sat down in the easy chair across from her. "Kristine. You must tell me what has happened. What is this all about?" This was some sort of nightmare. It had to be.

"Papa," she couldn't seem to find a place to get started. She held the cup in her hands, letting the warmth find her fingers. Finally, she calmed down enough to make a beginning. She nodded her head towards the letter her father was still holding. "I was working. It was last week. Early last week. Wednesday, I think. Yes, Wednesday. I was walking around the university, trying to find the right place to photograph Herr Himmler for the conference."

At the mention of Himmler's name, Gerhardt groaned. Himmler was involved. Kristine had been speaking for less than a minute, and his mind had already traveled from gathering information to how they would survive this and planning an escape, but she was continuing with her story.

"I was having trouble finding a place where the lighting was good, and so I sat down on a bench, and a man came up to me and handed me that envelope. He said his name was Dieter Weiss and that he was my brother." With that, she looked at her father who said nothing, but the expression in his eyes told her Dieter hadn't lied, and she fought back the tears. "He said that the letter and the picture of me would prove it. Of course, I had many questions, but he seemed so sincere and just said he had wanted to meet me before he left. He said that he had to leave, and that I could keep the letter and photo. He said he hoped we would meet again someday, or something like that. And then he left. So I read the letter and saw the picture, and he was right, wasn't he? I have—I had—a brother. Papa, why didn't you ever tell me?"

"Kristine," he began, and then stopped. "No. That is for another time. Tell me. What happened then?

How did you get from that to this?" He pointed in the direction of the car outside the door.

"Dieter found me again. I think he had followed me to find out where I lived. I was home, and I heard a big noise at the door. I opened it, and he was there. He had been shot. He fell into my arms, and I pulled him into the house. I tried to help him, but what could I do? He'd been shot," she repeated. "There would have been so many questions I couldn't answer. I was afraid. I cleaned his wound. The bullet had gone all the way through. I hoped he would get better, and he was getting better, until I had to move him before the press showed up for the party."

The press. Gerhardt groaned again. First Himmler, now the press. This could not get much worse.

"I made a bed for him in the darkroom so he could hide there, but when I went in to check on him after everyone had gone, he had died. All I could think of was getting him out of my home and somewhere safe. So, I came here." She sat back, still holding onto the coffee cup and waited for her father to say something, anything besides groaning.

Gerhardt Trautmann, as owner and general manager of the brewery, was used to handling small problems. A broken water line. A delay in the garbage collection. A work dispute. But this was not something he had ever envisioned having to deal with. People should not have to deal with dead bodies in the trunks of automobiles. Nobody he knew had ever had such a problem. Why was he having this problem? What had he done to deserve this? Dieter's mother had left *him*. He'd been perfectly happy with the way things were.

He hadn't hurt anyone. If Kristine's mother hadn't gotten nosy, everything would have stayed perfectly fine the way it was, and everyone would have been happy, but that was in the past. This was a different time. Kristine had finished her story, and so now, he once again reviewed everything she had said. He was, above all, a practical man. He had only one question.

"Think carefully. Did anyone see you with Dieter at any time?"

She frowned. "Well, I suppose it's possible that first day. I wasn't concerned about that. It was, at least for me, a chance meeting. It was out in the open. There was nothing secretive about it."

Her father nodded. "All right. At any other time? When you were taking him to your automobile?"

She shook her head decisively. "No, Papa. I am certain. As certain as I can be. Nobody saw anything when I was taking him to the automobile." Her father hadn't asked her about the time in between, and she was glad of it. He didn't need to know that Ilsa had been there. He'd never liked her and had told her as much to her face. Gerhardt Trautman could be a cruel man.

He nodded again and reached for his pipe. What should he do? He could call the doctor and say his son had been visiting him from America, had taken ill, and died unexpectedly. But travel was restricted, and family didn't visit from America these days. And besides, before the doctor would issue the death certificate, he would have to examine the body, and that meant he would see the wound. All gunshot wounds were reported to the authorities. Authorities could be bribed, but that opened a door that could not be closed. He finished lighting his pipe and then set it back down in the rack. Eighteen years. It had all gone by so fast, and yet it seemed a hundred years ago. Every possible course of action he considered kept coming up against a brick wall. There was no place for Dieter to go. No place except here. Except home. He took up his pipe again. He had made his decision. "Go get some sleep, Kristine. I will take care of everything."

She rose without a word and ascended the stairs to her old room, climbed into the feather bed, and wrapped herself in the duvet. Sleep came quickly.

Gerhardt continued to think. It was only six o'clock in the morning. Nobody was out and about. The front drive was secluded. The grounds were spacious, the flower beds in full bloom. He worked in them every day, always planting, moving plants from one place to another, cutting new beds. Finally, he put the pipe back in the stand for the last time. He had arrived at the only course of action open to him. Dieter would not be leaving his home again. And shortly, there was the soft sound of a spade working in the rose bed.

Kristine slept through the morning, and when she awoke shortly after noon and went downstairs, she found her father seated in his easy chair, his pipe once again lit, resting next to his coffee on the table beside the chair. She went to the kitchen, found some crusty rolls and cheese, poured herself a cup of coffee, and returned to the sofa to sit near her father. There was nothing more to be said. She needed to return to Berlin. She finished her meal and then walked to where her father was still seated in his chair. She hesitated and then embraced him. "I am sorry, Papa." She left him to his chair and his pipe. He was staring out the window at his roses.

Back in her automobile and on the way home, an overwhelming sadness filled her heart. She had told her father everything from the first meeting to her arrival here. Except for Ilsa. Except for the ring. Something had held her back. She didn't know why, and so her story had been as complete as she could make it. Except for Ilsa. Except for the ring.

Monday, June 17, 1940
France surrenders to Germany
The HMT Lancastria, transporting soldiers and evacuees from France is sunk by the Luftwaffe – the worst maritime loss in British history.

CHAPTER TWENTY-ONE

Conference, Day One

The central auditorium of the University of Berlin had been transformed almost overnight from a staid lecture hall to a showpiece of National Socialist Propaganda. The stage now resembled a Wagnerian production modeled after Bayreuth, and not by accident. This was theater where symmetry and order prevailed. Against the back curtains, at center stage, a rectangular banner proclaiming *Blut und Boden (Blood and Soil)* hung from the ceiling on golden cords. This banner was framed by three red streamers to the right and left, with the middle streamer of each adorned with a swastika.

Directly in front of *Blood and Soil* was the podium, from which the keynote speakers would make their remarks and the scientists would present their papers. Kurt Kleinschmidt was seated behind and to the left of the podium. Dignitaries were arrayed on either side, and the presenters occupied a block of seating in the foreground. To either side of the presenters, chairs had been reserved for members of the press.

For the audience, the farther out from the podium, the lesser the importance of the attendees. The first three rows were for those scientists who had not been selected to present but who were still expected to attend the conference, with the remainder of the auditorium's seating allotted to selected guests. Students with fathers active in the Party had been given the honor of seating the guests as they arrived. No opening night at the Bayreuth Festival had ever gone more smoothly than this extravaganza.

From the podium, Herr Heinrich Himmler, Reichsführer of the Schutzstaffel (SS), Reich Commissioner for the Strengthening of Germanism, and second only to Adolf Hitler in the National Socialist Party, gave the cue, and his first musical selection, *Deutschland über Alles,* filled the venue. With the final notes of the anthem, heavy and fraught with emotion, still resounding, a thunderous outcry of *Heil Hitlers!* brought the prelude to a close. Act One of Heinrich Himmler's production, *Vegetation Mapping for the Third Reich,* was about to begin.

. . .

There are good aspects to a front row seat and some not so good ones. The good aspects are that you have a good view of every part of the proceedings. The bad aspects are that you have a good view of every part of the proceedings. It was the latter that I was enduring while Herr Himmler rattled on and on about "removing the unharmonious from the German landscape." He was an expert in the way he used euphemisms and metaphors, getting his real point across while saying practically nothing of importance.

Physically, Himmler was not an imposing figure. He'd worn glasses since childhood, was slight of build, was always complaining about his stomach problems, and had adopted an odd haircut with shaved sides, believing that it made his head appear more Aryan, basically, bigger. It didn't. Regardless, his head was big enough, and getting bigger by the day.

The ideal Aryan male was big, strong, and blond, qualities that neither Hitler nor Himmler possessed. The ideal Aryan family was pure and consisted of mother, father, and at least four children. Himmler had left his wife to take up with his secretary. Hitler was unmarried, although carrying on with Eva Braun, whom he'd met when she was seventeen. Regardless, Hitler and Himmler had sold the country a bill of goods at the outset, and nobody had questioned the disparity. And now, nobody dared.

Himmler was building to a stirring finish, rallying the troops, as it were.

"As the Fuhrer has stated, 'Science cannot lie, for it's always striving according to the momentary state of knowledge to deduce what is true.'" He paused for effect and then gave a clear and explicit warning that more or less tossed the warm welcome of encouragement out the window for those who dared to challenge the prime directive. There had been some mild protests prior to the planning for the conference from scientists who had been working with their Jewish colleagues in the university. The closing line was meant to silence their protests once and for all.

"Our national policies will not be revoked or modified, even for scientists. If the dismissal of Jewish scientists means the annihilation of contemporary German science, then we shall do without science for a few years."

The words sent a chill through me, and the eruption of another *Heil Hitler!* chorus reinforced the horror of what he had just said. Himmler had finished, and the crowd was on its feet, as he strode purposefully from the podium. I jumped up to join everyone else. Then everyone sat down as abruptly as they had stood. It reminded me of cheerleaders at a football game. It was a well-trained crowd.

The silence that had followed from the academics after Himmler's last line, spoke volumes. Somewhere, someone dropped a piece of equipment, and the crash reverberated throughout the chamber. There was no applause from the scientists, no *Heil Hitlers!* even while the rest of the audience took up the expected and demanded cries. I, for one, was glad to see Himmler go. It's difficult to sit and watch someone who is pure evil hold sway over a captive crowd. I couldn't help but wonder how he and the rest of the Nazi warlords had gotten so far so fast. The beginnings of the Nazi Party hadn't, in any way, given a hint as to how soon they would cement their power over the entire country. They did it sometimes slowly, as with their own people, and quickly, when dealing with other nations that stood in their way. They were like a cancer gone out of control, eating away at the body that had given them life. It was a frightening thing to watch. I could leave and soon would, but others wouldn't be so fortunate. I wished someone would have opened the doors and windows and let in some fresh air after Himmler left. I didn't know any more effective way to deal with a bad odor. How the people of Germany would survive this, I couldn't begin to imagine. And then the proceedings resumed. Business as usual.

The most frustrating part of just sitting and not being able to do anything else *but* sit was knowing that the physicist I needed to find was sitting in one of the rows behind me, and I couldn't see him because we were all facing the stage, all eyes respectfully looking forward. So there I had sat, entranced with the sheer poetry of dear Heinrich's oration, stifling the yawns that kept coming, and hoping for a pause in the action. Our first break wasn't for an hour and was scheduled to last only fifteen minutes. With any luck, I could match one or more of the five remaining dwarfs and strike up a quick conversation, just long enough to make sure they saw the ring. I only had to vault over the five people hemming me in on the right, get past the press box, and screech to a halt before the physicists spread out in search of coffee or the facilities.

▪ ▪ ▪

It had just been an accident, dropping the backlights. It had made a horrible din, but, as she assured the students who were assisting her, nothing had been damaged. She had just tripped. It hadn't been an accident, though. Kristine had had enough of Himmler and his venomous speech. She just wished she'd been able to make more noise than she had. Finally done with filming all the power of Himmler's final exhortation, she turned to get a few shots of the audience as they saluted *der Führer.* She panned the auditorium, but she wasn't looking at the crowd. She was looking for one person, Fräulein Professor Doktor Katrin Nissen. She wouldn't be difficult to find, if you knew where to look, and Kristine easily located her, seated with the other presenters. Sure enough, she was still wearing the ring like a necklace. *Like an advertisement.* She wanted it to be seen. Why? What did it mean? Kristine lowered the camera and squared her shoulders. There was only one way to find out.

▪ ▪ ▪

Professor Kleinschmidt introduced the next speaker, Richard Darré, the Reich Minister of Food and Agriculture, which made me realize I was getting hungry. Still, Darré was only scheduled to speak for half an hour which was short by Nazi standards. I folded my arms across my rumbling stomach and prepared, once again, to endure.

Darré had, of course, written a book on the topic of blood and soil in 1930 and had given it the highly original title of *A New Nobility of Blood and Soil.* He spent part of his time slot not so subtly pitching the book, then retreated to his prepared remarks, a discussion of the virtues of the German peasantry as the cultural and racial soul of the Aryan race destined to fulfill the dream of *Lebensraum,* or the living space needed by Germany, by resettling in eastern Europe, having lots of peasant children, forcing the current occupants out or annihilating them, and making the Nazi dream come to fruition.

As he wound down with his enthusiastic recommendation of selective breeding, not only for farm animals and plants, but for the German population as a whole to ensure purity and strength, I prepared to jump up for the final *Heil!* before pushing my way to the aisle to tackle a physicist.

And I would have been successful, had the man next to me not fallen asleep during Darré's speech and become a veritable roadblock in my escape route. After nudging him gently twice, I finally kicked him in the shins. He woke with a start and a most unfortunate swear word, which, in the sudden silence after the *Heil!* caused all those in the immediate vicinity to stop and take a look at who was looking for early retirement. Finally, I climbed over him, while he was bending to retie his shoes that he had taken off so he could get more comfortable while he snoozed. Unfortunately, by the time I finally reached the aisle, the Physics Faculty had vacated their seats and melted into the throng heading to the bathrooms and the coffee. I was wishing there would be an easier way to go about this. As I proceeded to the foyer, trying to decide what that way might be, a woman shoved a piece of paper in my hand and was gone before I knew it.

I had gotten sidetracked and lost my concentration. Not good, not even for a single, solitary second. I gave myself a mental dressing down for being caught off guard. I unfolded the note. *The Blue Danube 7:00 tonight.* I refolded the paper and shoved it in my jacket pocket. All right. I didn't know who I'd meet or why, but The Blue Danube it would be—once I found out what and where it was.

Back to the problem at hand, however. There was a long table set up in the foyer with carafes of both coffee and also hot water for the tea drinkers. I took a cup of coffee and stood to the side. Patience paid off when I saw the tall, lanky form of Erich von Reichstadt making his way back from the bathrooms. When he paused for a cup of coffee, I walked over and greeted him.

"Guten Morgen, Herr Professor!"

"Guten Morgen!" Well, we had consistency, if nothing else. He peered at my name badge and brightened, the light of recognition shining his eyes. "*Ah*!"

He was promptly joined by two colleagues, and I set the coffee down on a table while the introductions were made. I played with the chain that held the ring, hoping to draw their attention to it and was successful. At least, I think they were looking at the ring. Regardless, Professors Wilhelm Waldvogel (with the bedroom eyes and hence, *Sleepy)* and Martin Albrecht (with the deep furrow between his eyes and hence, *Grumpy),* had a chance to see the ring. If one of them were the mole, he could find me if he wanted to. Four down, three more to go. Before we could get a conversation going, though, the lights dimmed, and we took our seats to be enlightened by the final speaker of the morning, Alwin Seifert, Reich landscape attorney, and another advocate of the *rootedness in the soil* concept.

Seifert's main area was making sure the German motorways were landscaped with native plants, and he worked with Reinhold Tüxen (tomorrow's keynote speaker) to ensure, that as Germany conquered eastern Europe, all the vegetation be "Germanized". That meant ripping out what had been growing for eons and replacing the removed plants with field hedges and other suitable, German native species. I wondered how they were going to handle the problem of those poor plants that had been forced to leave their native pollinators behind and might not have developed resistance to disease in their new digs. The Party hadn't thought this through clearly, but once again, the metaphor was clear. The Nazis weren't subtle, but they were determined. Finally, the marathon of speechifying drew to a close, and we were dismissed to attend to whatever needed to be done before the presentations began in earnest tomorrow.

What I needed to do was take a short drive using one of the automobiles provided for our use, so that we might tour the area in our free time and appreciate the visual accomplishments of Herr Hitler and his inner circle. While I appreciated the use of the automobile, I wasn't planning on a cultural appreciation tour of Nazi landscape design. No, indeed. I was planning a quick jaunt to the home and gardens of Karl Förster, a *Resistance Botanist,* if there were such a term.

It had only been two years ago, in August of 1938, that Berlin had hosted the 12th International Horticultural Congress. That one had been held in the Plenary Hall of the Congress Building, the old Kroll Opera House, and it had been a much bigger affair. There'd been more than fifty countries in attendance, and numerous day excursions to spots of interest were included on the schedule. The nurseries and grounds of Karl Förster at Bornim just outside Potsdam had been one option for attendees. This time around he had not made the approved list, so I made a list of my own. It only had one name, and it was his. Förster was a legend among botanists, and I knew this would most likely be my only chance to see his gardens and nurseries, and, if he had the time, speak with the man himself. I wasn't about to let the opportunity pass me by.

Some botanists work with annuals, some with biennials, and some choose perennials. Annual plants complete their life cycle in one year. They take root, grow, produce flowers, set seed, and then die. I like annuals, and they have their place in the garden, but they're not the foundation. They're more like accents. Biennials, such as hollyhocks and Sweet Williams flower their second year, set seed, and then usually die. Förster, however, worked with perennials, the plants that lived at least three years and often much longer. They set down their roots for the long haul and generally grew bigger and stronger each year. They're reliable and the mainstay in any garden. They are the foundation plantings around which designs are made, and Förster was heavily into breeding new varieties, from phlox to larkspur to asters to different varieties of grasses.

It was phlox that had drawn me into botany. One Christmas when I was a young girl, my Aunt Anna had given me a book about flowers. It hadn't been just a regular book, though. This one had had pages of stickers. There were stickers with pictures of flowers and stickers with pictures of the essential parts of flowers. From them I learned about petals, leaves, stamens, and pistils. Each sticker was to be stuck, for want of a better word, in various places throughout each chapter near the corresponding text. I'd become fascinated, and little by little, I learned about flowers and came to appreciate them. I loved phlox the most. Arguably the most fragrant flower in the garden, their color palette, ranging from white to pink to violet, makes them just about perfect, as had been that Christmas gift from long ago.

I didn't know what had drawn Karl Förster to this field, but he had begun his work in Berlin almost thirty years ago and then moved everything to Bornim near Potsdam back in 1912. The Nazis had their landscape architects and Förster had his, Hermann Mattern and Herta Hammerbacher. What they created was a testament to Förster's vision. The gardens held only the plants that he had bred, but what had made him famous was now putting him at odds with the Nazis. He wouldn't bow to the directive to propagate exclusively native plants. His criteria for plants were that, first and foremost, they be hardy. That meant they were able to withstand swings of temperature and moisture, be resistant to disease, and, above all, be true perennials. These plants included flowers, grasses, shrubs, and even trees, because trees are the most perennial plants there are. More than resisting the order to only grow native plants, Förster had Jews among his employees, and he refused to fire them simply because they were Jews. Förster was a man of character.

It was about 45 kilometers from Berlin to Bornim by Potsdam, about an hour or so in the car. It was a beautiful day, and everything was going well, at least for the first five minutes. Then I passed the smoldering remains of Wolff's Bakery. Sometime during the night, it had burned to the ground. I'd never heard the siren from a fire engine, and I had to think that the bakery had burned with the full knowledge and permission of the Nazis. Perhaps Helmut had given one too many chances at escape for the agents who had used him as a drop. Or maybe, and this thought chilled me, maybe my telegram to Gene warning that they'd been compromised had somehow caused this. I couldn't know. Just one more mystery that would remain unsolved in Nazi Germany. It was likely that both Ulli and Helmut were either dead or in prison somewhere. It's a dangerous game we play. With a bit of the shine off my morning, I motored on and did my best to put the fire out of my mind and concentrate on my driving. I could do nothing about what the Nazis had done. I could only do my job the best I knew how and hope.

The drive helped lift my spirits. Germany is a beautiful country. Having lived in the city for so long and working at the lab at the university, I had almost forgotten how beautiful the countryside can be, especially in the summer, when everything is green and blooming. It was mid-morning when I arrived at the gardens. I'd allotted myself two hours to stroll down the stone pathways, take a little time to sit on one of the benches, and finally reach the highlight of my visit, the sunken garden. The garden had been built on different levels, sloping gradually down to a pond at the base. At each level, there were plantings of flowers, so many flowers. This was not a highly stylized herb garden as one sees in England. The pond, landscaped with iris and daylilies, was a painting by Monet. I walked through a ravine bordered with ferns and woodland plants and strolled through the gardens filled with flowering shrubs. The trip had been a tonic for my soul. So much beauty, it was humbling. I had telephoned ahead to make an appointment to see Förster, and so, my last stop before returning to the university was Förster's study, where he greeted me warmly.

"Guten Morgen, Herr Förster," I said. "I am Fräulein Professor Doktor Katrin Nissen. It is an honor to meet you."

"Guten Morgen," he replied. "I hadn't been quite sure that I wanted to have this conversation."

I didn't know how to respond, and he must have seen the question in my eyes.

"You are here at the invitation of Herr Himmler. You are here as an advocate of Herr Jensen's beliefs, and those do not correspond with mine. However, I do respect your work. So, tell me about your current research," he said.

For the next half hour we spoke of flowers, and shrubs, and all good, growing things. I photographed his nursery and the variety of plants growing there. Leaving out many of the more delicate details, I told him about my short visit to Czechoslovakia to find the location where Heinz Hagemann, his chief gardener, had found the low-growing rudbeckia. Gradually, we were coming to an understanding, and I could see that, while he had questions, he had decided that perhaps I was more than I appeared to be. Finally, it was time to leave. Herr Förster handed me a packet of seeds.

"A farewell gift for you to take to America," he said. "Their future is not assured here."

I looked down at the label on the packet. The seeds were from the rudbeckia that was native to Czechoslovakia. They were *Goldsturm,* meaning Gold Storm. I accepted with thanks and promised they would find a good home with me. Those, plus the ones I'd gathered on my unfortunate outing, would join my research.

"We shall persevere and we shall, one day, emerge from this current storm," he said and winked knowingly at me. "We are the hardy perennials, I believe. They are annuals. Their time will be short, troubling, for sure, but they will not endure. Their kind never does."

The ride back to the university took a little longer with traffic, and once back on Unter den Linden, there was a delay at the site of the fire. There was an ambulance parked by the curb outside the remains of the bakery. It appeared they were prepared to transport a body, or the remains of one. Helmut would be spared a concentration camp. I set the morning aside. There was work to be done.

CHAPTER TWENTY-TWO

The Blue Danube

The three basic kinds of drinking establishments are nightclubs, cabarets, and bars; each has its own particular clientele and entertainment, and even the names give you clues. Nightclubs cater to the well-heeled. People dress to the nines for these and the Martinis, Manhattans, and fancy liquors from the top shelf appeal to the cocktail crowd as they listen to the big name bands and the major crooners and chanteuses.

The cabaret scene is more eclectic, and until the Nazis started closing them down, were famous for their decadence with their sexually explicit floor shows and thinly veiled political humor. Gathering places for the homosexual population, the crowd was generally younger, the dress more unconventional, and the booze and drugs far removed from top shelf. Since the 20s, they'd been theater where everything goes.

The Blue Danube was its own animal. It was a bottom-shelf bohemian bar and gathering place modeled after someone's idea of what a Greenwich

Village neighborhood bar might have looked like in the 1920s. It was dark. There was one glass chandelier with pendants a foot long that tried their best to reflect the one dim lightbulb housed inside. There was just enough light to show the way to the bar, the tables, and the door. If darkness equated with intimacy, this was the most intimate spot in town. The air was blue with cigarette smoke, and the noise level was high. Its clientele was working class with a splash of professionals who didn't buy into the fashionable or the political and students who didn't have the money to go anywhere else. The décor was best described as random. Modern art, probably the work of some of the university students, was nailed to the walls that had been painted a deep violet. The ceiling had been painted black. The choice of drinks made ordering simple. You either ordered beer or cheap, watered-down whiskey. The entertainment was whoever showed up with an instrument to play or a song to perform. On stage tonight, a young man with a saxophone was improvising poorly, but with enthusiasm, to an audience escaping from the troubles of the day and willing to put some cash in his tip can. I ordered my beer and stood by the bar, watching and waiting for the mystery woman to arrive.

The place was public enough to be anonymous, yet, as noted above, intimate enough for private conversation. It had been a good choice for a meeting. Perhaps I was dealing with a professional. Time would tell. And time did. At precisely 7 o'clock, a young woman entered the bar, and I recognized her as the tired-looking photographer from my picture-taking session at the university on Friday, Kristine Trautmann, sister of Dieter Weiss. Tonight, she didn't look so much tired as worried. Her attire was casual, trousers and a long-sleeved shirt, both of which were a light brown. She stood by the door, then made her way towards me.

And so, I thought, we meet again. She ordered a beer and motioned me to follow her to a small table recently vacated against the far wall near the back of the room. I checked out the hallway just to my left before I sat down. There was a supply room, broom closet, and bathrooms. The back door was down the end of the hall to the right. I took the chair facing the front of the room, my back against the wall. She took the other chair, facing me. Not a professional move. I was dealing with an amateur. The saxophonist had finished, replaced by a rotund, middle-aged man in lederhosen playing an accordion. Only in Germany. He would probably begin yodeling shortly.

I drank a bit of my beer. It was a Pilsner, actually quite good. I returned it to the table, my hand stretched across the opening. If she had a Mickey Finn, it wasn't going in my drink. She wasn't interested in my drink, however; she was visibly struggling with how to begin. I waited. She wrapped both hands around her glass. Not a good idea. It warms the beer, but she was working on an opening. She released her hold on the glass and began.

"We met at the university the other day. I am the photographer for the conference."

I nodded. I knew all that.

"I saw your ring."

Now it was on the table, but this wasn't unfolding the way I had thought it would. I had several questions that would need answers before I shared anything with her. Obviously, she wasn't the physicist I was seeking, so what was her connection? The first option was that my physicist had seen the ring, knew her, and had sent her to check me out. The question that followed that line of thinking concerned the nature of their relationship. She worked for Himmler. That added another layer of complexity. Now, I wondered if I could trust her. How much did she know? Was it a test? Was she really without a clue?

"Is that why you wanted to meet me?" This dialogue was sounding like a ping pong game. Somebody had to say something relevant sooner or later, but neither of us was prepared to be that somebody, and so we danced around the subject a bit more before she gave in.

"Can I trust you? I have to know if I can trust you." She inhaled sharply and then made her decision. "I've seen a ring just like that."

That was the safest thing she could have said. Point in her favor. "Go on. That's interesting."

"Yes. Why are you wearing it around your neck?"

Another good question. Why, indeed. I decided to relinquish a smidge of information. "It's a man's ring. It's too big for my finger."

"Where did you get it?"

She was settling in for a lengthy conversation, and we had time. There was no reason for me not to be here, unwinding after a long day at the conference.

Also, we had met professionally last week, so we were all right on that score. She was Himmler's photographer, and because of that, she'd have to come up with something of substance before I fed her anything that could hurt me. "It was a gift," I said.

She wanted to know if she could trust me, and I wanted to know if I could trust her. The chess match had begun. She studied my face, then took Dieter's ring out of her pocket and set it on the table in front of her.

I think my heart skipped a beat. I didn't move to pick it up, for fear she'd snatch it back and leave and I'd have nothing.

"Yes." Her expression was puzzled. "He must have given it to you. You each had one. Were you lovers?"

She'd let a little slip, so I answered. "No."

"I didn't think so. You're older. I mean, I'm sorry," she paused, running out of evasion. Finally, she let down the rest of her guard and blurted, "He was my brother."

Was. One little word that both answered one of my questions and raised new ones. She didn't know the physicist, but she knew, or had known, Dieter. Her use of the past tense somehow didn't surprise me. I think I had felt all along that Dieter Weiss was probably dead, and, if she were telling the truth, she most likely knew how he had died and when. "Tell me about him," I said.

Puzzled again, she said, "But the ring. You knew him."

"No, Kristine, I didn't know him, but I was trying to find him, and this was the only way I knew how. I was hoping that somebody who knew him would recognize the ring and ask me about mine and that would start a conversation that would lead me to Dieter. I'm sorry."

"Can I trust you?" She asked once again.

Heinrich Himmler's photographer wanted to know if she could trust a total stranger. In that moment, I paid attention. This young woman could be trouble, but she could also be *in* trouble. "Yes, you can. I think you know that, even though I'm not so sure I can trust you. It's a stalemate, but let's see where it goes, all right?"

"All right," she said, "but it's difficult to know where to begin."

"Begin at the beginning," I said. "That's usually the easiest."

I listened while she told her story that began with her meeting a man she found out was a brother she never knew she'd had and ended with her taking his body back to his birth home and their father.

"When Dieter showed up at my home, wounded, I put his arm across my shoulders to lift him so I could get him to bed, and that's when I felt the ring on his hand. After I'd gotten him settled, I looked at the ring and realized I'd seen it before. And then I remembered where I'd seen it, and so I looked through my negatives until I found yours. I knew the rings were the same. I knew I had to find you, find someone who knew him and who might tell me what had happened. He never got the chance. At first, I thought you might have shot him." She looked hard at me. "I don't think that now."

"I didn't shoot him, Kristine, although I think I can guess who did."

"Who? Who would shoot him?"

"The Gestapo."

Kristine looked totally bewildered. "Why would the Gestapo kill Dieter?"

"Why do they kill anyone? They kill anyone who disagrees with them or who may be a threat to them."

"And you think Dieter was a threat to them." It wasn't a question.

I nodded. "I know he was."

"Who are you? I mean, who are you, really? I'm not stupid."

"I am, in truth, honestly, Katrin Nissen, and I am here at the invitation of Heinrich Himmler to present my research at the vegetation mapping conference."

"But there is more, isn't there?"

"Yes, there is more, but you know what you need to know. Your brother was a good man, doing important work. You must remember him that way. He died doing that work, and I am sad for that but grateful that he didn't die alone."

Kristine picked up the ring and ran her finger across the griffin emblem. She picked at a speck and the griffin turned and opened. Startled, she set the ring back down and shoved it at me. "I don't want to know any more. This has all been, I don't know what it's all been. It doesn't seem real. A week ago, everything in my life was settled," she said, looking at the ring, "and now nothing is settled any longer. Everything has gone wrong, and it won't ever go back to the way it was."

"Kristine, this is very real, and I am truly sorry that you had to get involved. You did everything you could for Dieter. I don't know much about him, other than he was known for taking chances when caution would have been the safer route. Have you told anyone else about this?"

"You sound like Papa." She drummed her fingertips on the table. "Yes. Two people." She looked me directly in the eyes. "You must believe me."

I did. "Who did you tell, and what did you tell them?"

"Papa, but he needed to know. I mean, I showed up at his home with Dieter's body and asked him to help me. I told Papa everything, except I didn't say anything about the ring. Something kept me from telling him. I don't know why, but I held back. There's so much I want to know about Dieter. Papa never told me about him. He kept this a secret my whole life. I want to know why. He won't tell me anything."

"Kristine, we all have secrets, but you made the right decision about the ring. Who else knows about Dieter?"

"Ilsa. We are, I mean, we have been…" Her cheeks reddened and she paused. I nodded encouragement.

"Ilsa helped me take care of him," she said. "She knows Dieter was my brother, and she knows he is dead. She has seen the ring."

"Where does Ilsa work?" I asked. If I understood Kristine correctly, both of these girls were treading on dangerous ground.

"She's a staff artist at the Ministry of Propaganda. She designs their posters." There was pride in Kristine's voice. "I trust Ilsa with my life."

"I understand, but hopefully it won't come to that. If this meeting tonight or anything about Dieter should cause you a problem, get in touch with me. I can help you. I teach at Yale University." I took a small notepad from my handbag and ripped out a sheet of paper. I wrote my telephone number on it and handed it to her.

"Thank you for that." She looked down at the phone number. One brief line. A lifeline. "I don't know. I think I cleaned up everything, and I'm sure nobody saw me take him away. Everything will be all right, but thanks." She gave me a steady look. "How do you do this kind of work? How do you live with the constant fear that somebody will find out who you are? I have done one thing, and I am now always worried. I worry when I get out of my automobile. I wonder if I am being watched."

I took a last swallow of my warm beer, considering her question. "You just learn to live with it. You put your fears and your worries aside and do the job. I guess it comes down to believing that what you're doing is more important than you are. You understand that when you sign on. You do your best and hope. In a way, Kristine, you've also been recruited, and you're doing just fine."

"A week ago, I couldn't have imagined having this kind of a conversation with anyone. Now, everything is different. I thought I knew what I wanted, and then

Dieter came into it and now I just don't know." She seemed surprised at her words.

"That's what life does," I said. "Just when you think you've got it all figured out, it throws you a curve ball. If you catch it, you're still in the game. You caught this one. You did fine." I left her then, alone with her thoughts, while the accordionist on the stage played a folk song of the South Tyrol.

CHAPTER TWENTY-THREE

Marta's home

The beer, combined with a very long day, had made me tired. Granted, it had been a very large glass of beer, but it had been part of a business meeting. I was back at Marta's to review the day's events and make final preparations for my presentation tomorrow. After those sessions ended, I was free until the closing festivities late Wednesday afternoon. Two more days to complete the assignment. Perhaps the physicist I was looking for had already seen the ring and decided his contributions to our side were finished. After I'd had a chance to meet the final three, I would have my answer.

Reflecting on Dieter Weiss, I didn't know the exact circumstances of his death, and I never would. I activated the mechanism that opened the ring, and there inside was the microfilm he hadn't been able to pass on. It would come home with me. In the meantime, it would stay with me, and, when I got back home, I could tell Gene that Dieter had died in the line of duty and that his sister had unknowingly completed his assignment, which had also completed one part of mine.

I love spy films and murder mysteries, but they focus on the big picture and leave out a lot of the more mundane, necessary details that make up the fabric of our lives. Case in point, the microfilm. In the movies, after the heroine has found it, the next scene would show an airplane winging its way back to America, as the camera swept across the glorious mountains to the accompaniment of a musical score crafted to convey *The End.* But real life wasn't that abbreviated. I wasn't winging anywhere until Thursday, as my airplane ticket reminded me. I still needed to find the physicist, and I sure as hell wasn't letting the film out of my sight for a second before I winged. There was no way I was going to leave it on the dresser or the nightstand. My money belt was working overtime. I added the ring to the passports and the extra moolah and then readjusted my skirt. If this assignment got any more involved, I'd need to tack on an addition to the belt.

Secret compartments seem like mysterious, quasi-romantic places, when the truth is they are quite utilitarian. Another lesson from spy school. Hide everything right out there in the open. Well, almost in the open, but the point is a valid one. Take the inside pockets of my suit jacket, for example. They have zippers and are hidden, not only because they're inside the garment but also because of their placement directly behind the outside pockets. That means that anything the least bit bulky, say a Swiss Army knife, simply appears to be an item in the regular pocket, such as a pack of chewing gum, which, if you are carrying the knife, had better be there.

My handbag is my other hiding place, of course, for the stiletto. It's a myth, again blame it on the movies, that most of us carry guns, but they're bulky and difficult to conceal. They have to stay with you all the time, and they're noisy, which sort of goes against the *secret* part of secret agent. Silencers are also bulky and not easily concealed, especially by a female agent. That said, there are times when they're the best choice. So, the drama of the movies is entertaining, but I'll take my handy stiletto on *most* occasions.

As I wound down with the day, one minor issue was still niggling at me, and it was time to deal with it. I'd wanted to give myself time to decide what to do before I accused someone in the household of going through my personal items, but tonight had brought everything to a head. I couldn't be completely sure of the identity of the household snoop, but all the money was on Heidi, the maid. She wasn't very good at her job, in fact she was terrible, and the spur of the moment lies she told were quite bad. A six-year-old could have done better. Tonight, for example, when I returned to my room, she was coming out of it. She said she'd replaced my towels, but she didn't have any in her arms, just a pillowcase that she was carrying with the open ends all scrunched up in her fist. Little things like that can trip one up.

I thanked her and watched her scurry down the hall to the staircase. Who had sent her to check out my room, not once, but at least twice that I knew about? Whoever, they were certainly interested in my presentation. I checked the two clasps on my briefcase; they were both closed. I'd left the right one open. Most of my papers were there, but my slides weren't, and the section covering the genetics of propagation was gone, leaving a big hole in my time slot tomorrow that would need to be remedied tonight. I felt as if I'd been sucker-punched. My entire plan was now in jeopardy. It was time to deal with this, regardless of the fallout. The game was up. I went looking for Heidi.

On my way downstairs, a couple of thoughts came to me. Thought number one was von Reichstadt's missing papers. He'd never found them and was convinced he'd brought them home. Thought number two was Stefan Bauer's insistence that his research partner, Jürgen Winkler, had borrowed his notes and not returned them, even though Winkler swore up and down that he hadn't gone anywhere near them. It seemed a fair bet I wasn't the only one being targeted. There was an epidemic of academic theft at work in this house, and it was past time to put an end to it.

I first stopped at Bauer's door and knocked. He was in and listened while I shared my suspicions. Relieved that Winkler was in the clear, he agreed to join me, and so together we went downstairs to von Reichstadt's study where we found the door open. Von Reichstadt was stretched out on his sofa and seemed to be asleep, a glass of schnapps at the ready on the coffee table and Beethoven's Ninth in full swing on the record player. He awoke at hearing our approach, and we continued our little chat fest. United in our common purpose, the three of us set out for Heidi's quarters just off the kitchen. The door was ajar, and von Reichstadt pushed it open without ceremony.

Marta was standing in the middle of the room, looking for all the world like a cornered animal, which was a fair assessment, given the camera in her left hand and the slides—*MY* slides, or what was left of them—on the table next to her. Two of them had been cut to shreds, victims of the scissors on the table, and our unexpected entrance had prevented her from destroying the rest.

"Marta! What are you doing?" von Reichstadt stood, paralyzed.

The mystery of the missing items was solved. The room was full of stuff. And not Heidi's stuff. Jewelry in piles on the dresser, stacks of papers on the floor by the far wall, little ceramic trinkets on the table, a supply of hairbrushes. I had a feeling we'd found our pack rat or, more accurately, our kleptomaniac, as Heidi entered the room, saw what was happening, and burst into tears. She sank into the first available chair and buried her face in her hands, sobbing.

"I found these," was all Marta said, pushing past us to get to Heidi.

That didn't explain why she'd entered the room in the first place, or why she had a camera, or the reason why she was taking pictures, or why she was mutilating the *rudbeckia*. Von Reichstadt asked the first question, I asked the second, Bauer asked the third, and I completed the questioning with the fourth. She answered none of them. She just stood there, her arm around Heidi, defiant, silent.

It was apparent Heidi was a kleptomaniac, but Marta's role in this was far more macabre. Kleptomania is a mental illness. It mostly occurs in women, for reasons psychiatrists don't understand. Often, people who are kleptomaniacs are also compelled to put things in order, to straighten things that are crooked, or close things that are left open. That explained why she'd put the pages of my presentation back in numerical order on her first visit to my room and had closed the open latch on my briefcase during her return trip. Heidi couldn't help herself. She was compelled to steal, and so she took whatever struck her fancy. She didn't hurt anything she had taken, didn't have any use for what she'd taken, and couldn't even explain why she'd done it.

Marta was another story. Apart from reclaiming my property, I was more than willing to leave her to von Reichstadt. I just had one question, well, two, actually.

"Why are you photographing my slides?" Simple question, one would think, but Marta shook her head, refusing to answer. "All right, it's not that difficult to come to the logical conclusion. You're stealing my work—*our work*." I looked at Winkler and Bauer who both nodded, their expressions grim. "And that brings me to my second question, which isn't a question. You took advantage of Heidi's mental condition to get access to our research. Was it the price she had to pay for you not telling about everything else she had taken?" All right, that was more than two questions, but I was still puzzled. What was Marta planning on doing with our research, and why destroy my slides?

Bauer was hauling the stack of papers and folders to the table. As far as we could tell, most of what had been taken was there. I picked up the remnants of my slides and held them in front of Marta's face. "Why?"

She averted her eyes and once again shook her head. Von Reichstadt was beside himself and seemed unable to speak.

Bauer was furious, and I was more than willing to let him be. This was not over, that was a given, but I turned to the table and salvaged everything I could that belonged to me. I needed to run some damage control, and frankly, I wasn't sure how to go about it. Marta not only had been willing to overlook Heidi's kleptomania, she had actively channeled it into a form of academic espionage, and there would be serious consequences for what she'd done. Why had Marta done it? What could possibly have been worth her career?

Bauer and I left Heidi's room together, leaving von Reichstadt, Marta, and Heidi to deal with their mess. Marta's career was in shambles. I had no idea what would happen with her marriage. As for Heidi, she needed psychiatric help, but that was out of my control. I remembered my impression of how peaceful the house had appeared when I had first walked up the steps to the front door, but the flowers and the well-tended lawns were just a cosmetic overlay for evil.

Back in my room, I returned the remaining slides to their slots in the case and the pages to the folder. I sat on the bed, my mind in a turmoil. What could I do to salvage my presentation? There had to be a way, but at the moment I sure couldn't think of one. I locked the door and wedged a chair under the doorknob, just in case. As I've said before, one never knows.

Tuesday, June 18, 1940
From London, General Charles DeGaulle speaks to the people of France for the first time.
Hitler and Mussolini meet in Munich

CHAPTER TWENTY-FOUR

Conference, Day 2

I had lain awake for some time last night, thinking. Once the mind gets started, it won't stop. The house was silent. Whatever battles had been waged downstairs had been quiet ones. It was 2:45 in the morning when an idea came to me. It was a longshot, but it could work. I got out of bed, took a sheet of paper from my briefcase, and wrote a brief note. I removed the film from my camera and placed it and the note in an envelope, sealed it, and slipped it into my handbag.

I was nervous about tomorrow, today, actually. Regardless of my reason for presenting at the vegetation mapping conference, I was still a scientist, and addressing my colleagues on the direction and yield of my research to date was a matter of considerable importance to me and hopefully to my colleagues, as well. It was for that reason that I'd been careful to insert some *at this times* and *to dates* into my remarks, thereby keeping the research door open for some later mid-course corrections that would swing my findings back in the direction of their actual heading.

I was doing my best to think of today as if I were a pilot who had to abort a landing temporarily because of some obstruction on the runway, ramp up the throttle to get airborne again, make a wide arc, and then make the landing after the obstruction had been removed. It was an analogy that fit. All research is research in progress. Sometimes we get outcomes that don't ultimately fit into the model, and we need to find out why this is and what the next steps must be. Hitler and the Nazis and now Marta were the obstructions on my runway. These obstructions had to be removed, and I was doing my best to make that happen. I had to see this as just a temporary inconvenience, even though the Nazis were viewing the current situation as the beginning of the Thousand Year Reich, settling in for the long haul. Temporary, at least in historical matters, is a relative term.

Then my thoughts took off in another direction. The presentation was my cover, and I couldn't let it become my primary focus. I had only two more days to find the man who was the reason for my being here. I'd try the intercept routine again today at intermission. Three more men to get to see the ring. Was it one of them or one who'd already seen it and decided not to accept the invitation to continue? He might have been spooked when his contact failed to show, and after giving him a few days to reappear and still not seeing him, got the idea that passing on secret information might not be in his best interests. If that were the case, I would never find him. Restless, I opened the window to let in the cool night air. Some thought the night air was unhealthy. Foolish superstition, of course, but from somewhere in the copse of trees behind the house, an owl began its nightly recitation of *whoo, whoo.* I closed the window and climbed back into bed. Who, indeed? I had to find out.

The morning dawned sunny and pleasantly warm, although the weather inside the auditorium was going to be stuffy and hot before the day's proceedings concluded. I had dressed accordingly, my lightweight, pale yellow cotton jacket over a matching yellow blouse, a cream-colored, slightly gathered skirt, and my trusty low-heeled pumps. My jewelry was heavily tending towards rings. I sported the cheap costume jewelry model on my finger, wore Dieter's facsimile around my neck, and had the real McCoy zipped securely in my money belt. The necklace ring lacked a secret compartment, and that was to the good. No chance of getting them mixed up. It was those little details that I appreciated about Gene. I wasn't sure if he'd known that Dieter's ring had such a compartment, but if he had, there was enough complexity in the assignment without adding another level of potential screwup to the mix.

I was the first down to breakfast and selected the pancake. I was more or less trapped here until it was time to leave. There was no place else to go. As long as Bauer and Winkler remained with me, we should be safe, especially since Winkler had confiscated Marta's camera. *Insurance policy,* he had said, and I approved. His plan was to turn the camera with its film over to Kleinschmidt today at the conference, and we would then be effectively out of the immediate picture and harm's way. I doubted they would want my testimony at any disciplinary hearing for Marta, but Winkler and Bauer would be most willing to participate, and that would be enough.

There was no sign of Marta, and von Reichstadt was also absent. Heidi's sister had already come by and had taken Heidi back home. It was one less thing of concern. At least we weren't dealing with the Gestapo. Shortly, I was joined by Bauer and Winkler who just filled their bowls with Muesli, the standard German cereal offering. Mixed grains, dried fruits, and nuts. Very healthy, but boring. Also, the grains get stuck in your teeth. I added butter and powdered sugar to my pancake.

Conversation, what there was of it, came in dribs and drabs, as we were all caught up in our mental preparations and wanted to leave as quickly as we could. By 8 o'clock we'd all set out for the university.

▪ ▪ ▪

Kristine was setting up to take audience shots when I arrived at the auditorium. As she made her way up the aisle, panning left and right, I slipped her the envelope I'd prepared last night. We briefly locked eyes, and I let her pass. There was nothing else to be done. Von Reichstadt had gotten to the auditorium ahead of me, and I didn't bother him with idle conversation. I didn't envy him what lay ahead. He was still the only occupant of the physicists' row. His associates were either late risers or were tiring of the forced collegiality, but they'd show before the festivities began. They knew they had to.

I was looking forward to what the morning's keynote speaker, Reinhard Tüxen, would say, so I didn't need to feign interest. Tüxen's beliefs were the antithesis of everything the rest of us, or most of the rest of us held dear, but, as in any war, you must know the enemy if you are going to defeat him. As it turned out, there was nothing new to be learned from Tüxen. He was boringly predictable, just another Nazi spokesperson, but clever, nonetheless. We were subjected to a harangue on *potential natural vegetation.* As a scientist, I could not believe what I was hearing. Tüxen had had a traditional education. He was a botanist by training and a plant sociologist, and yet he had let the Nazis steal his honesty.

"It is possible to reconstruct developmental stages of a landscape in which the association of plants is in a natural state—that is, without human interference." The very words contradicted themselves. How on earth can people reconstruct an environment that existed at some point in time without human interference by interfering? They can't. These people couldn't even hear the nonsense they were spouting. *I will do something by not having done it* was the gist of the speech. But it got worse and more frightening. Tüxen proclaimed that it was necessary to cleanse the landscape of unharmonious foreign substance. This was an eerie parallel to Hitler's statement that the "German volk has to be cleansed". These guys were sure intent on doing a lot of housecleaning. Darré had noted that the Jews were "weeds". They were rootless,

not grounded in the blood and the soil. Bloody hell. It didn't take a botanical genius to see where these guys were going. Gerda was totally nuts, and Heidi needed psychiatric help, but this whole gang of crazies needed some serious time in a padded room. They were the real weeds, and if I'd had a can of Flit handy, I would have gladly pumped the first round into the core of this infestation. I just wanted to be done, go home, and lose myself in a rational world again. For now, though, duty first. I smiled, applauded, and did the *Heil Hitler!* routine.

My revenge, however short-lived it might be, was finally coming. It was my turn at the podium. I stood, pointer in hand, waiting for the student assistant to raise the screen for my slides and check that the projector was positioned correctly, while Kristine prepared to take yet another photograph of me to add to my steadily increasing portrait portfolio. She indicated I was to raise the pointer to a spot on the blank screen. I complied, although pointing at nothing seemed odd, but then she approached me and while repositioning the pointer in my hand, placed my envelope on the podium, and said those magic words once more. "Tonight, please. Same time. Same place. It is important." She backed up a few paces, so that the photo she took, while showcasing me and the pointer, merely caught the edge of the screen. She knew her stuff. Nobody would know there was nothing on the screen. People would see what she wanted them to see. It was the ultimate Nazi tactic. Now, however, I needed to focus on the task at hand, and so, pushing her request to the back of my rattled brain, I opened my folder and waited for the cue to begin my presentation. Kristine had made slides from the film I had taken at Förster's, and it took less than a minute to slip them in the waiting spaces in the projector. I had gambled on Kristine's willingness to help, and she had come through.

Kleinschmidt's introduction had been gracious and brief. His heart wasn't in the conference, after hearing Gerda's rambling confession, but at least we'd stopped Gerda before she'd had the chance to kill again. Of that I was quite glad, especially since I was the one she'd been planning to kill. I joined Kleinschmidt at the podium, he stepped to the side, and it was showtime.

I made all the usual acknowledgements, gave a professional smile, opened my folder, and began. The first slide, courtesy of Kristine, showed a field of *rudbeckia*, ablaze in the sunshine.

"I am pleased to present the results of our current field trials with rudbeckia hirta. Our work in the propagation of hardy perennials has taken on a new direction, in part based upon the find of a low-growing form of this plant, commonly referred to as black-eyed Susan, in Czechoslovakia. This has raised some interesting avenues of research, for we had first believed the rudbeckia to be native exclusively to North America. The question then that we must first consider is, what is a native plant? It's an intriguing concept."

At this point, my slide presentation displayed fields of *rudbeckia*, blooming in America, Holland, Germany, and Poland. All the same flower. Then I advanced to my next slide, which had come from the film I had taken at Förster's—a shot of the same flower, growing elsewhere.

"If we were to declare the Czechoslovakian rudbeckia a weed because of our ignorance of its natural habitat, we would not be operating according to the scientific method, for our task is not to destroy, but to learn. We are not the teachers, we are the students."

My next few slides were rather pedestrian in nature, focusing on methods of propagation. That had been my plan—to use the science to help me make my points. Then I fired my next round of ammunition. My next slide showed a rose in full bloom by a roadside. It was from a photo I'd taken in New York, where a rosebush that was approximately seventy-five years old had been spared when a new street was in the planning works. They'd used the rose as the centerpiece of a small traffic circle, eliminating the need for stop signs while keeping up the flow of traffic.

"A weed is just our way of referring to a plant growing where we wish it weren't. If I am laying out a garden path or a motorway or building a structure and encounter a rose where I wish to place a rock, does that transform the rose into a weed? This is a semantical issue, not a botanical one. Why blame the rose? We must step back and ask, 'How can I reroute my path?' Unfortunately, some have extended this analogy to people. 'You stand in my path!' Is this person a weed? What a ridiculous thought!"

I permitted myself a restrained academic chuckle, choosing to ignore the faint rumble emanating from the audience. My next slide showed a barren field, devoid of vegetation.

"A bird drops a seed while in flight. If the soil is suitable and the climate agreeable, the seed may take root and a plant may grow. This is God's work. Some plants, when introduced in this or another fashion, may become invasive, crowding out the plants that were there before. Planned management to protect the environment because of invasion is not the same as mass extermination of what we have decided doesn't belong, simply because it goes counter to our plans for dominance."

Several tedious slides examining my laboratory work followed until, finally, slide number 5 of my arsenal flashed on the screen. It was of a majestic Joshua Tree forest in New Mexico.

"Beautiful, isn't it? And yet there are those who would destroy it. Herr Jens Jensen, I believe, is one of those individuals. In his essay 'The Clearing' published in the 1937 issue of Die Gardenkunst, he states,

'The gardens that I created myself shall, like any landscape design, it does not matter where, be in harmony with their landscape environment and the racial characteristics of its inhabitants. They shall express the spirit of America and therefore shall be free of foreign character as far as possible. The Latin and the Oriental crept and creeps more over our land, coming from the South, which is settled by Latin people and also from other centers of mixed masses of immigrants. The Germanic character of our cities and settlements was overgrown...Latin spirit has spoiled a lot and still spoils things every day.'

"I wish to apologize for my countryman. My adopted homeland, America, is a strong nation because of its immigrants not despite them. On a lighter note, would this opinion have carried the day sometime in the past, our pantries would be less full, considering the potato, a staple of our diet, originated in the Andes of South America. Food for thought! And now, please let me share the results of our field studies."

I then proceeded through the rest of my technical and intentionally dull slide presentation, finishing to a polite outpouring of tepid applause, and then I was done, and I am sure that as far as Herr Himmler was concerned, done, soon to be gone, and never to return. It was a satisfying thought and almost as satisfying as the wink Kleinschmidt gave me as he regained the podium. He was a good man, and I hoped the future would be kinder to him than had the past.

▪ ▪ ▪

My exit at intermission today was less eventful than yesterday's, and I was able to greet von Reichstadt and the remaining three members of the nuclear research team as we made our way up the aisle. Professors Hans-Adolf Peters, Franz Fischer, and Horst Rupelt added their congratulations on my presentation, and von Reichstadt looked amused. They'd all now seen the ring, and I had nothing to do but wait and hope. Again, the beverages and refreshments had been set out for us. I doubted that my coffee had been poisoned, although I refused the cup offered me by the caterer and instead chose one from the selection already on the table. There was an assortment of pastries, and I pounced on a *Berliner*, the local name for an excellent jelly donut. I was feeling the predictable letdown after the adrenaline rush of the presentation, but this was not the time to let my guard down along with it.

I was a respectful and attentive audience member for the rest of the presenters which included my fellow houseguests, but the rest of the day crept by as I awaited my evening appointment with Kristine. What was the matter of importance? After my performance today, she'd be wiser to keep her distance.

CHAPTER TWENTY-FIVE

The Blue Danube

Two consecutive nights in a bar and you begin to think and act like a regular. It's a certain sense of familiarity, if not yet one of belonging, and the newness has worn off. You know the layout. In twenty-four hours, nothing had changed at The Blue Danube. The modern art was still nailed to the wall, the atmosphere was still smoky, the noise level of conversation still rose and fell. There was the clink of glassware from the bar, the musicians came and went from the stage after their gigs, trysts were arranged, and relationships were severed. But just outside the door, subtle change was coming. There was danger, and everyone knew, although they would never admit it, that soon the danger would become a nightmare from which there would be no escape.

I ordered my Pilsner at the bar and found a table close to where Kristine and I had sat last night. I didn't have to wait long. Kristine was German. She was punctual. She was also not alone. Her companion was a striking young woman with hair as blonde as mine and a figure that was considerably trimmer, a fact highlighted by the rather form-fitting charcoal grey skirt and powder blue sweater she was wearing. Kristine was still sporting the slacks and long-sleeved shirts she seemed to favor. They ordered their drinks and then found their way to my table.

"This is Ilsa," were Kristine's opening words, as she pulled out a chair, and we exchanged greetings.

"Ilsa Schlosser," Kristine's companion said, extending her hand.

Formality serves its purposes, in this case, helping us negotiate the awkwardness of first encounters. Kristine had called this meeting, so I took a sip of my beer and waited. Once again, it took her a bit to select her opening words, the right words, and I didn't rush her, although my curiosity was in overdrive. Was Ilsa somehow connected to Dieter, and, if she were, had Ilsa shared what we had discussed last night? That thought was troubling.

Kristine finally spoke. "You said last night that if there were something you could help with, you would."

"Yes, I did. If it's in my power, I will," I said. "I appreciate your help today."

"It was nothing," Kristine said. She and Ilsa exchanged glances. "If you can, though, I want you to help Ilsa get to America." Her voice was calm but tense. "She is not safe here, and she does not have much time."

Ilsa, so far, had let Kristine do the talking, but now she leaned across the table. "Kristine called me last night and said there might be a way out for me. I don't know if you can help, but Kristine says I can trust you, and so I agreed to come here to meet you and find out if you can help me."

I nodded. "All right. Fair enough. I'm here to listen. Tell me why you need my help. You've already told me what you want me to do." Here we were, three strangers who spoke of trust in a time when people no longer trusted their neighbors or even members of their own families.

"Yes." She took a steadying breath and launched into her story. "It begins some time ago. We," she tilted her head in Kristine's direction, "we met at university. I was studying art, and Kristine was in photography. That was," she paused to think, "nearly ten years ago. We've been together, more or less, ever since." She smiled, waiting.

"And," I prompted.

Taking my response as a cue to proceed, she did. "Our career paths intersected at times, during the next few years. You know about Kristine's work. I was also hired by the Party. It was an exciting time. My assignment was to design propaganda posters for the Reich. You've probably seen some of them."

Indeed. Using art to appeal to the emotions of the population was an inspired form of propaganda, and if those posters I had seen were Ilsa's work, she was a talented artist and propagandist. The posters were displayed everywhere. You couldn't miss them, but then that was the point.

"It's not difficult work. I am given whatever sentence the Party wants to use, and then I design a poster that conveys the message in a strong manner. For those who can't read, the picture has to say what the words do, and for those who can, the picture reinforces the message. The posters began as patriotic calls for people to increase agricultural production, support the National Socialist Party, and things like that. This is changing, and not for the better. The sentences I must illustrate are becoming more and more…frightening, I think, is the proper word."

Kristine took over. "It's been a steady progression the past few years, and the rate at which it's increasing is evident to anyone who's paying even the least amount of attention. It's no longer about national pride. It's about finding blame for anything and everything that might stand in *their* way. A year and a half ago, we knew it was coming to us." She looked at Ilsa who gave a slight grimace. "Kristallnacht in Rostock was no different from anywhere else. The synagogue on Augustenstrasse was destroyed by arson. Elsewhere, windows were smashed, paint was thrown on the walls of the stores owned by Jews, horrible things were written on the walls, merchandise was stolen or destroyed in the stores. Dozens of Jews were beaten or imprisoned, and all of it was encouraged by the Party. It was something almost beyond comprehension. And the fear—the fear was something that permeated everything. There was no escape."

I took a deliberate swallow of my Pilsner, watching both their faces, studying their eyes, and then I asked the one question, actually more a statement than a question, because they had already given me the answer. "Ilsa," I began, and that was as far as I needed to go. She bit her lip so hard it drew a drop of blood.

"Yes, I am a Jew. That shouldn't be such a difficult thing to say, should it? Just those four words." Her voice trembled with barely repressed rage. "I was adopted at birth. My adoptive parents couldn't have children of their own, and so a deal was made that benefitted everyone concerned. There was a doctor who could arrange everything. He saw to every detail. My adoptive mother confided about her unexpected and most welcome pregnancy to a few close friends, ensuring that the entire town would learn the good news. She also told them that it was a difficult pregnancy and she would be staying with relatives near Pappenheim, since my father was so busy with work. And then, after the appropriate length of time, she returned with me." Ilsa paused and Kristine took her hand.

"My new parents were Lutherans," Ilsa resumed her story. "I was baptized a Lutheran. I wanted for nothing, and my childhood was perfect, but when I went home to visit last year, they told me everything about my past, and my world turned upside down. It was almost too much to even think about. My mother was unmarried and pregnant, but she gave me life. She was also a Jew. None of this mattered to my parents. They have loved me. I am their child, and I love them. I also love the woman who gave birth to me, even though I don't know her. How can anyone love more than that? To give your child to strangers to give her a better life? Then the Nazis came to power. The world changed, and my world changed with it. My parents knew the records would reveal the truth, as the purges began, and they didn't want me to be unprepared." She gave me a hard look. "That is my story. I am a Jew. That, today, is an unforgiveable sin."

I looked at this blonde, blue-eyed German woman, now a target for the hatred of her own country. It defied logic, but it was terrifyingly real.

"The doctor has been arrested, my mother has told me. She said they are going through all his records, looking for anyone of *impure* blood. She is frantic, and while my father is perhaps not frantic, he is most definitely worried."

My radar snapped on. "Ilsa, when was the doctor arrested?"

"My mother said yesterday. Why?"

I did one of those little tuneless whistles that usually means the shit is about to hit the fan.

"And there's something else," Kristine said.

But I didn't need the confessional to continue. I already knew about their relationship. "Two reasons to get the hell out of Dodge." They looked puzzled. "It's a line from Western movies in America. It means to get out of town as fast as you can, while you still can."

"I will be all right," Kristine said, "but please, please help Ilsa. Once they find out, she doesn't have a chance."

On the surface, a simple request, but the actual logistics were a tad more complicated, and I went through some mental gymnastics regarding the best way to go about it. "All right," I finally said to their expectant faces. "I will help you. Just give me a minute." I excused myself and made a trip to the ladies' room, where I removed the Swedish passport from my money belt. Astrid Andersson had helped me, and now her assignment was to save Ilsa Schlosser. For a woman who didn't exist, Astrid was sure getting a lot done. And then, just as I was about to return to Kristine and Ilsa, I had another thought. It wasn't so much a thought as that *little voice* sending me a message. There was no denying what it was telling me. I had a sudden image of my husband clucking at me and shaking his head, but he would have done the same thing. Sometimes, you have to get involved. So, once again seated, I laid out what they needed to do.

"Kristine," I said, passing her the passport under the table, "here is Ilsa's new passport. It needs her photo. I'm sure you know someone who can take the photograph." I smiled at her. "Ilsa, you need to memorize everything written on that passport. Your name is now Astrid Andersson, and you are a Swedish citizen returning home from a visit to Germany. Destroy your own passport. Under no circumstances are you to use it again. Do you speak any Swedish?"

"No, I don't." She gave a slight shrug. "It's never been necessary."

"It is now." I took my notebook and pen from my handbag. "Tonight," I said as I scribbled on the paper, "learn how to say these words. It won't be difficult. *Good morning, good afternoon, excuse me, thank you,* and *I have nothing to declare* should cover anything that would routinely come up crossing into Sweden. Just say as little as possible and act as if you belong there. If the authorities in Rostock are diligent in their examination of the doctor's medical files, and given what the Party does, we know that they are, it won't take them long to find you. If the doctor listed your adoptive parents' names along with your birth mother's name, as he most likely did, the authorities already have yours. With just a few telephone calls, they can trace you to here. They've had this information since yesterday. I don't want to alarm you, but it's not in your best interest to go home tonight or to work tomorrow." I looked at Kristine. "Ilsa should stay with you tonight."

Kristine nodded, her lips pressed tightly together. The fear in Ilsa's eyes was noticeable, but it passed quickly. "I understand," was all she said.

"Book your flight to Sweden at the airport tomorrow morning and remain at the airport until your flight leaves. There are several each day. It shouldn't be difficult to get a seat. Talk to no one at the airport. Read a book, not a newspaper or a magazine. Books are more permanent. They convey a certain sense of ease and comfort. Newspapers are for spies and people trying to hide." I wrote down an address and handed it to her. Her little stack of paper was growing. "When you land, have a taxi take you to this address. You will be safe there. Just wait to be contacted by the person who will handle the rest of your travel." I saw the concern in her face. "Don't worry, Ilsa. Once you leave German air space, you are safe. And there is food in the house, I know. I have stayed there myself. In fact, the last time was just a few months ago."

In spite of her fear, she laughed. "I cannot thank you enough. You don't even know me, and you are doing this for me."

I ignored her last comment. "When you land in America, a man named Gene will meet you at the airport. He will be your guide to your new life. You'll like him. He taught me everything I know." I sat back and thought about the next thing I was going to do. First, I finished the Pilsner.

Kristine finished her own beer and moved to rise from her chair. "Katrin, thank you. I won't trouble you again."

"Not so fast, please," I said. "Sit down. There is more to be done."

Kristine looked confused. "You've thought of everything."

"I hope so, because this next part will take a little time. Ilsa's exit is pretty much cut and dried. Sweden is neutral, she's blonde. Getting you out of Germany is a bit more difficult, but it can be arranged."

The initial confusion on Kristine's face changed almost immediately to one of hope. "You've done what we needed. I can't ask you to do any more."

"You're not asking. I'm offering," I said and slipped the second passport under the table to her. "You are not safe, Kristine. You know it, and I know it. They will find out."

Her eyes held a question as she clutched the passport.

"Tereza Novak," I said, answering her unspoken question. "She's a Czech national but a German by birth. That is the way to handle it. There is risk, more risk in your exit than in Ilsa's, but if you're willing to take that risk, there is a way out. You know what will happen if you remain here."

She and Ilsa once again exchanged looks. "Yes. All right, but how will I know what to do?"

"First of all, don't break the beer glass. You're holding it so tightly, it's likely to shatter."

"Oh. Yes, of course." She set the glass down.

"Your passport is Czechoslovakian. They are occupied, and crossing borders into occupied countries requires a bit more preparation."

"I understand. What do I do?"

"Replace my photograph with yours. Then, wait. I know waiting is the hardest thing to do, but you must. I leave Thursday. When I arrive back in the States, I will make the necessary contacts. Just go about your daily routine. Beginning on Monday, however, you must be prepared to leave on a moment's notice. Have your new passport and your handbag with you at all times. You won't be able to take anything else with you. Don't leave your handbag unattended for even an instant. Guard it and your passport. One morning, there will be a car parked outside your home. It will have a white ribbon tied to the antenna. Open the passenger door and greet the driver as if he or she is a long-lost friend."

Kristine's brow was furrowed. "How will I know the car is the right car, and this is a person I can trust and not the Gestapo?"

I gave her my best deadpan expression. "Your driver will be eating a donut, and there will be a box of a dozen more on the passenger seat." They both looked as if I'd lost my marbles, but I reassured them the best way I could. "Look inside and check before you get in. If there aren't any donuts, just ask if they need directions. Then leave. In American films, the good cops are always eating donuts. It's an inside joke. But," I added, "no donut, no go. It might seem silly, but it's important. Understood?"

Kristine rested her hand on Ilsa's, and I placed mine on hers. Our mutual pact of honor affirmed.

I stood. It was time for me to leave. "Stop by and visit after you get to America. There's a lot of work available for good propaganda artists and photographers with our side, as you will find out." As I reached the door, I turned slightly and saw Astrid Andersson and Tereza Novak deep in conversation, making plans for a future that an hour ago wouldn't have seemed possible. It felt right, but then that's why we were in this fight, wasn't it?

Wednesday, June 19, 1940
Germany continues its march through France
From exile, General Charles DeGaulle speaks to his countrymen:
"Soldiers of France, wherever you may be, Arise!"

CHAPTER TWENTY-SIX

The Blue Danube

My third and final night at The Blue Danube and, confirming my observations of the previous night, I may not have achieved the status of a regular, but I was making excellent progress in that direction. The proof, if I needed any, came as I approached the bar. The bartender looked up, poured me a Pilsner, and slid it down to where I stood, about to place my order. I had earned my credentials. I was now a bona fide Blue Dube semi-regular, and I even knew the locals' affectionate name for their favorite watering hole. The conference was concluded, and the Dube was jammed. Tonight, I'd either find my physicist or be forced to limp home, defeated. All I could do was join the festivities and hope.

I looked around, almost half-expecting to see Kristine and Ilsa, and was seriously relieved when I didn't. If all had gone as planned, Ilsa would now be safely in Sweden and in the States by the weekend with Kristine soon to follow. While I didn't see them, I did see just about everyone else I had met and spoken with at the conference, and that included von

Reichstadt and all the physicists who were crowding the bar. Von Reichstadt had commandeered a stool, but the rest were standing.

Tonight's entertainment was a torch singer, belting out an Edith Piaf song about lost love. The Nazis might not have approved, but the clientele wasn't concerned. Edith was holding her own against the noise of the customers, and I slipped a Reichsmark in the tip container on the piano as I made my way to the guys. Tonight, just like the torch singer, I needed to find my man. My own was somewhere else, hopefully safe and waiting for me.

"Katrin! Over here!" That invitation came from Wilhelm 'call me Willy' Waldvogel, who raised his glass of beer in greeting. "Come join the party!"

Willy was one of those guys who was perpetually smiling. He was likeable enough, but the constant joyfulness was draining. Still, if he were the one I needed to find, I'd give him a few minutes to let me know. I took my beer and joined Willy and his cohorts. The party was in full swing, and the lines dividing Faculties had been breached, as I saw Otto Crump had also attached himself to the group. For a brief moment, I felt a little uneasy. There was no reason for him not to be there, of course, but it was one of those *feelings* nonetheless, and I kept it in mind, as I joined in the conversation and took the barstool next to von Reichstadt.

Once again, my mind traveled back to spy school, as it tended to do when I was wrestling with a problem. Our instructors had insisted there was no such thing as intuition, tending instead to focus on practicalities, but I, along with every other female there, disagreed.

I was back with that *little voice.* I wasn't afraid, but I was at a heightened sense of preparedness, to use the scientific term. I wasn't in a life-threatening situation, yet, but there was always that possibility. People who have been in life-threatening situations speak of fear as being palpable or something they could almost taste. Fear can seem to hover in the air, a remnant of someone else having passed by, even as we find ourselves alone or *think* we are alone.

Something told me not to get on that airplane. Something told me not to open the door. Something told me.... That *something* is the body's defense mechanism, and when it's activated, our senses are operating in an instinctive, primal, survival mode. It may seem to defy logic, but it's an essential part of our makeup. We aren't aware of it, but something about the odor or the sound of that plane's engine was wrong. Our ears picked up on the fact that someone had tried to turn the doorknob before knocking, or we saw that doorknob being turned ever so slightly, being tested.

Logic may try to reason with us and get us to dismiss that warning. Other people may scoff and call us cowards. This is the ultimate peer pressure tactic. Can we trust ourselves enough to resist that pressure? Sometimes, it all comes down to common sense. Being careful doesn't make you a weakling. It means you're in tune with your body, and it can also ensure that you keep on living. We ignore that instinctual warning at our peril. All that aside, I was here now and as prepared as I could be.

The ring had done all it could do. Everyone had seen it, and unless somebody tried to pull me aside for a private conversation in the next few hours, I would have failed. So, after a few words with Willy, I moved to where Fischer and Peters were enjoying a private joke that ended abruptly upon my entrance. It's the age-old story. Women can do their best to enter a man's world, but there will always be that invisible line that can't be crossed. Men and women are different. It's a simple fact of biology, but it makes professional advancement difficult, since there's a lot of work done outside the office in social situations where the sexes have their degrees of separation. I think it's why pillow talk has always had its place. Secrets shared in the bedroom can often help a woman advance in the boardroom. Pillow talk has been the great leveler.

I wasn't looking for opportunities to advance my career tonight, at least not my academic career, but I was doing my damndest to advance the espionage one and not having any luck. I wasn't sure what time it was, but it was getting on in the evening. Churches, casinos, and bars are the three places you'll never find a clock. None of them want you to know what time it is, and each has its own reasons for that. It's no oversight.

I did overhear a few raunchy lines, though, as I bided my time. Those physicists may spend their days consumed with mathematical equations, but it was obvious their nights were spent elsewhere. Finally,

Crump worked his way to where I was listening to Rupert share his thoughts on why we would soon be entering a new ice age. It had nothing to do with anything, and that's why I was finding his theory compelling. What would happen if the Thousand Year Reich should end up encased in ice? It was a pleasant thought.

"I suppose you're looking forward to getting back to your own work now," was Crump's opener. "Conferences can be energizing, but there comes a time to pack it up and get back to the daily grind."

There was a tiny prickle at the back of my neck, and I recognized it for what it was. "I am, although it's been wonderful for the most part," I said, "except for finding Professor Becker's body. That was not on the schedule, and I'm still puzzled by it and by all the rest of it." Crump knew exactly what I meant by *it* and started bobbing his head up and down like a ball on a spring.

"I've been working on my own theory," he said, inclining his head toward Rupert, who was still expounding on ice. "Do you have a minute to listen to what I've come up with?"

Did I have a minute? Damn straight. I had as many minutes as it took to get to the bottom of this and hopefully head for home with my mission completed. "If anyone is still in danger, you need to let them and the authorities know, but there's just so much you can do," I said. "Filling those empty positions isn't going to be easy if the candidates think there's a serial killer on the loose."

"Let's get a breath of fresh air. I can't hear myself think, and it's best nobody overhears us. They'll think I'm crazy." Crump moved away from the bar.

Crazy is not a good word to say to someone who is in the least bit suspicious of those around her. Still, fresh air sounded good, but the dance floor was now jammed, and there was no way to get to the front door, where I'd be safer, as Edith Piaf had retired from the microphone and a five-piece swing band was in full cry. The band was good, and my toe was tapping. "Why don't we head to the dance floor?" I asked. "We could talk and still enjoy the music." If John were here, we could cut a rug, but he wasn't here, and I wasn't back in the States. They could play the music, but they couldn't make it *home*. Home is where you're safe. Nobody was safe here.

"I don't dance."

Well, that settled that. I followed Crump down the hall to the back door, and we stepped outside where the air was indeed fresher. It was humid, but it was a fresh humid. I took a deep breath to clear the smoke from my lungs. Cigarettes foul the air. They can also impede your thinking, because now, in the cleaner air outside, I knew that what I had suspected was true, and that events were beginning to escalate. All the waiting had quite suddenly come to an end, and I found myself at the point of no return.

I had found the killer, but having just interfered with his plans for his next victim, I needed to make sure I didn't become collateral damage. Crump, having preceded me out the door, now turned to face me. It was one of those *I know that you know that I know* moments. I took a step backwards, putting myself just slightly beyond his reach. "How were you planning on killing Erich von Reichstadt?" I asked. My tone was pleasant, conversational, and had the desired effect.

Crump stared at me, not believing what his ears had heard.

"Was it time to give the final, fatal dose?" I asked.

He pulled a small vial of pills from his trousers pocket and waved them at my face, as if I were some sort of mental defective who didn't understand the obvious. "How did you know? How could you have known? It was supposed to be finished tonight. Now you've set me back." He shoved the pills back in his pocket and took a step towards me.

My heart was pounding so hard he surely must hear it. "Such a pity, but you waited too long." I took another step back, but it would be the last one, as the door had swung shut, cutting off my only escape route back into the bar. "You missed the best opportunity, right after he'd had that heart attack. That was the time, but you didn't want that. You wanted to enjoy watching him die." I was keeping my voice steady and my gaze steady as well, even while my ears detected a faint rustle somewhere off to the left. A rat in the garbage, perhaps, or something bigger and more dangerous. I couldn't know. Crump was dangerous enough, although I was still certain he was acting alone.

"It was research. Humans are excellent research subjects, and I was interested in what the increments would do."

I had one chance, and that was to move directly into his left side and get him off balance. He was a lefty—the way he'd held his beer had told me that. The closer I could get to his left side, the more my advantage would increase.

"Research," he repeated, as if that was all that mattered.

That was the angle. Research. There was only one way out of this, and I was sure hoping it was going to work. "How much did you use? To begin with, I mean?"

There was a slight relaxation of his jaw, which I took as a positive sign. "Not all that much. A few grams gave me a good baseline. Then, increasing it over the next month produced some interesting effects. The tremor, of course. That was expected. I hadn't anticipated the fatigue, though, and the loss of appetite. That was fascinating." He paused.

I could sense him wondering what else he would want to share before he decided he'd said enough and turn his attention to me. I threw out my last piece of ammunition. "I'm surprised at your choice, though. Amaryllis isn't a native plant."

"Do you really think I gave a shit? That's why I used it. Von Reichstadt wasn't part of the Faculty. He didn't belong with the others. There has to be order. They were all the same. He was different, and so he got different treatment. Is that too difficult for you to understand? Why are you here, anyway? I thought you'd be packing to leave."

"Yes, well, I'll pack when I get back to Marta's. Does she know your plans? I mean, she's been helping you all along." There it was again. A sound that didn't belong. Something was close by. My mind was racing, along with my heart. I could use a little help here, if we were going to get to the happy ending part of this little drama. Human or animal? A cat stalking a rat that happened to jump out from the garbage cans and impale itself on Crump's face, while it tried to escape, would be welcome. Wishful thinking, but Crump was talking again.

"Marta? Another stupid woman." He stared at me, daring me to disagree. "She was useful, of course, helping me with my research. Other than that, I'm just tying up loose ends. She and I will have plenty of time to talk when this is all over and done with. Her husband was the last obstacle. But, I am curious. How did you know? Was it something I said?"

So, there was the explanation for Marta and the camera. She was doing it for him, continuing the theft of others' work in an attempt to advance Crump's. It occurred to me out of the blue that most people live their entire lives without encountering one psychopathic killer, let alone two. I mean, what were the odds? Regardless, just as with Gerda, conversation was the only way to stall him. Just one little movement that would let me keep on living. All that flashed through my mind in a second or two. Dammit, I was going to see John again, and this nutcase was not going to prevent that from happening, so I sallied forth.

"Actually, Otto, it was *everything* you said. You said way too much, and you relished every word. You gave me every detail of every death, and it was a bit of overkill, if you will pardon the pun." It was my turn to do the slow, deliberate head shake. "I wondered what the victims' connections were to the other members of the Faculty. For a while, I thought it had to be their areas of research—you know, not being what the Party approved. That was plausible, but it didn't explain Amelie Kleinschmidt, and it always seemed to come back to her, especially after Emma's death. There are no coincidences, you know. There didn't seem to be any common thread, until I considered what their connection was to each other, to Professor Kleinschmidt, and to you. Once I discovered that, the rest fell into place."

Crump made a noncommittal grunt. "They never understood my genius. None of them did. They were pedestrians. At least, two of them were." He laughed at his little double entendre.

"What about Gerda?"

"Gerda? She was convenient, easily persuaded to do whatever I told her to do to make Kurt's life easier. She was in love with him, the stupid cow. I kept the Amaryllis on her desk. She tended it so carefully." He scowled. "I hadn't realized she was so unstable. That was an error on my part. But this has gone on long enough. We need to take a walk."

"All right, Otto, but just one more question, please. It's a simple one. Why did you kill so many?"

Crump was getting restless, and my own adrenaline level was reaching a critical point. We were heading to some sort of climax, and I offered a silent prayer. This would be the last question, but I pushed harder, because the unmistakable sound of footsteps was getting closer. "Von Reichstadt was the one you wanted."

"Of course. You're as stupid as the rest of them. With him gone, I had easy access to Marta. After a respectable time, we would marry. Manipulating women is easy. You're all the same. Then, it wouldn't take long before her accident, and I would inherit everything. Her home, her fortune, and the greenhouse as a bonus. I didn't build it for her, you know, but then I realized that getting rid of the others would serve me two ways. They would confuse anyone looking for Erich's killer, if indeed they discovered his death wasn't due to natural causes, but it was also payback."

"For what?"

"This has gone on long enough." Crump's agitation was increasing, and that was what I wanted. Anything to keep him from getting me away from here. His eyes now darted left and right before returning to glare at me. "All right. I can answer that. You need to understand. They were, or most of them were, on the committee that denied me tenure, and Kleinschmidt was the head of that committee. They dragged up some of my papers they said had been plagiarized. Fools. I didn't plagiarize, I improved on inferior research. The Faculty put me on probation, while they continued their investigation. They said I'd never be tenured, and that if there were any more instances, I would be fired at the end of the term. I couldn't have that. My work had to continue. So I did what I had to do." His voice was increasing in volume, a sure sign he was just about at the end of his explanation. "It was a simple research problem. The others that had to die were just laboratory work. They didn't mean anything." He'd finished with his story. "Let's go." He reached for my arm.

My handbag was in position, and all I needed was one second to activate the spring. One second is not much time, for being the portal between life and death, but in that one second, my fingers closed around the stiletto, and Crump saw what I now had in my hand. He stepped backwards to reposition himself. He had the advantage of strength and size, that was a given, but I had the advantage of agility and a weapon I knew how to use. For another second or two, maybe three, we faced each other, waiting. Then he lunged at me and managed to deflect my hand just enough that I lost my balance and fell backwards, hitting the ground hard. Unlike Gerda's fall, I was unhurt, and the stiletto was poised to strike, even as he came at me.

I believe he saw the flash of the stiletto silhouetted against the light as I thrust it up under his ribcage, sliced through his liver, and punctured his diaphragm just before the blade entered his heart. This time it was Crump who hit the ground, the silent scream of death on his face.

The stiletto had done its work. It is a nearly bloodless instrument, neat and tidy. In a way, the expression on Crump's face mirrored Augie's, and I found in that a sort of poetic justice. I wiped the blade on Crump's trousers. It was a symbolic gesture more than anything, and a last salute to Emma Trupp. After all, it's important to keep the equipment clean. I returned the stiletto to its case, took one last look at

Crump, and informed his dead face, "Easy to manipulate? No, Otto. You were dead wrong on that. Not *all* women." I stepped back and turned to see Professor Martin Albrecht regarding me with an amused expression.

"I followed you just in case you might need help." He looked at Crump's body. "I can see that I worried needlessly."

I assured him that his help had been most welcome. His movements toward us had given me reassurance. Then he said what I had been hoping to hear for the past week.

"I believe you have been looking for me."

The relief that flooded over me was almost strong enough to counteract the aftertaste of having taken a life, even one as evil as Crump's had been. "This is not the best place for a conversation," I said. "Let's go back inside and find a noisy space on the dance floor."

The band was still going strong, but their choice of a slow dance number signaled their intention to wrap it up. Albrecht and I found a slot among the crowd to finish our conversation.

"I thought you might be Gestapo," he said. "Dieter just stopped coming around. Nobody knew what had happened, but I didn't want to take any chances. And then you showed up with his ring. I wasn't sure how to find out who you were, but after seeing you deal with Crump, I figured I'd try my luck. You aren't, are you?"

"Gestapo? No. Not by a long shot. I'm with the good guys. I came to find Dieter and, failing that, to find you." The band increased its volume. They were gearing up for the finale. "Dieter is dead, but I have the microfilm. He didn't divulge anything about you to anyone. You can rest easy on that." I looked around at the rest of the dancers. How many of them—of us—would be able to rest easy any time soon? Our time here was winding down, along with the band. The last notes were hanging in the air. I asked the final question. "Are you willing to continue?"

"Yes. Believe me, I am no hero. I am afraid, but that isn't important. They cannot be permitted to win. The work must go on, and it must go on in America."

Why is it that the real heroes never think of themselves that way? "All right then," I said. "Your new contact will be named Rolff. Same procedures. Nothing else will change."

"Very good." The music had ended. He released me and gave a slight bow. "Safe travels to you."

"Thank you. Oh, by the way, do you and Kleinschmidt ever cross paths?"

"Occasionally, why?"

"Next time you see him, let him know the killing has stopped."

"Roger that, as you Yanks say." He bowed, kissed my hand, and returned to his colleagues at the bar.

Dancing with an oversized handbag is an acquired skill, and I was quite happy to once again have it dangling from my hand as opposed to resting on Albrecht's back during our talk. I considered stopping by the bar and saying good night to von Reichstadt before I left but thought better of it. With a final look around the Blue Dube, I made my exit—this time out the front door and into the clean night air.

I took my time strolling back to Marta's. My last night in Berlin had been a humdinger. Tomorrow, I would be winging back to the States. I just had to survive the night, and with Crump no longer in the picture, my odds of survival had increased substantially. Still, before crossing the street, I checked for oncoming automobiles, buses, trucks, bicycles, and even pedestrians. I wasn't taking any chances.

Wednesday, June 26, 1940
French Volunteer Legion formed by General Charles DeGaulle in London

CHAPTER TWENTY-SEVEN

Katrin and John's Apartment
New Haven

It was morning on my fifth day home, and I was finally feeling human again. Sleeping in my own bed and being able to totally relax, even for just a little while, had been pure luxury. Remembering what John had said when all this had begun, though, I'd simply unpacked, done my laundry, repacked, and set the Gladstone down by the front door. Still no travel stickers, however.

I'd had my debriefing with Gene on Monday. He'd hoped Dieter's story would have ended differently, but he knew, as I did, you get just so many chances, and Dieter was always looking for one more. At least, Gene could rest easy knowing Dieter hadn't been turned, and the microfilm had ended up in the right hands.

Ilsa was in D.C., undergoing her own debriefing. Gene would be involved in her future propaganda assignments for the cause, along with those of Kristine, whose ride with the donut-eating cop was scheduled for tomorrow. She'd be in the States by the weekend and would meet Gene shortly thereafter. Ilsa had brought along several rolls of film Kristine had shot—a head start on her American professional portfolio. Gene had been suitably impressed and had taken an intense interest in her photographs of Becker's corpse. I had no idea where that was headed, and I didn't especially want to know.

I'd told Gene about the murder investigation I'd conducted on the side, and he'd been quite intrigued. I left it there, but early this morning, apparently after he'd done some digging, he telephoned to let me know that Otto Crump's body had been discovered by the garbage collectors making their early morning rounds. There were no witnesses to the murder. No leads, no suspects. I wondered if Marta were grieving the loss of her love, and I also wondered if Erich von Reichstadt had suspected anything. He'd never know how close he had come to a second, and assuredly fatal, heart attack that night, and I was glad he was still alive and kicking. I liked him. His health should be improving over time, Gene had informed me, with the exit of Crump and his amaryllis extract poison.

I'd also told Gene about Amelie Kleinschmidt's accident and injury, and it seemed that Gene's connections knew no borders. He told me that Kurt Kleinschmidt had been contacted by a specialist in Switzerland who had agreed to see Amelie. Perhaps there was help for her and Kurt. I hoped so.

Professor Martin Albrecht would meet his new contact, Rolff, next Monday. Albrecht's contributions to our nuclear research program and intelligence community would continue.

Gene was still battling with Hoover but seemed to be making some headway. His clothes were still rumpled, but he'd vacated his car office and was back in his regular digs.

As for me, I was back home and enjoying the peace and quiet. I'd be back at the university tomorrow, but for now, I was enjoying my breakfast—a cup of coffee and an apple pancake that I'd made for myself. The pancake wasn't as good as Barbara made, but it was passable. If I kept at this cooking thing, one day I might even get good at it.

I had the morning paper propped against the sugar bowl and was looking at the real estate listings. There was a beautiful home in Bethany, out in the country a ways, but close enough to drive to Yale for work. It had a decent-sized lot with room for flowers, a greenhouse, and chickens. I had just gotten up to get the scissors to cut out the advertisement to show John when he got back home, when the mail cascaded from the front door letter slot onto the floor. I went to retrieve the assortment of bills and letters, and then, one last item, the familiar yellow and black envelope of a Western Union telegram, fell from the slot, fluttered to the ground, and settled at the top of the pile. I looked at my real estate ad and then back at the telegram. I gave one of my theatrical sighs, although there was nobody there but me to hear it. I took the telegram to the kitchen table, slit open the envelope, and scanned the message.

Librarian needs assistant. Driver waiting outside.

Once more into the fray. John was waiting for me in London. I took a quick look out the living room window. Sure enough, there was a taxi parked by the curb. I took a deep breath and went into the bedroom to collect my handbag, fully restocked with yarn and books. I hesitated only briefly before adding my service revolver to the contents. I didn't know where I'd be going, what I'd be doing, or when I'd be back. In those situations, it's best to think of all contingencies. One never knows.

POSTSCRIPT

Whether you suffered through history classes in school or were fascinated by what you learned, history is simply the written record of what has happened since we've been able to carve it into rocks, ink it onto papyrus, use a quill pen for an illuminated manuscript, tap it out on a typewriter and, eventually, a computer. From this record, one word, one idea, is always, for a writer, the starting point for an adventure into the human mind and spirit.

The recipe for historical fiction, at first glance, seems simple. Take an event, toss in a few characters who might or might not have lived during the time that event was happening, add some obstacles to thwart them in their quest to achieve whatever it is they are seeking, and, in the process, create a world that might have been, came to be, or never was. There are so many directions to go. It's not for the faint of heart.

Europe uses the 24-hour clock. Since Katrin is operating as an American, however, I have used the American system of time-telling. For those who would wish to convert to the 24-hour clock, add 12 to any hour after noon. For example, 1:00 p.m. becomes 1300 hours.

We can't escape history, and the stories of our lives are fodder for any writer with the desire to tell a story. In telling this one, I drew upon the stories of many people who lived during the WWII era. Katrin's exploits are, of course, fiction, but the reality of her circumstances is very much fact.

The propaganda conference that Kristine Trautmann alludes to is a reference to *First course for Gau and Kreis,* a training course for party propagandists that was held from April 24-26, 1939 at the Ordensburg Vogelsang in the Eifel Region. The words attributed to specific Nazi figures in attendance there are accurate.

The Central Office for Vegetation Mapping of the German Reich was founded in 1939 and headed by Reinhold Tüxen. "*Cleanse the German landscape of unharmonious foreign substance*" was its mission. I used this office to develop the name for the fictional conference Katrin attends. The conference that Katrin alludes to that occurred in 1939 did actually take place.

The conference created for this book serves as a venue for gathering prominent Nazi figures of the time in one place and finding a way to use their exact words to show the depths of the evil that drove them. All historical figures of the Nazi Party quoted at the conference in this novel said the words attributed to them, however far-fetched and bizarre they may seem today.

The native plant obsession was quite real for the Nazis. All of the agencies mentioned in this novel existed, and their mission of extermination of both plants and people was all too real.

Karl Förster was an historical figure of the time. While the conversation he and Katrin have is fictional, Förster's description as an honorable man who employed Jews at his nursery is accurate.

The University of Berlin is loosely modeled on Humboldt University of Berlin, an institution where Albert Schweitzer did indeed teach until the growing Nazi movement forced him to emigrate.

What are referred to as *Departments* in American colleges and universities (Department of Physics, Department of Biology, etc.) are referred to as *Faculties* in Germany (Faculty of Physics, Faculty of Biology, etc.) Those who teach at these institutions are referred to as *faculty* in the United States. Their counterparts in Germany are referred to as *staff.*

Professional titles (honorifics) are important in Germany. During the time frame of this novel:

A male university professor is *Herr Professor Doktor Schmidt (for example)*

A married female university professor is *Frau Professor Doktor (Schmidt)*

An unmarried female university professor is *Fräulein Professor Doktor (Schmidt)*

. . .

As this book is written, it is 80 years since the bombing of Pearl Harbor by the Japanese. That occurred on December 7, 1941 and marked the entry of the United States into what became known as World War II. The United States joined the Allied Forces, fighting against Hitler and Japan. Russia had originally been on their side of the equation but later shifted to the Allied side, a move that many would later come to regret. That is material for another time.

To get a feel for the time period of this novel, it's important to understand how language changes over time. The best example is the German word, *Fräulein.* Today, it is considered to be a term of condescension and is no longer commonly used. Literally, it means *little woman.* Originally, it referred to any unmarried woman, regardless of her age, and was a title of respect. Since the 1970s, the term has fallen out of favor and is now seen as a tool for identifying women by their marital status, or even, in a darker interpretation, by their profession, implying prostitution. Regardless, many older women who lived during this time of transition insisted on keeping the title (or honorific). They were comfortable with the tradition and did not wish to embrace the change that was thrust upon them.

This evolution extends across languages. It is no longer considered polite to refer to a French woman as *Mademoiselle,* a Spanish woman as *Senorita*, or an

American woman as *Miss.* As Katrin notes in one passage of the book, men have never traditionally been identified by their marital status, but women have. Those times have changed, but for purposes of the time period of this novel, the current, correct, and respectful terms of the time period are used.

Katrin is operating as an agent of MI6, the British intelligence organization, in this novel, since the OSS, the Office of Strategic Services, didn't come into being until June 13, 1942. It was, as Gene explains, a donnybrook among Donovan, Hoover, and Roosevelt, but ultimately, President Franklin D. Roosevelt signed the papers, and the OSS, with Wild Bill Donovan at the helm became the focal point of wartime intelligence gathering and operations. It was disbanded on September 20, 1945, after formal termination of the war, and much of its activity was taken over by the CIA.

One other note, before I leave you. *Kristallnacht,* or the *Night of Broken Glass,* was the beginning of the Holocaust, a time of such evil and terror that sane minds cannot and *should not* be able to understand it. It was real, as was the burning of the synagogue in Kristine's home town of Rostock. I have been to Rostock. It is a beautiful place, but as with so much of Germany, it has a dark past from which we must learn.

Katrin's adventures will continue. She lived and worked in one of the most interesting periods in history.

ABOUT THE AUTHOR

Karen K. Brees is the award-winning author of *The Esposito Caper,* along with *Headwind* and *Crosswind* *(The World War II Adventures of MI6 Agent Katrin Nissen* series). She holds a master's degree in history and a doctorate in adult education. She is also the author and co-author of seven nonfiction titles in the health and general interest field, including *Preserving Food* and *Getting Real about Getting Older.* She has been a bookmobile librarian, classroom teacher, university professor, cattle rancher, and goat herder. She currently resides in the Pacific Northwest where she is at work on the third Katrin Nissen novel.

NOTE FROM THE AUTHOR

Word-of-mouth is crucial for any author to succeed. If you enjoyed *Crosswind,* please leave a review online—anywhere you are able. Even if it's just a sentence or two. It would make all the difference and would be very much appreciated.

Thanks!
Karen K. Brees

Made in United States
Orlando, FL
16 June 2024

47957880R00203